MW00958998

THE COMEBACK PACT

WARNER UNIVERSITY BULLDOGS
BOOK 1

E. M. MOORE

Manufactured in the United States of America
First Edition June 2023

Edited by Chinah Mercer of The Editor & the Quill, LLC

Cover by 2nd Life Designs

Huge thanks to my beta readers: Jennifer, Shawna, and Jorden!

Special thanks to Courtney H. for Kenna's name, and Ashley who gave me West. Much love to you both!

ALSO BY E. M. MOORE

Uppercut Princess

Arm Candy Warrior

Beautiful Soldier

Knockout Queen

Crowned Crew (Heights POVs & Stories)

Finn

Jax

The Ballers of Rockport High Series

Game On

Foul Line

At the Buzzer

Rockstars of Hollywood Hill

Rock On

Spring Hill Blue Series

Free Fall

Catch Me

Safe Haven Academy Series

A Sky So Dark

A Dawn So Quiet

CHAPTER ONE

Kenna

IF MY LIFE had a theme song right now, it'd be "Sunshine" by OneRepublic.

Sweet baby Jesus, I'm back.

I almost skip through the pool area to Coach's office, the chemical smell of chlorine assaulting my nostrils in the best way. God, I missed this. I missed the echo my teammates give off in this cavernous room. The way the divers' splash into the water sounds like an orchestra coming out of surround sound speakers.

A little bit of sunshine..., I sing inside my head, trying to keep my footsteps steady even though all I want to do is dance with joy.

The note in my hand feels like a hot poker zinging electricity up my arms and into my chest. A rush. A surge. A feeling I haven't been that familiar with these last few months because of the damn football team. Bulldogs, my ass. They suck. No loyalty. No strength. I hope they—

"Kenna!" a voice shouts.

I take a deep breath, evening out the Niagara-Falls worthy waterfall of anger that suddenly overtook me.

Welcome to the eighth wonder of the world... McKenna Knowles's rage.

I have issues of the mad kind. The injustice variety. The kind that makes you want to spit swords and slice through dumb, asshole jocks.

I lift my hand to wave at the teammate who called my name, plastering a smile on my face, and for a few seconds, it feels like everything is back to normal. I'm at the pool. Soon, my hair will smell like chlorine again.

Then her gaze flits, almost imperceptibly. A quick peek. A tiny slide of the eye, really...

And my world comes crashing down *again*.

I clasp the note in my hand and turn around, stomping toward the locker room. Things will never be the same, but I wish I didn't have to wear my past on my face for everyone to see.

Unlike the pool area, the swim and dive team locker rooms are quiet, secluded. Just what I need. I lean against the door, taking a deep breath. My mom's new recurring words hit me. "They don't mean it. Curiosity is normal."

Yeah, well, curiosity killed the cat, and I'm about to grow claws à la Wolverine.

As usual, the anger doesn't get me anywhere, so I close my eyes and do my breathing exercises. That's right. I'm *that* kind of screwed up. I'm a twenty-one-year-old college student who needs to utilize breathing techniques for anger, depression, anxiety... You name it, I probably got it.

A little bit of sunshine...

A little bit of sunshine...

I keep repeating the OneRepublic lyrics until they come out fast and happy again. No matter what, I have this note. No matter what, I'll be back on the dive team as of today. This is what I've been waiting for. The only thing I've been striving for.

Mission fucking accomplished.

It's almost like a puzzle piece clicks into place, and I'm off again, skipping for good measure.

Fake it 'til you make it and all that jazz.

Nothing should break me from this good mood. I'm getting my old life back, and that's all I want.

A few steps away from Coach's office, I spot movement from the corner of my eye. I drag my gaze from Coach's short, blonde hair pulled into her usual half-up do, Bulldog-blue collared shirt, and khaki shorts to the small frame staring into her locker. Her long, thin arm resting on the metal.

"Girl!" I shout, bursting with excitement again.

This time, it isn't even manufactured. "Did you get my texts?" My voice goes up several octaves, shocking even me.

Laney jumps, and I laugh.

She doesn't match me, though. Her face drains of color as she glances at me, and my stomach squeezes.

I'd been calling and texting her all morning. I wanted my dive partner to be the first to hear my amazingly incredible news, and I was even hoping we might tell Coach together...

"Kenna, hey," she says, glancing down. She drops her hand from the locker and then stares inside it like there's a tunnel to Narnia she can crawl toward.

Life won't be the same again. You just have to make the best of it.

I plaster a smile on my face, even though I don't feel like it. Laney's my best friend. We went to high school together, won state together in synchro diving, and then we both got accepted to Warner University three years ago to dive for the Bulldogs. Up until the incident, she was also my roommate. She would never not answer my calls or messages. "I have great news," I try again, echoing the rambling messages I left on her voicemail, but it falls a little flat.

Her whole face is in the locker now, a bright-red blush creeping up her neck. "Yeah?"

Warning bells go off in my head.

I stop my slow steps toward her. Something's not

4

right. It's almost as if she's avoiding me like I'm the putrid-smelling D&D nerd that tried hitting on her at Starbucks our freshman year.

My fingers curl into my palms, the note in my hand crinkling. She was there at my hospital bed. She freaking was there after my first surgery, and my second surgery, and—

The door to Coach's office swings open with a creak, and I turn toward it. She gives me a big smile. "McKenna. How great to see you!"

I return her smile. I'll deal with Laney later. Who knows? Maybe a guy she was seeing broke up with her. Or maybe she had a bad practice.

The world doesn't revolve around you, McKenna.

The excited grin that grows on my face isn't fake. "Coach, I'm so happy," I singsong.

She ushers me into her office and shuts the door. As usual, manila folders are piled everywhere. She calls it organizational chaos, but to me, it just looks like stacks of folders and papers strewn about with no purpose whatsoever. She moves them around on her desk, but honestly, it doesn't look like there's a reason for her madness. She just transfers everything from one side to the other, almost like a nervous tic.

"I'm so glad you wanted to meet," she says. Her fingers flex, and she finally peers up to meet my gaze.

Fuck.

I see it there: nerves. Apprehension.

But that's okay because she doesn't know what I'm holding in my hot little hand. The piece of paper that's about to change everything.

My foot taps against the tile of its own accord. It feels like if I don't rein it in, it might grow wings and take off tap dancing out of pure joy.

Coach takes a deep breath and opens her mouth, but I don't let her get a word out.

Okay, maybe the world does revolve around me. At least for right now.

"I got it," I tell her, slapping the note down on her desk and sliding it over like it's the missing page of some historical treasure. The words written on this note are valuable, just not drape-myself-in-gold-and-diamonds valuable.

Honestly, it's even more.

She glances up, and I nod, smile pulled so taut the muscles around my mouth start to ache.

"McKenna..." She sighs.

I open the note for her. "It's all right here." Once I get it unfolded, I point at my doctor's poorly scrawled signature. "She's okayed me to dive, Coach. I'm back."

The area behind my eyes heats. I've been trying to tamp down the emotion that's been building like a pressure cooker ever since that day six months ago, and it feels dangerously close to boiling over now.

All of the pain I endured—physically, emotionally,

mentally—it all comes down to this moment. The one I worked so hard for.

Coach picks up some manila folders again, taps them against the surface of her desk, then moves them back to the other side, her fingers flexing and straightening. Is that a...tremble? A shake?

For a moment, my heart stops beating. Then I go cold. A metal box slams around my heart, and I sit back.

"McKenna, I agreed to meet with you because I've come to some difficult decisions lately."

Difficult...

I want to tell her that I don't think she knows what difficult actually is. It's unfair, but the bullshit I've had to go through these past months because of a bunch of reckless douches makes me want to scream into the abyss for eternity.

"I got the note," I tell her, feebly. This doesn't look like it's about to go my way.

"The truth is, you're out of practice, Kenna. You haven't been able to get into the pool for months. You're out of shape. We don't know where your conditioning is. You know as well as I do that time off can severely hurt athletes. You're such a good diver—"

"Were, you mean," I say bitterly, not meeting her eyes. Instead, I flick imaginary lint off my athletic pants.

She huffs, leaning back and crossing her arms as if *I'm* the one who's doing something wrong here.

"I know you can come back from this, but not this season. Not right now. I was able to keep your scholarship in place." She leans forward again, her arms gesturing as if that was a feat in itself. She's quiet for a long time, and she doesn't talk again until I peer up to meet her eyes. "We can't hold it forever, though," she says, gaze teeming with sympathy. "This note is a good step. It gets you back in the water. But the reality is, I can't put you on that platform, and deep down, you know it."

My stomach clenches. All of the work I've done, and it feels like Coach just tossed it in the toilet and flushed it.

"But Laney," I say half-heartedly, my heel digging into the tile at my feet. I'll use any excuse at this point.

"Laney's been partnered with Taylor. They've been practicing together for a while now, and they'll be diving synchro together this season."

Laney...and Taylor? No wonder she didn't even want to look at me.

Coach beckons someone forward through the glass window of her office, and I turn to see my best friend standing outside the door, her dark hair wet to her shoulders. She steps in, and my heart sinks when the door closes behind her, the lock clicking into place with finality.

"You and Laney have been partners for a long time, so she wanted to be here when I told you."

I turn back around to face Coach.

Did she? How righteous of her.

"I'm really sorry, Kenna," Laney's unsure voice sounds from behind me.

I shrug, not knowing what else to do or say. Everything that comes to mind sounds angry and bitter.

"It was my decision," Coach says. "You were out of commission, and Laney needed a partner for synchro."

The world just kept on spinning... Leaving me behind.

After several moments, I ask, "What do I need to do to get back on the roster?" The truth is, I can sit here and feel sorry for myself, or I can do something about it.

Coach finally picks up the note that only a few minutes ago I'd thought was my golden ticket. She reads through everything. "This is great, Kenna. Really. You can come back and practice with us starting immediately. Let's see where you are physically and make a plan from there. I want you back on this team."

She stands abruptly and moves over to my side of the desk. Laney steps out of her way as I gradually get to my feet. Coach places her arms around me, squeezing slightly. She smells like pool chemicals with a hint of fruit.

I've had a Coach hug before, and it was better than this. Stronger.

Everyone thinks I'm going to break.

"I'll make it back on the team," I vow, speaking the words aloud so she hears them, too.

"You will," she says, stepping away, her hands squeezing my shoulders.

"This year."

Her smile thins. "Kenna, I need you to have realistic expectations."

Oh, realistically, I understand exactly what happened here. They gave my spot to Taylor. If I don't have a synchro partner this year, who am I going to dive with? It takes months and months of training with a partner just to sync up. Laney and I had been partners for years. We were practically twins up on the platform.

"You'll see," I tell her.

Right now, I have no idea how I'm going to pull this off, but I don't care. I can't come this far and just stop.

She nods, and I spin to leave the office. Laney steps out of my way, but her footsteps follow as I march through the locker room.

"Kenna?" I don't slow down. "Kenna!"

Nope, not today. Today I get to be the best friend whose heart got stomped on.

They've been practicing together for a while now...

She never said a word. I sprint past the pool and

practically lunge out of the double doors. Instead of breathing in chlorine-free air, I smack right into a wall of muscle and inhale the scent of sweet cedar.

Strong hands on my shoulders right me, and I'm so angry that I turn a scowl at my savior. When I see who it is, that scowl deepens.

West Brooks. All-star football player. Big man on campus that all the girls fawn over right along with the rest of the stupid jocks. He's drop-dead gorgeous with dark hair and green eyes. He's always wearing a stoic face that says he's miles above everyone else, his prominent chin shoved into the air like he's a god and we're all just his puny servants.

I don't care who he is. If he wears a football jersey at Warner's, he's my enemy.

"Fuck off," I growl, shoving away from him. Not sure if I'm actually mad at him because he's here to witness my little meltdown or because I had the momentary thought that he was good-looking. Or maybe I'm just projecting my hatred for Laney onto everyone else.

One of the jersey chasers hanging onto the crook of his elbow laughs incredulously as I walk away. "Well, that wasn't very nice."

Well, it's all I can muster from someone who belongs to the team who completely ruined my life.

CHAPTER TWO

West

THE MOMENT my hands touch McKenna's shoulders, a possessiveness takes hold of me. My fingers dig into her skin, and a dormant voice in my head growls *mine*.

She is fucking beautiful, I think, as the tips of my fingers begin to tingle, followed by shockwaves of darker, covetous thoughts that would get me shot down if voiced. Her hair lies in honey-brown waves past her shoulders, and once the pungent chemical aroma from the pool subsides, all I smell is her. It's a sort of sweetness, a tease that makes me want to eat her up.

Her slight frame stiffens. She's at least half a foot shorter than me, and I dial back to retreat, but for some reason, I can't get my hands to let go. They stay where they are, righting her on her feet as she pegs me with an angry glare.

The scar on the right side of her face is inflamed, but my eyes don't wander there. They only see her. The complete package that is McKenna Knowles.

Everything about her screams "get the hell away from me," but I can't heed my body's base impulse. Her very nature calls to me. Like a cactus, her thorny edges are fucking gorgeous.

"Fuck off," she seethes, tearing herself away.

I blink. In my head, that was going differently. But I know better. Kenna has every right to hate me.

Off my left shoulder, one of the girls who hangs on every word I say spouts something that makes my back stiffen. I don't even hear the words, it's the tone of her voice directed at Kenna's retreating form that sets me off.

I unwind the girl's arm from around mine and turn the other way, my heart still beating in my chest like the roar of the crowd at championships. How can just one touch from Kenna give me the same feeling as thousands of others chanting my name?

She's an enigma.

I make my way toward the exit, and my phone feels like an anvil in my pocket. Whenever I see Kenna in person, this is how our interactions start and end, but through my phone, there's a whole other world of possibilities.

"West," the girl complains behind me.

I know her name, but it's like one of those useless facts we learn in science. I wish I could unlearn it to make room for more important stuff. Like whether Kenna prefers french fries or tater tots. Does she prefer Marvel over DC? And what does her skin taste like... Don't get me wrong, jersey chasers have their merits at the right time and place, but this is not one of those times.

I walk off with a determined stride, and the hallway parts for me. Some girls peer up at me and blush. Others meet my stare with a seductive look as if they're trying to lure me to their side.

A male voice starts chanting, "Hulk, Hulk, Hulk!"

I raise my fist in the air because that's what they expect of me. I'm their Bulldog poster boy.

Someone else calls out, "How's practice, Big Man?" I turn toward the voice with a smirk on my face. The guy laughs. "That's right," he shouts as I continue the other way.

I've learned I don't have to say anything to the attention directed my way, which suits me. However, sometimes, I feel like a caricature of myself. A cartoon that eats, sleeps, and shits football all day long, but I'd do it all for the game, anyway. That's how much I love it.

Once outside, I round the corner of the building and step out into the sunlight. A breeze lifts my hair slightly and presses my Bulldog-blue shirt against my pecs as I take an alternate route to the football building for my meeting with Coach Thompson. We've been on campus practicing for weeks already, and everything is going exactly as it should for our opener, so I'm nervous as all hell that Coach called a meeting.

To distract myself, I pull up a pair of doe-brown eyes in my mind to fascinate over. She seemed upset, then angry.

She plowed into me, that's why I felt that protectiveness over her.

That's all it was. No other reason whatsoever. When people run into me, it never ends well. Just ask my opponents on the field. She's already been hurt, and I didn't want her to get hurt again.

On autopilot, I traverse the campus and enter the football building that houses the coaches' offices plus the gym and training rooms. Off the back, there's a practice turf that we run drills on with all kinds of equipment. This is my favorite building on campus. It's dubbed The Bulldog House, and the air smells like the new leather on a football all the time. I get stoked just setting foot in here.

Checking my phone for the time, I find I'm a little early, but Coach is sitting in his office, so I knock on the door.

He peers up, squinting through the glass before gesturing me inside. Coach Thompson is a goddamn legend in Warner country. He recruited me from high school, and he's done more for me in these past three years at Warner than any other male influence in my life.

"There you are, son," he says, and I pull out a chair. It wouldn't matter if I was thirty minutes early, Coach always greets his players the same: as if he's been expecting us and our absence has let him down.

I nod in silent greeting as I sit in the royal-blue leather chair across from his stark-white desk. The building and its contents are almost brand new. The newest structure on campus, actually, built by funds from alumni and the community.

We bleed blue here.

Coach leans back, appraising me. I know better than to guess why he asked me here, so I just wait for him to start talking. When he does, he says everything in a rush, like he hasn't the time to even have this meeting, let alone discuss at length what he wants, but I don't take offense. He's always like this.

But what he says nearly knocks me on my ass.

My brows raise.

"You know her, right?" he asks, face scrunching.

I nod because everyone does. The whole damn campus does. Hell, the whole town and surrounding counties know her name. What happened to her was everywhere.

Because of us...

My heart starts pounding so hard in my chest it feels like a rapid tremor. This is a bad idea. "Me?" I finally get out, and the question is strangled, like I'm choking at the thought because I absolutely am.

He fucking knows I'm not the player for this job.

He glares at me, his eyes narrowing to slits until it appears I'm about to get one of his verbal beatdowns. "Are you too fucking good to do something I ask you to do?"

I shake my head, my lips pressed together. I don't bother arguing that he's got it all wrong. That's definitely not what I meant, but my mouth gets me in trouble when I use it.

"Every single one of you players"—he points at me, his finger shaking—"who were involved in that mess with Hamilton will do exactly what I fucking tell you to do, when I fucking tell you to do it if you want to stay a Bulldog. You understand me?"

My muscles flex. The past few months, it's been the same verbal berating, all of which we deserve, but this one hits home a little more since it's completely directed at me, and we're talking about McKenna Knowles here.

He cups his hand around his ear, waiting. Expecting.

"Yes, sir," I call out.

"Good," he says, sitting back in his chair, steepling his fingers in front of him.

"You're a damn good player, Brooks," he finally says. "I have a whole team of amazing fucking players, but let's face it, we're in a bad press situation here."

I swallow the lump in my throat. It's died down now, but the horror of what happened and who was to blame was so thick around here that it was difficult to wade through.

"You get me?" he asks when I don't respond.

"Yes, sir." I know he wants me to say more, but my mind is careening. He wants me to get McKenna Knowles to our games. To our practices.

But she despises us. She despises me. Hell, she just told me to "fuck off."

"Let her know this isn't to parade her around. She'll absolutely be put in every position of respect. She'll be like Charlie," he finishes, eyes gleaming as if he's found the perfect reasoning.

I shift uncomfortably. That's what every girl wants...to be compared to a dog.

To be fair, Charlie the Bulldog is our faithful mascot, and he's definitely put on a pedestal of honor and respect, but someone outside of football won't see it that way.

But I get what Coach means. Morale is down around here. Our rivals, Hamilton, won our homecoming game last year, and then when we faced them again in the playoffs, they kicked our asses. To make matters worse, they escalated the stakes by pulling prank after prank to rub it in our faces—and one went too far.

McKenna was a casualty.

And now, we're not just dumb jocks, we're dumb, reckless jocks with no compassion for anyone else.

Leaning forward, Coach turns the paper on his desk around and faces it toward me. It's the *Bulldog Gazette*, and the headline reads "Football Season Approaching, Will We See Change?"

Coach sighs. "I'd love to say this was written by some pimply faced, athlete-hating nobody, but it honestly doesn't matter. I've seen more bad press about the football team these past few months than I've ever witnessed in all my years here. Hamilton will be working with suspensions for the first few games, and my wife loves to remind me that it could just as easily be my guys riding the bench and screwing up our season. We need to do better, and she's our reason. Our fucking pillar of strength. Our moral compass pointing due north. Whatever we do this season, we do for her."

Whenever Coach talks like this, I get pumped. I find myself nodding along and saying "Yes, sir" at the appropriate times, but as soon as he dismisses me and I walk out of his office, an ice-cold dose of reality hits me.

The football team might need McKenna, but she sure as hell doesn't want anything to do with us.

We tried rallying around her after everything happened, but her parents shooed us away—and they were the loudest calls for change, too. They did countless interviews with all the local and state papers. The news even hit big media outlets where the underlying theme was how college athletes were treated differently than regular college students. And the bigger the program, the more leeway their athletes were given.

They paraded out numbers of student athletes who were failing. Statistics that showed athletics had taken precedence over academics. Even exposés where college professors, hidden under anonymity, told the world that they were pressured to give student athletes better grades so they could play.

And the crux of it all was that football players were the worst offenders.

Coach is right about bad press, but McKenna Knowles doesn't want to be our remedy. She'd rather stand triumphantly on the mountain of our downfall.

And who could blame her?

The pain and suffering she's gone through because of our rivalry with Hamilton is astronomical.

But Coach gave me a challenge, so I'm going to do it.

How? No fucking clue.

My phone *pings*, and I pull it out. My heart does a bit of a gallop in my chest when I see who it is, even though I feel like a damn bastard.

McKennaK: You ever just want to eat Cheetos and binge Baywatch?

Smirking down at the screen, a thrill shoots through me until it quickly turns to an avalanche of guilt.

NoOne: I don't see how those two go together. *laugh face*

Yep, NoOne is me. I've been messaging her in secret for months. If she only knew who she was talking to, she'd hate me even more...

CHAPTER THREE

Kenna

I SMIRK down at my phone when NoOne's response to my question comes in.

> McKennaK: What shows and snacks do go together, then?

> NoOne: Zombieland and Twinkies. Obviously.

> McKennaK: *laugh face*

> NoOne: But if you really want to watch Baywatch, maybe Jell-O?

> McKennaK: Jell-O? Really?

> NoOne: I don't know what you watch it for, but I watch it for the boobs.

I snicker. Of course. What a guy thing to say.

> McKennaK: And to you, boobs are Jell-O? I'm questioning this convo now.

> NoOne: OK, what are boobs to you?

Hmm. I bite my lip as I stare down at my screen. My lunch tray is pushed to the side with a half-eaten chicken patty sandwich on it. The rest of the room is filled with other students talking and laughing, but my complete focus is on the conversation I'm having with a person I don't even know. Over these past few months, I can say I'm certain he's a guy. The boob comment aside, I've straight up asked him. Unless he's catfishing me—which is possible, but meh—I like my chances.

Also, he has to go to Warner because he's messaging me within the school's app. What I don't know is how he got a username that's not his name. We're all supposed to be first name, last name initial, but instead, his is NoOne. Definitely increases the mystery factor.

Honestly, it doesn't matter because this texting relationship has been a nice distraction, and one I've desperately needed.

I grin as I come up with the perfect answer.

> McKennaK: Whipped cream

He doesn't respond for a while, and my stomach

clenches. We've never taken our messages in this direction before. Little bubbles pop up, like he's typing, but then they go away.

I tap my foot against the cafeteria tile, wishing I could unsend my response, but he's obviously seen it. Out of the blue, a voice sings, "I... I just died in your arms tonight." Gazing up, I find my new roommate with a clear plastic water bottle to her mouth, belting out those lyrics like she's on stage in front of an enormous crowd. "It must've been some kind of kiss."

She struts toward me, then sits, dramatically crossing her legs and lifting her chin in the air in an end pose that has me laughing.

After a brief pause, Sydney slides her gaze my way while still keeping her diva pose. "How was it?"

I open my mouth to tease her, but she's already up and out of her seat before I can get anything out.

"Hold up," she announces, pointer finger straight up in the air as she walks away. She moves about four tables down before spinning toward me again. Her black ponytail whips from one shoulder to the other, showing off her long, dangly earrings shimmering in the light. She has a shit-eating grin on her face, the bottle of water still clenched tightly in her fingers. Taking off, she runs the first few feet before dropping to her knees and sliding until she's right next to me, all the while, her head tilted back as she sings into the bottle-turned-microphone, "I... I just died in your arms tonight."

She pauses, not moving, and while I shake my head at her, more than a few people clap and someone even gives a high-pitched whistle. Before taking the seat across from me, she stands and bows, like she does this every day for her adoring fans. "Well?" she questions with a hopeful smile.

Jesus. What can I say about Sydney other than she's a hell of a lot of fun? "The second take was definitely more dramatic. What year did that song come out?"

"Oh, come on. Are you trying to tell me you don't know that song?" She takes a big gulp of water and then sets it down in front of her. "I need to be unique, and I feel like an oldie but goodie will help me stand out."

Ever since I moved in with Sydney, she's been obsessing over this year's Lip Sync Contest. The winner performs at halftime during homecoming, but not just that, the boosters go all out. There'll be a legit stage, a great sound system, pyrotechnics, lasers, whatever the winner wants to bring their show to life. It's good fun and just another thing that sets Warner football apart from everyone else.

Ugh. I hate how everything at Warner University is centered around football.

My phone finally *pings* with NoOne's answer.

My fingers itch to type *do you want a cherry to be
involved?* but that's crazy. I don't even know this guy.

I make myself put my phone away so I don't say
something I'll end up regretting. However, as soon as I
do, I feel the doctor's note that had me so hyped this
morning.

"Sorry," I tell Sydney. "I'm just being a downer.
Coach said I won't be diving this year. She gave Laney
a new partner. But don't worry," I say sarcastically.
"They're holding my scholarship for me as long as they
can." I stop there, hopefully giving Sydney the same
implication Coach gave me.

What if I don't have a scholarship next year?

"What?" Sydney exclaims. It rings so high and
shrill that several people turn to look at us. She knows I
don't like attention being drawn to me, so she grimaces
as an apology and leans forward like we're co-conspira-
tors. "That's bullshit. The note," she whisper-yells,
referencing again what I thought was going to be a
done deal.

"She said I can start practicing with them, but she
thinks I'm out of shape and definitely won't be ready in
time to dive this season."

"Dude," she declares, eyes wide like she's as astonished as I am.

26

"I know." The sting of it hits me again. Telling someone makes it worse because it feels real now.

She blows out a breath. Out of everyone, she knows how much I was counting on this win. I may have just moved in with her at the end of last semester, but we became fast friends. My parents didn't want me in the dorms anymore after what happened, and Sydney was on the hunt for a roommate. It's only a bonus that we actually get along and that her house is super charming and perfect.

"So, what are you going to do?" she asks, clenching her water bottle.

"She says they'll evaluate me to see where I'm at, and we'll go from there." I shrug like it's no big deal, but I'm still devastated. The cold shoulder from Laney felt like a bigger betrayal. She should've been keeping me updated on what was going on, but instead, she was already diving with a new partner for crying out loud.

Sydney stays quiet as I fall down the rabbit hole of self-loathing. She gnaws on her bottom lip like she does when she's nervous about saying something. When I first moved in, she did it a lot until I told her she didn't have to be reserved around me. Before the incident, I was actually a lot of fun.

"Spill it."

"I'm saying this with heaps of love and unicorn sprinkles...but I wouldn't wait on your coach." As soon as it's out of her mouth, she rushes on with the rest of her thoughts. "She gave your spot away already. She told you there wasn't a place for you even before she evaluated you to see where you were at. Sounds like someone who doesn't care if you make it back on the team. I say you take matters into your own hands."

"So...like, do what?"

"I don't know. Dive shit. What do you need to do to 'get back in shape'?" she asks, using air quotes with her fingers.

"Conditioning, strength training, extra practice time..."

"Cool. Do it." When I just blink at her, she puts her serious face on. "Kenna, you need this. Diving is what kept you motivated during the surgeries and everything else. Don't let them take this away from you. Do you think Einstein just sat back and let someone else come up with his relativity theories?"

I think I know what she's saying, but—

She groans. "Okay, do you think David Booty just—"

"Boudia," I correct her. "David Boudia." Honestly, I should be surprised she even knows the Olympic diver's name.

She glares at me. "Do you think David Boudia just sits back and lets things happen to him? No, he goes out and gets it. He sees a problem and fixes it."

"Okay, okay," I say, trying to cut off her rant before it ramps up. She's absolutely right. Coach isn't doing me any favors, so this is all in my hands. I need to make a comeback plan on my own.

I need— Shit, I need another coach. Or someone like a coach. A trainer.

I'm trying to come up with a plan of action when Sydney's stare skates past me a few times. Finally, she locks gazes with me. "Don't look now. Football players are eyeing you up."

My body automatically stiffens. I remember the interaction I had with West Brooks earlier, and a sheet of ice freezes my spine. Sydney knows all about my past, my hatred for that team, and how they get away with freaking everything. They took part in the antics that permanently scarred me and none of them got so much as a suspension.

The dean even had the audacity to tell my parents that the rivalry with Hamilton went back to when both universities were founded, like it was a legend he wasn't going to apologize for. I was just an unfortunate bystander to kids who went too far.

"They're walking this way," she says under her breath.

"Who?" I gasp, my muscles locking up.

Her gaze flicks up. "West and Aidan."

I groan internally. West freaking Brooks *again*, and Aidan, the new hotshot starting quarterback after our old quarterback graduated and got drafted to play professionally.

"They're not coming *here*, are they?" I whisper, my foot bouncing up and down. My stomach churns, and I feel like I'm going to be sick.

"God, they are fine pieces of meat," Sydney states, her stare drifting to the floor like she's taking them all in. I kick her under the table, and she snaps out of it. "Fine pieces of type-A arrogance, I mean."

I roll my eyes. The truth is, they are unfortunately handsome with their big muscles and strong jaws. However, their disregard for others is abhorrent. If you have nothing to do with football, you aren't even on their radar. I've only caught their attention because of what happened.

The right side of my face burns at the memory. I'm suddenly super embarrassed and pissed at the same time, so I prop my head on my clenched fist and look the other way, simultaneously covering up my scar. Maybe if they don't notice it, I won't be an unwanted beacon for them.

Sydney suddenly freezes, and I peer over to find her gazing at me in surprise. She eeps out an "I'm sorry" two seconds before a masculine throat clears.

Fuck me. Just fuck me. This is exactly why Mom and Dad didn't want me living on campus anymore, but I have to eat, don't I? I can't avoid every communal space on campus.

"McKenna."

The voice is low and gravelly, almost like it's

underused. Right away, I know it's West. Aidan is a lot louder, and he wouldn't just say one word to get my attention.

My name on West's lips gives me a chill, and not only the kind that solidifies the ice around my heart, a different kind, too. I don't want to look his way. In fact, it's the last thing I want to do, but I also don't want to be seen as someone who's afraid of them. They should be cowering from me.

So, I pull up my big girl panties and turn their way, giving them the coldest stare I can muster, which comes rather easily.

My gaze flits over Aidan, but it stops on West. God, he *is* a fine piece of meat. His dark hair makes his green eyes look out of place, but in a sexy kind of way. He's all quiet and mysterious. We've had several classes together, and I don't know if I've even heard him string together a complete sentence in the years we've been going to school here. He certainly has never said my name before.

And damn, the sound of it still lingers in the air, giving me goosebumps.

I'm so mad at myself when my mouth won't make words. I'm just staring at West like I'm one of his groupies, and he's just staring right back.

Aidan sighs. "Hey, Kenna. How are you?"

I drag my gaze away from those taunting green eyes and size up his teammate. Aidan's about as tall as West, maybe a little taller, but he's not as wide. He's still bigger than the average male on campus.

Listen to me, *average male on campus*, like the football players are in a league of their own. This is exactly why they're allowed to get away with everything... because people think they're gods or some shit.

"It's *Mc*Kenna, actually. Kenna is reserved for my friends."

Aidan doesn't skip a beat. "Okay, *Mc*Kenna." He smirks. "How are you?"

"Fine," I say, but then I shake my head. I'm not having a cordial conversation with them. "What do you want?" I bite out.

The QB's lip twitches a little, like he's refraining from laughing. My gut tightens at his reaction.

Is he making fun of me?

"Listen..." Aidan peers at West, but he's just standing there like a statue, still staring at me intently. "Coach thinks it's a good idea if you come to practice."

I blink. Before my brain can catch up with me, I laugh. It comes out so sudden that even Sydney looks at me like I've lost it. "I'm sorry," I say, trying to rein it in. "It sounded like you invited me to your practice."

"I did," Aidan responds, keeping a jovial expression on his face.

Indignation swamps me. These guys couldn't even be bothered to see me when I was in the hospital, but they want me to come to their practice?

"For what?" I snap. "So you guys can all stare at me?" I deliberately tuck my hair behind my ear to show off the scar that mars my cheek, but surprisingly, neither of their gazes wander there. "So I can be some sort of disfigured—"

Aidan interrupts me. "Hey, I'm sorry. It's nothing like that. Coach just thought it would be good for you and the team to come together. To boost morale or something." He glances at West for some backup, but the big guy just stands there, his expression never wavering from me.

"So, he wants me to be your scarred mascot? Parade me around a bit. Or, I know," I say, my voice shrill enough to catch everyone's attention near us, "he wants to make it look like I'm okay with what happened? Like if I come to your practice, everyone will forget that your actions had consequences?"

Aidan grimaces like I kicked his puppy. "I'm so sorry. No one thought Hamilton would have taken it that far. We're all pissed. It won't—"

West's face morphs into an angry shade of red. He pulls on Aidan's shirt and then immediately spins and stomps away. Aidan walks backward, frowning at us before turning and catching up to his friend, who is already by the exit doors.

"What the fuck?" I mutter, glaring at West's retreating form. My whole body is vibrating, like I'm one second away from erupting. I should be the one walking away in anger.

Sydney reaches over, clasping her hand around my forearm. "Hey, it's okay. They're stupid. They don't get it."

I watch West push open the doors.

Why come all the way over here? Why say my name and then just look on while Aidan speaks?

What is his problem?

My gaze drifts back to his tight backside for a moment—a very brief moment—until I want to gouge my own eyes out.

West Brooks is a meathead football player, and therefore, not for me.

CHAPTER FOUR

West

EPIC CRASH AND BURN. It's the only way I can describe it.

"Dude," Aidan complains as we exit the cafeteria, "what the hell was that?"

I close my eyes and sigh. I shouldn't have told the guys about what Coach wants me to do, but the odds of them not finding out were slim.

Fuck.

I'd had eyes on her since the moment I walked into the cafeteria. I watched her message "me" over the app. The way she'd smile down at her screen at our conversation...

It gave me false confidence.

When her roommate came singing into the cafeteria and the guys finally noticed she was there, they'd talked me into doing Coach's bidding right then.

Epic crash. Epic burn.

I shrug for Aidan's benefit and peek over to find him holding the bridge of his nose. "She fucking hates us."

And I don't blame her, but that's a conversation for a different day.

The moment she turned those fiery eyes on me, I fucking froze. Panic swept over me like I was an eight-year-old boy again. I clammed up. Let's get real, this whole thing was going to be a challenge because I'm me, but the fact that she hates my guts is taking me to a place I don't want to be again.

I shudder.

"You could've said something," Aidan remarks.

"I...blew it," I manage to get out.

"Understatement." As a quarterback, Aidan is cool under pressure like you wouldn't believe, but he can't stand when people don't like him—which admittedly is few and far between because he's Aidan. People love him. "You might have to tell Coach that this isn't feasible," he says, turning the corner as we make our way to the weight room.

My stomach flips. That isn't an option. We've let down Coach enough.

I make a noise of disagreement, and Aidan peers over at me. "I mean this in the nicest way possible, dude, but you can't just grunt at this girl and expect her to show up. Jersey chasers are easy. They'll fall at your feet just for being you." He shakes his head. "I don't understand how you're a completely different person on the field."

When I have a jersey on, it's my suit of armor. Since I was a kid in peewee football, wearing that uniform...it felt like it gave me superpowers. Being a football player placed me in a different reality. I could do anything. I could *be* anything. I didn't have to hide in the corner anymore.

And now I'm the best fullback Warner has ever seen.

"I just am," I say, cutting through the silence.

Not many people know about my past. I don't go announcing it because I'm the 200-plus pound "Hulk" on the field. People don't want to hear about the scared boy with daddy issues. They want me to be the tough man all the time.

"Okay, you don't want to let Coach down, I get that," Aidan says. "You need a plan of action, then. Just like football, you can't call plays out of the blue. You need a route. If your end goal is getting her to practice, you have to find the path there, and I hate to break this to you, but I'm coming up blank."

My lips thin.

Thanks for the vote of confidence, man.

"Don't get me wrong, I'll help. You're my number

one on and off the field, bro, but I'm just saying, you got your work cut out for you."

I let that sink in. Why can't I be the guy I am with Kenna when we chat? NoOne. Him, she likes. Me, she despises. The simple truth is that if she knew I was NoOne, she'd hate him too, so she can never find out.

When I'm him, the anonymity gives me that armor back. I can be myself. I don't have to worry about how the relationship is going to work out because it's fake anyway. It's like hooking up with jersey girls. They only want to add me to the list of players they've slept with. They're not looking for the real thing.

Lately, though, I've been talking with Kenna more, and it's started to feel like the real thing. Today, our banter turned almost sexual. *Almost.*

I should pull back. Real feelings never get me anywhere good.

"So?" Aidan asks as he tugs the door open to the weight room. We've had to use the general weight room because the one in the football building is getting a revamp. Players from other sports have complained that we're taking it over, but when you have a bunch of guys that need to get their workouts in, I'm not sure what they expect us to do.

"I'll figure it out," I tell him.

Right now, I want to lose myself in the routine. Sweat cures a lot when you're me. Working out is when I can shut my brain off and focus on the present.

I grab my weightlifting gloves and belt from my bag before I toss it onto the ground next to a rack. It's leg day, so I search up my Heavy Lifting playlist and put it on repeat. It's an eclectic mix of music from "Eye of the Tiger" all the way to "Lose Yourself" by Eminem.

Aidan and I rotate in and out. I rest while he lifts and vice versa, and then we both spot for each other.

We've been doing this since he was QB2, so we don't even have to talk as we get our workout in. A few sets later and sweat already starts gliding down my temples. My muscles tense and push, then rest. Every once in a while, my mind will wander to Kenna. How she felt when I steadied her in front of me in the hallway outside of the pool. The douse of heat and electricity that rang through me when we touched. The smile she put on my face when she said boobs were whipped cream. Of course, my mind had immediately gone to *Varsity Blues* with the iconic whipped-cream bikini scene, but I couldn't tell her that. If she even got an inkling that she was talking to a football player, she'd crucify me.

I put the bar up on the rack, breathing heavy.

"You only did nine," Aidan says.

Shit. This incognito relationship I have with Kenna is a distraction. A distraction that won't go anywhere because no one will ever be able to penetrate my armor. Hell, no one will ever *want* to penetrate my armor, and especially not football-hating McKenna Knowles.

From this moment on, she's just the girl Coach needs me to get to practice. That's it.

I turn the volume up and double down on my focus.

It's just me, the music in my ears, and my screaming muscles playing a tense dance for the next hour.

I lift the bar for my last squat and grit my teeth, my legs shaking uncontrollably. As soon as I get it up, I move it to the rack. Aidan's right there, a fist outstretched. "Yeah, man."

I fist-bump him and then grab my sweat towel to wipe my face down.

"Leg day," Aidan calls triumphantly.

I take a step, and my legs give out a little. You know it was a good lift day when your muscles feel like Jell-O afterward.

My water bottle comes sailing through the air toward my head, and I snatch it before guzzling some down. Aidan grins at me. The dude will throw anything—footballs, water bottles, towels, condiments when we're out to eat. Literally anything that's not bolted to the ground.

His gaze flicks up, and he grimaces, immediately turning toward me. "Oh shit. Walking ball of rage just outside the weight room..."

I peer up to find Kenna's thin frame pulling open the door. My stomach tenses. Hope builds in my chest, but it dashes as quickly as it came when she sees me peeking over at her and rolls her eyes before changing direction.

For a brief moment, I thought maybe she was coming in to see us. Hell, I thought maybe she was coming in to see *me*.

She makes a straight play toward the bulletin board hanging in the corner of the room. People post shit there, but I've never really bothered to look since this isn't our usual workout spot. She takes one of the small papers and uses the pen that's attached to a string to write something. After a second, she shakes it, then tries to write again.

A cute, small growl escapes her throat before she flings the pen and searches for something else to write with but comes up blank. She's about to walk out when I march toward my gym bag and take out a pencil I have in the side pocket. I meet her just at the door. "Here," I say, offering it to her.

She looks at the pencil and then at me. I only have it because I used to be really meticulous about writing down my workouts, but I've been on the same routine for about a year now that's really working for me, and I know it by heart.

"No, thanks." She sniffs.

"It's just a pencil," Aidan speaks up from the other side of the room. "It won't bite."

She sneers at him and then back at me. I'm well aware that sweat is still dripping down my face and there's a massive wet mark on my collar that darkens the front and back of my shirt. Adrenaline from my workout is coursing through me, and my mind is telling me to say more. Joke with her. Tease her. For fuck's sake, flirt with her.

But I don't do any of those things. Instead, I move the writing utensil closer to her and lift my brows like I'm goading her.

She takes the pencil from my hand, but she does it in a way where it's abundantly clear that even being near me is like an ice pick to her brain. Without a hint of thanks, she leaves me standing there while she goes to the bulletin board and quickly scrawls out a note, then pins it to the cork.

If I were normal, I'd probably ask her what she's doing. If I was a guy trying to get with her, I might even tell her I could help her with anything she needs and let the innuendo hang in the air.

She marches right up to me and stares down at my hand that's still outstretched. After placing the pencil back in my grip, she mutters a thankless "thank you" and then walks away.

There's so much I don't know about her. Is she the type to hang out in weight rooms? She's on the dive team, but those guys don't weight train, do they? Plus, I know she had to take a hiatus because of the injury to her face. She couldn't very well get in the water and risk infection before it healed.

Seriously. What happened to her was fucked.

Aidan steps over a few benches and walks to the bulletin board as soon as she's out the door. "What are you doing?" I grind out, peeking at Kenna's retreating form. She turns the corner, and I relax a little more.

"Seeing what she wrote."

I want to tell him to knock it off. It's a violation of her privacy to see what she's up to, but I'm also curious as all hell.

Aidan lifts the hem of his shirt to wipe the sweat from his eyes and then snatches Kenna's paper off the board. The top of it rips.

"Dude," I snap. She's totally going to know we messed with her note.

"Dude nothing," he says, grinning at me. He moves my way. "The universe just smiled upon you, man."

He walks over with a little swag in his step and hands me the square piece of paper.

In small, delicate handwriting is:

Trainer Wanted. If interested, message me at McKennaK.

Aidan strides over to his bag, chuckling. "The way this dropped in your lap."

"She won't want to hear from me. Or any football player." I walk over to the message board and start to pin it back up when Aidan steps behind me and tears it out of my grip.

"You're messaging her, and we're sure as fuck not putting this back up. She'll be forced to work with you because no one else will know." He wads the note into a ball and stuffs it in his training pants.

I just stand there, shaking my head while he grins.

"You can thank me later."

Thank him nothing. No good can come from this... except actually making Coach happy.

Fuck, I have to do this, don't I?

CHAPTER FIVE

Kenna

AS LUCK WOULD HAVE IT, the sky opens up as I walk home. I shouldn't have stopped at the campus café to grab a coffee, but I really needed a pick-me-up. The rain starts to come down in pelts, and I start jogging, but the hot, brown liquid splashes out of the tiny sip hole and scorches my fingers.

It's nice that my apartment is so close to campus that I don't need my car, but that's backfiring on me at the moment. My foot catches on a sidewalk lip outside Alpha Sigma Phi, and I'm pitched forward, flailing for balance. The cup flies from my grip.

Coffee. Goes. Everywhere.

If anyone saw that...

With a quick look around, I stand up straight. At my feet, the contents of my Styrofoam cup are being washed away by the rain in the blades of green grass where it landed. I snatch the empty cup off the ground and trudge home, just past Greek Row, raindrops catching on my lashes the entire time.

I run up the front walk and barge inside, grumbling. The house is close to campus, but not as close as when I lived in the athletic dorm. I would still have a delicious hot coffee if I lived in the athletic dorm.

Loud music blares from Sydney's room in the back of the house. I hang up my jacket in the entry closet to the closing notes of a Christina Aguilera song. In the dead air before the next song begins, my sneakers squeak out their own tempo as I make my way to my room at the front of the small, two-bedroom house. Sydney's parents rented the place for her starting her freshman year at Warner and, lucky for me, her last roommate graduated. This place was a Godsend when I returned to school after the incident. My own little oasis. It removed me from campus and everyone's stares, which I desperately needed.

I change into a pair of sweats and an oversized sweatshirt before looking at my phone. Mom texted earlier, wanting to know how the meeting went with Coach, and I haven't written her back yet. I'm the one who wants to get back on the dive team and resume a normal life. My parents would be happy to wrap me up in a safety blanket for the rest of my life. If I tell them Coach isn't going to let me dive this year, that's all the ammunition they'll need to reinforce that I should focus on something else. "The future" is a concept my parents keep parading in front of me, and their version of it doesn't involve me diving. It almost didn't involve me returning to Warner.

I mean, sure, I'm probably not going to dive at the Olympics, but can't I just soak up the rest of my collegiate athletic life? I *love* diving.

While I stare at Mom's text, wondering how to word what I want to say, I get a notification from the school's app. I click on it, wondering if NoOne got back to me, but when the name pops up, my teeth gnash together. WestB.

Seriously?

Was I not clear enough earlier when I said I didn't want to go to his stupid football practice? I can hear my parents' shock now. They dragged all of college athletics through the mud after my incident, but football was their main point of contention. After all of that, I don't even know why any football player would want to talk to me. The amount of criticism the program took was substantial, though in hindsight, it didn't do anything.

In order to read the message he's sent, I have to accept him as a contact. I tell myself not to, but I'm too damn curious why he would be reaching out again. Does West Brooks actually talk through text, unlike in real life where he just stares at everybody? Is he the type to send a one-word message? Or even worse, has he sent something like a question mark because he expects me to know what he wants? That sounds exactly like something a pompous football player would do.

I have to admit, he has that mystery factor. And the body. Jesus. I'd have to be visually impaired to miss all of his muscles through his sweat-drenched shirt earlier.

I suck in a breath as realization strikes. They read my message on the bulletin board, didn't they? He and that stupid quarterback.

My face flames at the thought.

Before I can mull it over, I click on his name.

WestB: Hear me out.

The little bubbles are up like he's still texting, and I lie back on my pillows, clutching the phone. One would think he'd have put everything in a single message because I could just as easily block his ass before he writes anything else. Then again, maybe he didn't expect me to accept him so soon.

Shit, I should've waited. This looks too eager, and I am definitely *not* eager.

I can always block him later...

Since he left himself wide open, I type out a quick response.

> McKennaK: No.

I smirk. I bet West Brooks doesn't hear that word a lot.

He should.

The rest of his message comes in a few moments later, and my eyes widen at all he's written. I scroll down and then back up. It's a block of text, and even though my intuition tells me this is about to piss me off, I read it, anyway.

> WestB: Don't be mad, but I read the note you left on the bulletin board. I can train you. I gained twenty pounds of muscle my senior year of high school, and I've gained more each year while here. I use a combination of cardio and strength training, heavy on the strength training. Lots of the guys ask me for help coming up with their own routines. My major is exercise science. Tell me what you need, and I can help.

That was very...car salesman-y.

> McKennaK: Why?

The question flits through my brain and stays there like a concrete barrier. I was never on his radar before. What the hell is going on?

WestB: Because.

I growl in frustration. There's only one reason he would be trying to be nice to me right now.

McKennaK: I'm not going to your stupid football practice. Tell your coach I decline.

WestB: Did I say anything about that?

McKennaK: If it's not about that, what's in it for you?

I mean, he's a football player. They don't just do nice things for people.

WestB: What do you need training for?

I groan in frustration.

McKennaK: For diving. Football isn't the only sport Warner has, in case you didn't realize.

I sit there, waiting for a reply, but when a few minutes comes and goes, I go back to my mom's text to try to figure out how I'm going to word my response. I could lie... I'm technically not off the team, Coach just isn't going to let me dive...right now.

Like Sydney said, I can't wait for everyone else. I

have to show Coach how badly I want this. And so what if my mom thinks everything went back to normal? It will be, eventually.

I bite my lip. West's proposal keeps nudging at me. He isn't called the Hulk for nothing. It's tempting to let him help. I didn't know his major was exercise science, but it makes sense. You'd have to be an idiot to not see that he takes care of his body.

But he's just not an option. I'm sure I'll get other hits on my post on the bulletin board. If not, I can always go to a member of the exercise science faculty and have them recommend someone.

I shoot off a text to my mom telling her everything's good. I figure I can put her off for the first couple meets, but I'll have to get back in the dive rotation soon so she'll never know my spot on the team, or my scholarship, was in danger. As soon as I hit send, I get a response from West.

> WestB: Listen, you hate us. I get it. I don't need to be your friend. You don't even have to like me, but I'm offering you a good deal here. I know what I'm talking about.

The arrogance in his text makes my skin crawl. He's offering me a good deal? Please. Spending any amount of time with him would be torture.

I'll do it without him.

Instead of giving him the courtesy of a response, I

yell down the hall to Sydney during a break in her music. "You want to go for a run?"

A few moments later, her door opens. I can picture her now in her rolling chair, staring down the hallway toward my room. "Sorry, did you say run? I probably misunderstood."

I laugh. "No, I said run." I pause, waiting for a response. "A little cardio might help your lip sync routine," I offer, hoping to goad her into it. I never liked running, but it was always more fun with a friend. "Especially when you win and have to be on the stage in front of everyone at homecoming."

"I know you're just using my goals as an enticement, but I accept. Only because I love you. And because I want you back on the team. And because I think once you go with me, you'll never ask again."

I chuckle at that, but it turns out she was right. We only make it a couple of blocks before she's holding her side. I'm not the best runner by any means. Dive practice and competition season have always kept me in relatively good shape, but I'm feeling it now.

I'm just not feeling it as much as Sydney.

"Stop," she exhales, bending at the waist. "I'm going to die."

I don't need to tell her how few steps we've actually taken. If I look behind us, I can still see our cute fence in front of the house. When she glances over her shoulder, her body melts. "Seriously?" she gasps.

A laugh bubbles up my throat, and then I can't stop. I grab her shoulders for a hug. "You're a good friend. You can go back."

Standing straight, she throws her shoulders back. "No, I can do this." She jogs in place, her ponytail bouncing from one shoulder to the next. "I got this."

"Sweetie," I say, giving her a look.

She pouts, feet landing on the sidewalk once more. "Yeah, you're right. Chances are I'd only make it another couple of blocks." She grimaces. "But I don't want you to run on your own. Here." She pulls out a slim canister from her pocket that has a keychain attached to it. "Here's some mace. Do you have your phone in case you need to contact someone?"

I nod. She makes me give her all the details about where I'll be running and how long I'll be gone before she starts walking back home, promising to check in with me if I'm gone too long.

There's a trail only a couple blocks away, so I head there. Before I even make it to the start, my chest is straining, and I'm gulping in air. Maybe Coach had a point about my current state. But I bet I could get on top of a dive platform and nail it. I've been diving since middle school. It's in my blood.

It doesn't matter. I'll show her.

My running on the paved trail isn't pretty. I have to stop and walk a lot, and I'm mad I didn't bring music because I'd originally thought Sydney and I could run and talk, so it's just me, myself, and the commentary in my head about how weak I am right now and the reasons why I'm so out of shape. Replaying the last several months does me no good, but I can't stop. It always happens when my mind isn't preoccupied.

The first thing I remember about that night was being woken up out of bed with a loud bang, and then the purest burning sensation I'd ever felt on my right side.

Chaos ensued from there.

Images flick by, and I'm not even sure they're in the right order. When I first hear my name being called, I think it's from the memory, but then it comes again, louder and more clear. I turn to see West Brooks running toward me.

What in the...

"Are you stalking me now?" I shout, before turning around and continuing to jog. My heart slams in my chest, but I try to push it to get away from him. Of course, his stride eats up the distance between us in no time.

He settles into a cadence beside me, and I peek over. I'm a sweaty mess, but he's barely glistening. I try slowing down, and he stays with me. I speed up, and he's still by my side. We're coming up on the mile marker on the trail, designated by a wooden bench, so I stop.

When he does too, I glare at him. "No, we're not doing this."

"I'm not stalking you," he says, barely a hitch in his voice. His delivery is so monotone, like the epitome of casual indifference.

It's infuriating.

"Oh, we just happen to be running the same trail?" I challenge. "How did you even know I was out here?"

He shrugs, but when I keep my heated expression on him, he says, "A couple of players saw you turn down the trail and let me know."

"Oh, wonderful." I'm on *all* their radars now? This is a nightmare.

I get to my feet, my calves flaring in pain with the stretch of my muscles. I definitely shouldn't have taken that break. I need to push on.

"Don't run with me," I call out over my shoulder before taking off again.

He doesn't listen. His surprisingly light footsteps start off after me.

"I have mace," I throw back as he nears.

"Is that supposed to stop me?"

"Something has to," I snap.

"Just agree to let me help you."

Exasperation takes root. "Why?" I yell, spinning on him. He stops where he is, and we face off on the paved trail surrounded by trees.

He stares at the ground. For my own ego, I'm

happy to see that his forehead glistens with sweat. He brings his gaze up to meet mine finally. "I just want to help." The wind lifts his dark hair, and my stomach clenches.

His eyes are so open, so vulnerable in that moment that it stuns me to silence. It's not the reason I expected, which makes me want to lash out even more. "Because I'm deformed? Because you feel guilty about what happened to me?"

His jaw tenses, and suddenly, I know what it feels like to line up across the field from him. Fear spreads through me with a jolt.

"Fine." He peers away. "It's because I want to get you to practice." The vulnerability is on hiatus. He's back to his monotone words.

I knew it.

"You said you needed training for diving, so I'm going to guess that you haven't been able to work out lately. Maybe your coach said you needed to get back in shape?"

I blow out a breath, surprised he even thought that much about my circumstance at all. "I got a doctor's note that I can get back in the water and start practice again, but Coach took my synchro partner away and told me she's going to bench me this year because of my conditioning."

I don't even know why all of that comes out. It feels good to unload it somewhere though since I didn't tell my mom the truth earlier, and Sydney cares, but she's not much into sports.

Anger sweeps across his face, but it's only there for a split second before he returns to his normal noncommittal expression. "So, let's make a deal. I'll help you get back into shape. If I can get you back on that dive team this year, you come to practice with me. Only once. I don't care if you just show your face for a second."

My shoulders slump. It really is all about football for him, isn't it? I don't even know why his response makes me so disappointed.

On the other hand, one second of showing my face at a football practice could get me back on the dive team. That's...enticing. Right? Hell, I could even spend that time telling them I think they're a bunch of coddled bastards. He didn't say in what capacity I had to be there.

"I'll think about it," I tell him, but even I don't believe my own words. I'm in. I guess.

But all this is only proof of how desperate I really am to have everything back to normal.

When I turn to run again, he follows.

CHAPTER SIX

West

AIDAN PAUSES his video game when I walk in. He's leaned back in his desk chair, his left leg propped up on his bed. He scans me from head to toe, smirking. "So?"

I shrug. I really don't know what to think about the last couple of hours. Well, all day actually. When she jogged back to her place at the end of her run, me hot on her heels, she walked right up the walkway without looking back. I called out that I expected her to be in the weightlifting room at seven a.m. tomorrow, but she didn't respond.

She didn't...respond. That never happens to me.

I don't know where I stand with McKenna Knowles.

Aidan tilts his head. "You couldn't pull it off? You're West Brooks, dude."

I flip him off, then go to my closet to grab a towel. This will be my third shower of the day, but once again, my shirt is sticking to me with perspiration.

"Before you do that..." Aidan hedges.

The tone of his voice has me peering over my shoulder. He runs his hands through his hair. "Your mom called. She wants you to call her."

My teeth grind together. An avalanche of emotions hits me all at once. Love for my mom, of course, but at the same time, there's a hesitancy there, too. "You shouldn't have given her your number," I remind him.

"What kind of awesome roommate would I be if your family didn't have access to me?"

"Normal?"

"Just call her."

"Yeah, yeah." If my mom's calling instead of texting, something is up. Checking my phone, I see she tried to call me while I was jogging with Kenna. Well, jogging behind her while she ignored my existence.

I picture my mom all alone in that two-bedroom trailer, stressed out and chain smoking. It could be worse. She could be stressed out, chain smoking, and dealing with my father.

My stomach clenches as I walk back out of the room I share with Aidan in the athletic dorms. The long hallway is lined with doors on the left-hand side that lead to other athletes' rooms. On the right, though, is where I'm headed. Pushing the bathroom door open,

I can hear at least one shower running, so I let the door close and head to the lounge area instead. Luckily, no one else is in it, so I sit in an empty chair next to the small table and dial my mom.

The room smells like burnt toast. Don't get me wrong, it's cool they have a little kitchenette with a seating area on this floor, but it always smells like burnt food because college students are the worst cooks.

Mom answers after three rings. "West..."

It's not her panic voice, but it's not her just-checking-in voice either. "Hi, Mom. You can't keep calling Aidan," I say stiffly. "I was just out for a run."

"He told me."

"Okay..."

She takes a deep breath, and there's a waver in it. Instantly, I'm on high alert. I've watched this woman go through some shit, and I'm overly protective of her because of it. At the same time, I'm dealing with my own shit *because* of her, so it's this weird mix of responsibility and wanting to put distance between us.

"He called me."

My jaw snaps shut. *He* can only mean one person. My abusive, fucked-up sperm donor. I don't even like to use the word *father* because that would mean I'm actually related to him. That a part of him actually lives on in me, and I cannot deal with that.

The mere mention of him puts me right back in that tiny, dingy trailer. There wasn't enough room for all three of us with his anger acting as another entity, taking up all the available space.

My world closes in, vision blurring, heart pounding. I take a deep breath and hold it, releasing it slowly.

"He said he's tried to call you. He's blaming me for the fact that you're not calling him back."

When a number kept popping up on my phone, I wondered if it was him. The majority of people close to me understand I don't talk on the phone, so they don't even try. He wouldn't know that because we may be blood related, but we're far from close.

"Why are you answering his calls?" I shoot back.

"I didn't know it was him."

On the other end of the line, I hear the flick of her lighter, and then she inhales deeply before blowing out a breath. I can only imagine the toxic cloud adding to the years and years of nicotine and smoke already stuck to the grungy walls.

I want to ask her what she wants me to do about it, but I already know. She thinks if I talk to him, he'll get off her back, but this is what he does. He just wants to come back in so he can fuck things up some more and then leave us in shambles again.

"I'm not talking to him. Block the number," I tell her. "It's on you if you talk to him again."

"He's blaming me!" she scolds.

My heart pounds recklessly. It's as if I'm physically getting smaller and smaller. In my head, I'm in a closet with my fingers pressed into my ears so I won't hear them fighting.

"Mom..."

"West." Her voice comes out frantic, and I feel like I'm going to fucking explode.

I can't be her savior anymore. Sometimes I don't even think I can save myself.

Wave after wave of anger laps at me. My hands start shaking. My leg starts bobbing up and down. I can't stop it. It's like a tsunami that's about to over-power me. My fist closes around my phone so hard I'm worried I'll damage it.

Without saying a word, I pull the phone away from my ear and end the call.

I push the phone away and rest my head on the table. Closing my eyes, I breathe in that burnt toast in long, exaggerated breaths. My white-knuckled fists stay on either side of my head for minutes and minutes until they finally relax.

Relief pours over me then, and it's enough to knock me out of it completely.

I'm not him.

I'm not him.

When I've gotten myself under control, I grab my phone and my towel. Luckily, no one else is in the bathroom when I walk in, so I don't feel anxious about taking a long, scalding shower to help rinse the reminder of my past off me.

After walking on eggshells my whole life, even just going through the motions of living is hard. Am I going to get yelled at for taking all the hot water? Will he scream at me for using up all the shampoo? What if I take too long and don't realize he wants to get in the bathroom after me? Even breathing seemed to set him off, and I can't fucking shake it sometimes.

I don't know how long it's been when Aidan messages me.

You okay?

I turn off the water, towel dry, and shoot him a message telling him I'm fine.

One very, very fucked-up night when I was loaded and vulnerable as fuck, I spewed out all my shit to Aidan. I have to give him credit, he didn't shy away, and he's been nothing but a true friend since.

He's still playing video games when I stalk back to the room. He gives me a once-over, as if checking if I'm okay, but doesn't ask questions. Probably because he knows he won't get an answer.

He gets me, more than anyone else does.

Aidan offers to let me play, but I shake my head. There's an assignment for my lit class that I have to get done, but as I open up the book and start to read, my mind starts to wander.

McKenna Knowles.

I thought she was beautiful before Hamilton threw that firework into her dorm window, and that hasn't changed. Don't get me wrong, what happened was fucked up, but with her scar, she gets to show her past upfront. With me, everyone acts like I'm this all-American football player who was born with a silver spoon up his ass, but that couldn't be further from the truth. Everyone has a goddamn story. Some of ours are hidden underneath the surface, like mine. McKenna wears hers on her face, and there's something so fucking freeing and sexy about that.

I see her try to hide it all the time. First there were the bandages, then makeup. Now, she kind of just lets it out there for everyone to see, and I get this sort of thrill, hoping she's being true to herself and not caring what anyone else thinks.

I wish I was like that. Why the fuck can't I be like that?

But then I see her pull her hair over it, or turn her face when someone stares, and I wonder if maybe we're the same.

The reason why is so apparent to me, but I push thoughts of my father away. That's a one-way ticket to a descent into madness, and I've already played that game one too many times.

Aidan's video game makes a *ping* that sounds like a notification on my phone, so I end up peering at the screen. Nothing's there. Wishful thinking, maybe.

I push my book away. My earlier encounter with Kenna as myself left a bad taste in my mouth, but I know who she actually likes...

> NoOne: Hey, whatcha doing?

> McKennaK: You know me. Just living it up with my calc homework.

I scroll through where our last conversation ended and see my remark about the cherry.

> NoOne: I hope my cherry comment didn't freak you out.

My fingers fly across the on-screen keyboard, and it feels so good to put my thoughts out there, even if it is under anonymity. Aidan mostly gets the moody, doesn't-want-to-talk, athletically gifted Hulk, but Kenna, unknowingly, gets to see the real me. Or the me I wish I could be if I could just get my brain to understand that not everything has negative consequences like my past.

> McKennaK: Yeah, I kinda dropped the ball on that one. Sorry. Been dealing with some stuff today.

Stuff. That can only mean me, I'm sure. Part of me wants to pry and get her to say what she really thinks about me, but I'm pretty sure I already know. She is not impressed with West "the Hulk" Brooks.

> McKennaK: Question. It's a big one.

I worry my lip. Flexing my fingers, I ignore the hollow sensation in my chest. It feels a bit like she's about to ask if NoOne is West, and I'm scared as fuck to get found out. How would I even explain it?

> NoOne: I'm ready.

It's the only thing I can think to text, but the truth is, I'm not ready. This girl means more to me than she should, and that freaks me out. Everything I've ever enjoyed has been taken away from me. Even football for a time.

> McKennaK: You know who I am, right? I mean, it's no secret what happened. How come you've never asked to meet up?

> McKennaK: Or is that not what you want from this?

A pit opens up in my stomach. I just stare down at my screen, reading her words. I don't know what it's like to be Kenna, but I do know what it's like to go through something traumatic. Approaching her today must have brought back all the memories of what happened.

Her words remind me of why I first messaged her. I'd had to bribe a student worker from the tech department to make me a username that wasn't attached to me in any way whatsoever. Then I told him if he snitched I would kick his ass.

NoOne: The truth? I don't know.

It's a lie, but I've been lying to her, so what's one more? I knew if I approached her as myself after what happened that I'd never be able to say what I wanted to. So, I went about it this way, hiding under the guise of someone else, a secret pen pal. An admirer of sorts. Her parents had isolated her. She needed a friend. At least, that's what I'd told myself.

My phone *pings*, and I stare down at the screen in a panic.

McKennaK: Is it my scar?

My stomach doubles over, and I shoot a text as quick as I can.

NoOne: NO

My heart races. There's so much more I want to say. My brain tells me not to, but this is why I'm NoOne, right? I can say whatever I want without thinking.

> NoOne: I love your scar. That might sound weird, but…scars are like warpaint everyone can see. No one can doubt how badass you are.

My chest is heaving as I wait for her reply. Next to me, Aidan's shooting a pretend gun and throwing fake grenades, and this feels as life or death as that. I just lobbed the ball into her court, and now I have to sit back to see where I stand.

Seconds go by that feel like minutes. I start typing again…

> NoOne: …and being a badass is sexy as fuck.

After sending, I wait for her response, but it doesn't come. After half an hour, I end up turning over and falling asleep to the sounds of Aidan's video game.

I dream about loud bangs and sharp noises and my father's voice booming off the walls.

It makes me glad Kenna didn't write me back.

I don't fucking trust myself not to be like him.

CHAPTER SEVEN

Kenna

SCARS ARE *like warpaint everyone can see.*

Those words scroll through my mind as I walk to the weight room. This morning, while I put my hair up, I stared at my scar in the mirror and saw something I hadn't before.

Evidence of a survivor.

The scar represents that tragic moment, but it also goes beyond that, too. The surgeries. The pain. The recovery. The fact that I'm walking my ass to campus so early in the morning just so I can show everyone—especially a football player—that the incident didn't break me.

Being a badass is sexy as fuck.

I grin to myself, but as I walk into The Hub, it's not lost on me that West Brooks awaits me. He doesn't say things as beautiful as what NoOne said to me yesterday.

Actually, what am I talking about? He doesn't say anything at all.

This is going to be the most awkward workout ever. Last night, I wasn't even sure I would show up, but NoOne's texts convinced me. Turning West down would be shooting myself in the foot. I'll take what he's offering and use it to my advantage.

The overhead lights in The Hub flicker on as I walk underneath. Soon, the whole hallway is lit, and I stop in my tracks, frowning. A note on the weight room door says Reserved.

What the hell? Leave it to a football player to not realize they're not the center of the universe. The room is already reserved for someone else.

With a frustrated groan, I turn on my heel and almost walk straight into a wall of muscle...again.

West.

His commanding presence overwhelms me, making me feel small as I barely come up to his shoulders. Blinking up, I can't help but to take him in. The way his sleeveless tank shows off his shoulder muscles. His corded neck. The strong line of his jaw that gives way to his dark hair and enticing green eyes.

It's no wonder this guy has girls hanging around him all the time. I bet they don't even notice he doesn't talk.

His mouth moves, surprising me. "Where are you going?"

The sound of his voice does something to me again. I swallow. There must be a reason he doesn't use it very much. It's like an aphrodisiac, calling women from miles around.

Shaking off all those thoughts, I cross my arms. "The note says it's reserved."

"Yeah, I reserved it," he says simply, brushing past me. "For us."

Spinning, I watch as he walks toward the weight room and breezes past the sign. My eyebrows hitch into my hair.

Wait, what?

I take off after him, not letting the door close behind his formidable body. I catch it just in time and step inside. "Can you even do that?" I ask, voicing my initial concerns.

He shrugs, making me bite my lip. Frustration nips at me.

"It must be nice to be the popular man on campus," I snark as I drop my bag inside the room.

Out of the corner of my eye, I see his back stiffen. "I thought you'd be more comfortable if no one else was here. You know, so you wouldn't have to be seen with a dumb jock."

My muscles lock up. I guess it was a nice gesture. Not only because I don't want to be seen with him, but because I'm a little rusty and having people looking at me while I suck is not high on my to-do list.

The words taste sour, but I say them, anyway. "Thank you."

He peers over at me, dark shadows muting his eyes like he didn't sleep very well. They make me want to ask if he's okay, but he immediately nods and then bends to grab some papers from his bag, breaking the moment.

Walking over, he hands them to me. "I made you a training plan." I skim over the first page as surprise jolts through me. It's very detailed. Every workout for each day of the week, including weights and reps, plus cardio. He even has tiny notes on the side about good nutrition and percentages of protein vs carbs vs fats.

"You did all this?"

Without looking at him, I move to the next page. There are more schedules here. Trampoline. Pool time.

Now I'm truly flabbergasted. I just keep blinking at the pages. Surely West Brooks had no idea how divers trained before this...before me.

"Is there a problem?" he asks, concern etched in his eyes, as if he'd hate it if he'd missed something.

"How do you know about all this?"

"I Googled it yesterday."

"Yesterday? When you didn't even know if I would agree?"

He lifts his shoulders again, and I swear to God, that must be his go-to response for everything.

"If we can't get pool time here, we can ask at the town's rec center. Then there's that trampoline park on Route 3, just outside of town."

"You seriously Googled how divers train?" Astonished is the only word I can use to describe how I'm feeling right now, and I'm stuck on that one emotion. West Brooks is taking this seriously. I hadn't even thought as far ahead as his notes and calendars. I figured I'd talk to Coach and see about pool time, but I wasn't sure if I wanted to do that. Of course, I'll be attending regular practices, and— Holy shit! West even has those practices on the calendar already. What did he do? Sleep with one of my teammates to get the information?

Even as I think it, I scold myself. Our schedule is on the Warner University's Athletics page, just like everyone else's. Football, basketball, baseball, wrestling, swimming, diving. Warner has a great athletics website, and someone on the social media team keeps the socials updated as well.

"I looked up videos of you diving, too. You're good."

Those words hang in the air like precipitation on muggy summer nights. Turning toward him, I half smirk. "How would you know?"

He presses his lips together, but his face brightens,

like he's trying to hold back a smile. "It looks hard, and you did it, so you must be good."

How in the world is this happening right now? I'm having an actual conversation with West Brooks, Warner University's golden boy.

We stare at each other for a beat too long before West peers away. "Let's get to work."

...*And that was short-lived.* His abruptness nearly makes me laugh.

But that's short-lived as well. West kicks my ass in the weight room. It isn't long before sweat is pouring down my face and I'm demoralized. Coach was right. I am weak. I hadn't realized what being sidelined would do to the built-up muscle from years of training.

"You're doing good," he states as I rack the barbell with frustration after a failed squat. I didn't get all the way down, my form was terrible, and worse yet, I'm no longer surprised Coach benched me and recruited another partner for Laney. I mean, I still hate it, I'm just not surprised.

While I was recovering, the world kept turning. I'm the only one who stood still. Who got held back.

"Another," I demand.

"You've done enough for today," West reassures. "You don't want to overdo it."

"Are you saying I'm weak?"

He turns his head toward me, sizing me up. I'm fully aware I'm picking a fight, but I'm just so damn pissed at myself. "The opposite, actually." He stands to his full height. "I see the same competitiveness in you that's in me, and I know damn well I can overdo it sometimes. It'll only set you back in the long run."

He turns his back, and I don't listen. I get under the barbell again, ducking my head to rest it on my shoulders. I press up—but it doesn't go anywhere.

"Kenna..."

Fuck me. My legs tremble. His voice, his fucking real voice. Not the one where he's barking out orders or the way he perfectly crafts his sentences before he even says anything, I'm talking about his raw voice.

"Trust me."

I groan in frustration and push away. Spinning, I find his hand on the barbell. That's all he had to do to keep me from picking it up. The guy is a beast.

He eyes me, and it's as if I can see him compiling what he wants to say before he says it. He does that a lot. So, now he actually talks, but everything is calculated and measured. Like he's thinking about every consequence of his words before they even leave his mouth.

"I know you're mad. I would be, too. But you're going to come back from this. You're not going to get there in a day, but you will."

"How long?" I say, hands on my hips, breathing heavy. Right now, there's nothing I want more than to throw it in their faces. Yeah, I was held back, but I didn't quit. That's not who I am.

As usual, it takes him a long time to answer. "The good news is you have a solid base. Your muscles know what to do, you just have to get them back."

"But how long?" I insist.

I miss just being able to do things. Maybe I could step up to the platform right now and dive. However, if the fatigue I'm feeling at this moment means anything, I'd probably drown.

West doesn't answer. He goes back to his bag, taking the training schedules he made for me with him. He folds them carefully and then tosses them in before zipping it up. Even though he's dressed for working out, he didn't do a damn thing. He watched, he tweaked, he pumped me up, and my gut tells me I wouldn't have done this well if he wasn't in this room with me.

Standing, he turns toward me. "You should talk to your partner about pool times. Let me know and I'll put it on the calendar."

My stomach clenches. I didn't tell him I no longer have a partner. I don't know what getting back on the rotation will mean for me. Another partner? Will I get Laney back? Do I even want Laney back? Or maybe I'll switch to singles?

"You don't have to worry about that. I don't have a partner."

He narrows his gaze. I avoid him by going to my bag and grabbing my water bottle before taking a big gulp. Yanking my shirt up, I wipe the sweat from my face, pointedly avoiding him.

"Your coach partnered her with someone else, didn't she?"

I bite the fabric of my shirt momentarily and then let it go, tugging it down to around my hips again. "Yes."

"Okay."

I zip my bag and hike it up around my shoulders before spinning with my water bottle in my hands. He says *okay* like it's nothing. "She's been my partner for years. We were so in sync."

"Where is she now?"

"With—"

"If she's not here," he interrupts, "she's not important. So you don't have a partner. Do you want another one?"

Taking a page out of his book, I shrug. I've been a synchro diver for so long, it never really occurred to me to dive by myself. But now that it's in front of me, there's no reason I couldn't do it. Also, it takes a lot of practice to get in tune with someone else. At this point, I'm probably better off trying to go it on my own.

I shake my head, and he nods like that settles the conversation.

He walks past me, his bag in tow. Opening the weight room door, he holds it for me as I scoot past.

"Come to the cafeteria with me," he orders before I can walk away without him. "I'll show you what to eat after a workout."

I stop in my tracks. I would never go to the cafeteria after a workout. I'm a mess. Sweaty. My hair is probably a tangled nest, and my scar is most likely bright red from exertion. Plus, there's this whole thing about eating with him. Right there in front of people. It's like I'll be holding up a billboard saying what they did was okay.

He strides past, his tree-trunk legs eating up the distance in the hallway. I'm pretty sure I see the hint of a scowl forming. "At least go through the line with me."

I stare at his strong back as he retreats. Was that disappointment I heard?

Interesting.

CHAPTER EIGHT

West

DIVE INTO THE ABYSS...

I didn't even know Kenna had a tattoo, then there it was when she turned to squat, peeking out below the barbell as it sat across her shoulders.

I don't know what it means to her, but I like it. There's something about the word *abyss*, like a gaping, mysterious hole. The idea of diving into something like that is terrifying and exhilarating.

She could've just had the sentiment written out in pretty handwriting, but it's not. The words "Dive into" are rounded and then drop off, like the trail someone would take while diving. Then "the" is just under the *o* in "into," while "abyss" is shaped like a gaping chasm, the *y* scooping to the bottom. It has to be a diving reference. Or at least partially a diving reference.

I press my lips together as I make my way to the cafeteria, hearing her soft footsteps behind me. I wonder how long she'll stay there, and if she'll even do as I asked. If she even should do as I asked. All I know is that I wanted to keep being around her, so instead of asking her to breakfast, I told her I'd show her what to eat like she's a toddler.

She probably won't come with me.

To my surprise, she does. She follows me into the line and puts on her plate what I put on mine without me having to say anything.

My mouth feels dry. I talked a lot more this morning than I usually do, and the interaction is leaving me spent. I'm tired of thinking about what to say and analyzing it to death to see what the ramifications of every word are, a habit I had to pick up when I was a kid because I never knew when some innocuous thing I said would set my dad off.

When I was five, I announced I had to go to the bathroom while we were sitting down as a family to watch TV, and my father berated me for half an hour until I peed my pants in the living room, and then I had to sit through another hour of his tirade until my piss turned cold and stuck to my skinny legs. Afterward, my mother wordlessly put me in a bath, and I stayed there until my fingers looked like I was eighty years old and I was shivering from the water having long gone cold.

I'm still in my own head when I stride to the football table. Aidan's there as well as a few of the other guys. Cade Farmer, a super senior. Plus, Colt and Zo. When I sit, Aidan glances behind me, and his eyes immediately widen. I turn to see what he's looking at when Kenna comes into view. Shit, she absolutely did follow me.

My chest constricts. I want her to sit with us. I want to be normal for her, but I'm not quite sure what to say. She's not like a jersey chaser. She won't let me get away with just being the Hulk and not having to work for anything.

Aidan jumps in. Sometimes, I swear it's as if he can read my fucking mind. "Kenna, what's up?" He nods at the open seat next to the one I was going to take.

She hesitates. Peering down the table, her gaze stops on all of the guys. They all stare back at her, some of them inclining their head. Cade smirks because that's just who he is. He loves women.

Aiden pauses after seeing her waver. He holds up his hands. "*Mc*Kenna, I mean. We're not friends. I remember." The bastard can't help but be charming.

He disarms her though. Her shoulders relax, and she lifts her gaze to mine.

"Please?" I ask.

She bites her lower lip. The flyaways framing her face have curled out in this cute way, and her skin glows from the workout.

"I don't actually like you guys," she says, as if she can't even believe she's standing next to our table.

Cade bursts out laughing. "Not like us? That's impossible."

Aidan shoots him a look before I can.

I realize I've mostly been calling her Kenna in my head, and she didn't call me out for calling her by her nickname when we were in the weight room just now. It's easy to fall into easiness with her because I know her. I've been talking to her for months as NoOne. We've developed a relationship that she knows nothing about, but I do.

"Are we sitting here?" a female voice interrupts my thoughts. "Cool."

The girl Kenna always sits with approaches our table. She stands next to Aidan, motioning for him to move to the next seat down. He scoots over, his brows pinched, making two of the other guys move down as well.

Kenna groans, sending her friend a look that she promptly ignores. After the girl is already settled in the seat next to Aidan, Kenna sighs and sits. I have to fold my large body, making sure I don't graze her while I take the spot next to her.

"I'm Sydney," the newcomer says. "Kenna's roommate."

She's bubbly and has dark hair that lands past her shoulders.

"So you can call her Kenna?" Aidan points out. He's clearly not going to let this go.

"Duh," her roommate responds.

I watch as Aidan appraises her, his lips twitching like he can't wait to have fun with this one. "Well, since we're all sitting together all nice and cozy, that means we're all friends, right?" He shifts his gaze to my right. "I can call you Kenna then?"

Kenna shifts in her seat. Sydney notices her discomfort and speaks up. "It means you're getting warmer, but not warm enough, Football Boy." She turns her full attention toward her friend. "How was the training this morning?" She peeks at me before sliding her gaze back to her friend. She looks hopeful, brows raised.

"Training?" Zo asks, then it seems to dawn on him. "You fucker." He throws a ketchup packet at me. "I went to work out this morning, but the weight room was signed out."

"And it will be until further notice." I glower at him, sliding the packet off my tray with my pinkie. They can find another time to work out until Kenna feels comfortable having other people around.

When I dig into my oatmeal, I sense her stare on me. Out of the corner of my eye, I see her watch me intently with a curious expression on her face. My stomach knots.

"I think I see a muscle already," Sydney jokes, pushing her finger into Kenna's bicep.

Kenna actually laughs, relieving the tension inside me a little. "I think that's a shadow."

"She did good," I remark. My words quiet the table, and I have to stifle the embarrassment that creeps up. I'm West Brooks. I don't get embarrassed. I mow defenders over on the field. I growl in their faces and force them to the turf, all while barely breaking a sweat.

But McKenna Knowles unnerves me.

Aidan leans back, narrowing his gaze at me. To my left, the other players start talking amongst each other, but Aidan keeps staring at me quizzically. Sydney and Kenna start talking about the Lip Sync Contest, and soon, Aidan joins their conversation, suggesting songs for Sydney, which she either immediately denies or tilts her head to think about. Some of his suggestions make them laugh.

I envy my friend. He talks so easily. Just when I get up the courage to say something, they're already on a different song or a different topic altogether.

My head hurts. I'm emotionally exhausted and furious with myself.

The reason why I'm so good at tackling people on the field is because there are rules. Run this play. Run that play. Block this person or wait for the handoff and run as many people over as I can on my way to the end zone.

Sitting next to Kenna is dark and scary, yet thrilling at the same time.

Like diving into the abyss...

"You guys should come to the contest," Sydney says, smiling. In the next second, she flinches. "Ow." She glares daggers at Kenna, who scowls right back at her. "I mean, wow"—she peers down at her naked wrist where a watch should be—"I should probably get to class."

Aidan snickers. "Thanks, I'd love to come. The Hulk and I will be there."

"What's this?" Cade asks, always all ears when it's something social.

Aidan nods toward Sydney. "She's going to be in the Lip Sync Contest. I said we're going."

"Sweet." Cade grins. "Sounds like fun. What song are you doing?"

That prompts Sydney and Cade to have a conversation over Aidan. Kenna falls silent, and I peek over to find that she's only eaten the bacon and the fruit she placed on her plate. A spoon still sits in her oatmeal. "You don't like it?"

"Huh? Oh," she says, following my gaze. "It's okay."

I get up, leaving all of the talking behind me, and head back to the food line. People say hi to me as I pass, and I give them my normal bro nod. I grab some honey and put it in a little dish for Kenna before walking it back over.

Placing it next to her, I say, "Try this. It should sweeten it up."

She pours it over top of her oatmeal and then stirs it briefly. Before scooping a spoonful in her mouth, though, she closes her eyes. They stay shut while she chews a few times. "That's better." She turns toward me with a small smile. "I've never been a big fan of oatmeal."

"You can put fruit in it, too. Bananas. Blueberries."

"Can I keep the honey?"

Jesus. She can do whatever she wants.

She's taken her hair out of its ponytail and is running her fingers through it. It's wild around her full lips and high cheekbones, the color nearly matching the honey I've just given her.

I can't help but take the rest of her in as I watch her movements, mesmerized. She may have a slight frame, but I saw pops of muscles come out when she was lifting. Lean with nice, long legs, she's full in all the right areas.

My breathing slows. A few times in the weight room, my hands had brushed hers, and electric shocks shot straight to my toes.

Shit. I might be obsessed with this girl. The cruel

part is I don't even know what to do about it. I'm...inept in everything except football.

She lifts her brows, and I realize I haven't responded to what she's said. "Yeah." I shake my head, as if to knock me out of the spell she's put me under. "You can keep the honey." My gaze drifts to the neckline of her shirt that's shifted low, showing off her cleavage. Her whipped cream comment flits through my mind, and I swear to God, she'd look amazing in a whipped-cream bikini. Two cherries where her nipples should be.

Damn...

A swift kick hits me under the table, and I immediately straighten and turn to find Aidan glaring at me with wide eyes.

Shit. I don't know how long I was staring at her. Long enough to make it awkward, I'm sure.

Kenna stands. "I need to shower and get to class."

Sydney follows right after. "Same. See you guys later."

Kenna doesn't say goodbye, and the two of them walk their trays to the alcove. Once they're out of sight, I stand, too, feeling stupid. Aidan falls into stride next to me after I place my tray with the other dirty ones.

"Dude, way to make it weird." He smiles to soften the jibe, but he could hand me a trophy while saying it and it would still hit hard.

"I don't know what the fuck I'm doing," I admit.

"You like her?"

I shrug, which is as good as saying yes.

"You couldn't have picked someone easier?" He shakes his head, that quintessential bite of sarcasm that's uniquely his dripping from his words. "Just be yourself."

What if I don't know what that is? I've been trying to be someone else most of my life. I wanted to be the kid that didn't make Dad yell. I tiptoed around the house like I wasn't even there because I never knew when I was going to step on a landmine.

Who the fuck am I?

The football part of me, that's easy. I'm West "the Hulk" Brooks. I know how to be that person.

But who am I off the field?

Am I really this quiet, introspective guy? Maybe I should talk more? My stomach clenches. Maybe I should talk less?

"It's useless," I say aloud.

Aidan pulls on the back of my shirt until I stop. Someone calls out his name, and he turns to high-five a passerby before spinning back to me with a serious face. "This is going to sound like those cheesy as fuck self-talk podcasts Coach asks us to listen to, but you need to be yourself. If she doesn't like you for you, then that's on her. Not you. Once you fake it, you have to keep up that façade for the rest of your life, and it's goddamn tiring, dude. So, if you're the sulking Big Man who only talks some of the time, cool. That's you. She either wants to jump on that dick or not."

"You've been hanging around Cade too much."

He grins. "At least he talks."

I punch him in the shoulder. "Fuck off."

He throws his arm around me, and we start walking down the hall together. "She's cute, man," he tells me. "You should scoop her up before someone else on the team decides to."

"I think she's self-conscious about her scar."

He grips my shoulder. "Probably. But is it me or does it look a little badass?"

That's what I said, I think. Aloud, I just grunt, causing him to snicker.

"I'll put the word out on the team that McKenna Knowles is yours."

It feels a little caveman, but I agree to it. Well, I stay silent, which means I agree to it.

Teammates don't fuck with another player's girl. It's Football 101.

CHAPTER NINE

Kenna

"CLEARLY, you're changing your mind about football players," Sydney states with a laugh.

I give her a look. *The* look. Even though, deep down inside, I know she's right. Framed by the forest, she stares back at me as if challenging me to deny it. If I'd known she was going to tease me about West again, I wouldn't have agreed to go on a walk with her.

The Loop Trail circles the entire campus, starting and ending at the main entrance to the university. We've only just started and I'm already thinking about nopeing out of this.

"You've been training with him for two weeks now. We eat breakfast with *them* every morning." Her thought lingers in the air with no follow-up. She's trying to drive the point home, as if I don't already see it.

My stomach churns as I think about the last couple of weeks. We did start eating with them after training, and I don't know how to feel about it. It made sense at first so West could look at what I was eating, but...we just didn't stop. It's our pattern now. It's expected. Of course, it doesn't help that Sydney sits there waiting with the rest of the team, even when West and I are late getting out of training.

When I don't say anything, she continues, "You should see the way he looks at you. Girl," she breathes almost excitedly. She's got a bounce in her step, and suddenly, I feel like I'm in an intervention where everyone attending is looking out for my best interests.

My skin tingles when I think of him.

West Brooks...

I can't deny that there's something there. An attraction at the very least. But then my mind hits a brick wall, slamming down from out of nowhere. "He never talks," I point out.

"Who needs him to talk?" she says with clenched fists. I'm not sure what she's doing with her hands exactly, but she's talking animatedly. "He goes with you to Jump Zone. He's signed out the weight room for you guys every morning, and you told me he showed up at your dive practice."

"He only stayed a few minutes," I remind her. My mind is telling me to deny, deny, deny.

"Because he had to get to his own practice," she insists. "Damn. I've dated guys for six months who never did that much for me."

"Yeah, he's really trying to get me to his practice," I state, but it feels hollow. I'm not exactly sure what West is doing, but he hasn't mentioned our pact since we started training together. In fact, we haven't talked about him much at all. It's always about me, training, and diving. Even then, there's not *much* talking. Maybe a "one more rep" or "how does that weight feel?", but his training notes are so good that there's really no reason to discuss things.

Sydney huffs. "I'm trying to decide if you're being intentionally blind, or if your hatred for the team runs so deep that you can't even see what's right in front of you."

I look straight ahead, peering at the spot where the concrete trail curves toward the trees. After sitting with the team at breakfast and watching them interact, it's hard to make them fit into the box I'd labeled for them. Yeah, they're horndogs, but what college guys aren't? The truth is, they talk about football like I talk about diving. They're competitors who love the sport, and the only time West really gets animated is when he's talking about the game, even if it is only in three-word sentences. It's as if a light ignites inside him.

"Both," I eventually tell her. Being obtuse seems like the smart path to take right now. I've felt West stare at me. I've even seen him check me out, most notably that first day at breakfast when he was staring at my breasts and I had to turn away because my nipples were turning into traitorous pebbles.

Worse yet, I can feel my reaction to him all the time. I like it when he looks at me...and that feels like a problem.

"I just don't see West Brooks being a bad guy," Sydney remarks.

"Well, his mouth won't ever get him in trouble, that's for sure."

She snickers and elbows me in the side. "That means it can be put to better use."

I cackle. "We've been sitting at their table for too long. You're starting to sound like that one senior."

"Cade Farmer," she sighs, her voice taking on a dream-like quality. "Freaking hottie. Of course, they all are."

"Cade? Really? I thought you were into Aidan?"

She shrugs like it doesn't matter, then she's quiet a while as we walk. The sun is setting, and the sky has a pink haze to it on the horizon. It's super pretty, and I'm about to point it out to Sydney when a harsh whistle cuts through the air.

Turning toward the sound, I stop in my tracks. We've wandered toward the practice field, and the football team is currently lined up. Fuck. Why is it that all roads lead to Warner football lately? It's like a bad penny.

"Oh shit," Sydney says as she stops next to me. "I didn't know they'd be practicing out here. Of course, the first game is in a couple of days, so it makes sense."

We literally can't go anywhere on campus without the start of the football season being thrown in our faces. It's spirit week, and the halls of every building on campus are decked out in royal blue and white. Streamers and banners and life-size posters of the starting lineup. In West's, he's holding his helmet in his hands, straight in front of his midsection, his knuckles white as he glares into the camera lens. Two black stripes under his eyes complete the look, and even thinking about it gives me chills. He's a complete badass.

Despite his size, he doesn't give off that vibe in real life. He's kind of like a mute teddy bear. I have a feeling if he ever did get heated, he'd turn those wild eyes on his target, though. Lord help the other person if he did.

Giggles sound, and my stare moves up to the metal fence. A few girls stand there to watch practice, clinging to the chain-link. Coach blows the whistle again, and I can just see where the lined-up players connect in a cacophony of pads hitting pads and helmets hitting helmets. The girls gasp, then fawn over them.

"He really is the Hulk." A petite blonde-headed girl turns toward her friend. "Don't you think?"

Jealousy ping-pongs around my insides until I push it away. I have no reason to be jealous if another girl thinks West is hot. He is.

"We should go watch," Sydney offers after eyeing me.

I gesture toward the fence with a sneer. "Like them?" There's no way I'm going to act like a Warner Bulldog jersey chaser. I just can't. I'm morally opposed.

"Of course not. We can hide and watch."

I shake my head. "For what?"

"So you can watch West. Don't tell me you haven't thought about his ass in those football...pants. Or whatever they're called."

I tug on the sleeve of her shirt as she starts to walk up the little knoll toward the practice field. Where we are, they won't be able to see us easily, and that's how I'd like to keep it. "Come on. We're not going to watch them. That's weird and creepy, and you sound like a stalker."

One of the girls at the gate squeals when a player gets laid out on the turf, and I peer over at Sydney with an *I told you so* stare.

She grimaces. "Yeah, okay. You're right."

We start forward again, but I'm preoccupied with

what's happening on the practice field. West walks into view. He's easy to pick out because he's practically behemoth-size.

The royal-blue-and-white practice uniform is cut in such a way that it shows off his tapered waist, tree-trunk legs, and wide shoulders. He's holding on to his helmet in his right hand, the sweat dripping off his face getting caught in the edges of his hair. Tilting his head back, he squeezes water into his mouth from a green and orange Gatorade bottle, and pours some on his face. Then, I swear to God, he shakes his hair out like he's in a shampoo commercial, and instead of it looking cheesy as fuck, he's drop-dead gorgeous.

He's. A. Specimen.

My foot catches, and I fly forward, almost hitting the pavement face first. Cheeks flaming, I glare back at the smooth, flat sidewalk. Surely, there was just a rock there or *some* culprit that took me down. It isn't because I was too preoccupied watching the god-like football player.

Sydney steadies me, holding back a laugh. "Break your neck why don't you. I knew there was something there. I knew it."

"Okay, so he's hot as fuck. There are plenty of guys that are hot."

"Yeah, celebrities, maybe. How many celebrities have you ever met?" She stares up at the field and shakes her head. "You know how they say everyone goes to Florida to die since it's, like, the retiree capital of the world? I swear all the sexy football players go to Warner."

Life isn't fair, I think, because I know exactly what she's talking about. I don't know where the football coach got all these players from, but they are all freaking ballin'...and West Brooks is... Shit, he's jaw-droppingly handsome. The kind of guy you want to jump on because a ride on that might make a girl's life.

"Come on," I tell Sydney, shaking my thoughts off. I can't keep thinking about these things because I have to work in close proximity with him nearly every day, and I don't want to make it weirder than it already is. Taking off, I start speed walking, hoping to clear the practice field sooner rather than later.

I'm a girl on a mission because I don't even hear my name being called until Sydney yanks back on my arm and points toward the field. It's not West—West doesn't shout names—but it is Aidan.

Shit, shit, shit.

We weren't fast enough. I keep trying to speed ahead, and Sydney sighs. "Girl, I don't know what you're doing, but that boy is calling my name, too, and I am here. For. It." She punctuates each word, and when I turn, she's not even looking at me, she's staring off toward the field where Aidan is jogging our way in all of his football glory. His sweaty hair bounces off his head, and he moves in just a way that I spot West behind him.

My heart flips in my chest. It's so fucking cliché. He's not running, he's just striding across the field in our direction, that look of stony determination in his eyes that I'm all too familiar with now.

My body electrifies, the skin on my arms practically buzzing. I've never had this reaction to a guy before. It feels like my first kiss. That moment just before when expectation hangs around you.

That's how I view West Brooks.

An expectation.

He holds my gaze the entire time it takes him to cross the green grass that's littered with the occasional fallen leaf. When he gets near us, my mouth goes dry. I've never been this close to a football player in his jersey, and I have to say, it's...something. The pads only accentuate his build.

"Spying on us?" Aidan grins as he slows to a stop.

"We were just walking," I spew out, my stare still on the giant closing in on me. I take a deep breath to steady myself.

"I mean, I was spying," Sydney says, in full-on flirt mode. "Kenna wanted nothing to do with it."

"Aw, you're going to hurt the Big Man's feelings," Aidan teases, the corners of his mouth tipping up. "Please don't do that. It always sucks for me." He chuckles, rotating his shoulder as if he'd been hit hard today.

West finally gets to us. He eyes his friend. "You could've gotten away from the tackle. You've gotten lazy."

"Who needs to be active in the pocket when I got you?"

Some of these words don't compute, but my attention keeps being drawn to West's lips, then down to his stubborn chin.

"What are you ladies doing in a little bit?" Aidan asks. "Once we take showers, a few of the guys are heading to the ice cream shop in town."

"I'm always down for some ice cream," Sydney says, peering over at me with wide, begging eyes.

Suddenly, I can feel everyone's gazes on me, and I squirm. I don't know what to do. Follow this attraction to West to see where it leads? I can't imagine anything good will come from it, and I'm not even sure if he—

"You should come," West states. He closes his eyes briefly, his lashes fanning down.

Dear God.

"I don't know," I tease. "Am I allowed to have ice cream?"

I bite my lip. My words came out all breathy and... well, flirty. Fuck, I'm flirting with West Brooks. How did I get into this mess? My body is a traitor, and it's sending the wrong kind of signals right between my legs.

"Rewards are always good," he muses.

Sydney claps her hands. "Good, I hope they have delicious dick."

I peer over at her, my mouth open, but everyone else is making plans, and it takes me entirely too long to realize she said "I hope they have delicious *dip*."

Dip. She wants dipped ice cream, for crying out loud.

Jesus. I must have dick on the brain.

CHAPTER TEN

West

JERSEY CHASERS HAVE FOLLOWED us to Scoops. They sandwich me into the interior of a booth, and my only consolation is that I get to look at Kenna the whole time, which is why I know she's hating every moment of being here. She gets flavored hard ice cream and stirs it with her spoon until it gets soupy, hardly even looking up.

At one point, she reaches for her phone, and I see her type something out. Kenna and NoOne are still talking. Kenna and West don't talk very much at all, so when my phone *pings*, I hesitate to bring it out in case she's messaged NoOne—except, I'm not logged into that account right now. I'm logged into my own.

I peer down and smile. Kenna has actually messaged *me*.

> **McKennaK:** Do you think they notice you don't talk?

My stomach tightens. The jersey chasers are pressed against me from all sides like I'm a quarterback in the middle of a collapsing O-line, and she's right. I haven't said one word to them, even though they talk to me as if I'm responding.

I peek up at her, and she's grinning. She'd pulled her hair over her scar as soon as the other girls sat with us, and it's still lying that way now. I wish she hadn't. I wish she'd let it out like she couldn't care less what they think, but I'm well aware that some of these girls can be bitches. Especially when they think they're in a competition for attention.

If they only knew. There is no competition when it comes to Kenna.

I type out an answer on my phone.

> **WestB:** No

After I hit Send, I berate myself for it. I can't just unclench when I'm West. The few things I have said to her in person sound foreign, like I'm wobbling on toddler legs every time I attempt to talk to her like a normal human being.

> McKennaK: It's weird, don't you think?

> WestB: Very.

She stares at her phone with a frown, and I panic. I'm completely uninteresting. I want so badly to be the guy who puts a smile on her face—hell, even a scowl. I'd be happy with any emotion right about now.

Being the guy that bores you to death is the worst.

Quickly, I type out:

> WestB: I might have to enlarge the doorway to our dorm if Aidan's head gets any bigger.

She reads the message and glances up at me. I nod toward Aidan, who's also wedged between two jersey chasers and Sydney, who's practically leaning across one of them so she can keep him engaged in conversation.

> McKennaK: lol Just watching him is exhausting.

> McKennaK: So, how do you do it? Do you use the whole sock on the doorknob trick when one of you is hooking up?

I read the message and look up at her again. She's biting her lower lip, smiling at the screen. She's moved her hair behind her ear, and I'm trying to decide if this is a test or not. How much should I tell her?

Before I can think of an answer, a gasp rings out, and the girl to my right cries out, "Oh my God, what happened to you?"

My heart pounds. I'm going to be sick.

For a moment, Kenna doesn't know the girl is talking to her. She's still staring down at her phone, but when the table goes quiet, she finally peers up, her face in the initial stages of blushing.

The girl points to the side of her face, indicating Kenna's scar.

How can this girl be so fucking oblivious? It's like the time I had to stay with my grandparents for a little while when shit got bad. I came down the stairs with a huge zit in the middle of my forehead, and my grandfather exclaimed, "What the hell is that?" as if he'd never seen a red dot on a pubescent boy's face before.

My mind races. Kenna's eyes begin to water, but her face doesn't look like she's about to burst into tears. It gets hard. It gets weary, and it reminds me so much of an expression my mom wears so often now. She's tired and pissed all the time.

All the damn time.

"You got it from wrestling a tiger, right?" I ask, staring at Kenna. She moves her gaze to me, and I will her to keep it there. It's like I tell her in the gym: focus. It's just you and the weights, nothing else.

Right now, it's just me and her.

I stare so hard it feels like I'm reaching across the table and holding her cheeks, making her stay here with me.

I can see the moment she relaxes, and it's like a gasp of much-needed oxygen for me. A breath just seconds before oblivion. She holds my gaze like a good girl. "Actually, it was a jaguar."

"Bitch, you told me it was a black bear," Sydney says, elbowing her friend. Then, she peers over at the dumb girl next to me. "And if you want to see someone go all Mama Bear, keep spouting nonsense and watch where that gets you."

"What?" the girl asks, indignant, pulling her shoulders back. "I was just wondering."

"Oh, really? How did you get to be so tactless? I was just wondering," Sydney mimics with the girl's same inflection.

The girl huffs before turning toward me. "I don't know what the big deal is. Do you want to go somewhere else?"

I don't look at her. Frankly, I'm pissed I have to put up with this nonsense when all I really wanted to do was spend time with Kenna outside of training. "Actually, I was just about to ask Kenna if I could walk her home."

I wasn't. I would never...except the words just fell out when I opened my mouth. They were already being heard by the entire table before I could turn them over in my mind again and again, searching for the repercussions. Once they're out there, though, I can't take them back.

Panic engulfs me. She could turn me down in front of everybody.

"Yeah," Kenna squeaks out, gaze locked on mine. "Yeah, let's go."

The girl next to me stares, dumbfounded. I start to scoot the opposite way and make two girls and two players stand just so I can get out and meet Kenna without having to go anywhere near the other girl. When I unfold to my full height, we immediately walk away. I open the door for her, and she leads me to the parking lot before stopping next to Sydney's car and spinning toward me.

"Thanks for getting me out of there. I can wait here for Sydney to be done."

My newly acquired confidence takes a hit. "Oh, you don't want me to walk you home?"

"You were serious?" she asks, tilting her head, staring at me.

I want to wash that uncertain expression off her face. I would kill to have Aidan's talking skills right now. Or, hell, any of the guys'. I nod, gesturing toward the sidewalk. The good thing about Warner is that it's relatively small. The town is pretty upscale. The street-lights are bright, and the parks and roadways are well-manicured. It's clear that the people of Warner have pride in their city.

It's a far cry from the trailer park I grew up in with the broken chain-link fence around our small piece of land that's mostly dirt with the occasional weed here and there. Even better is that you don't hear the sounds of poverty all around you. Wailing kids and screaming adults. Everyone fed up with their circumstances, yet stuck with no way out.

Except...I found a way out.

We've walked two blocks when Kenna finally breaks the silence. "I can't tell if you're trying to be mysterious, or if this is just how you are."

I chuckle. "It's how I am, unfortunately."

"Yeah?" she asks as if she doesn't quite believe me. "But you turn into a dick on the football field?"

"I let my actions on the field speak for themselves." There are guys on the team who talk endless shit. Your Mama jokes and anything to hype themselves up. Those kinds of players get under my skin, but I never talk back. I just make sure to get a hell of a tackle on them play after play so they remember my face and they know they don't want the Hulk coming after them next time.

"Huh," she says, looking away.

"That surprises you?"

She grins. "Yeah, a little. I mean, you're one of the best players on the team. You—"

I know where this is going... "Get away with every-thing because we're Warner's pride and joy?"

"Yep."

"I don't know," I tell her honestly. I hate the stereo-type, and I hate even more that there's some truth to it. "I just want to play football."

Football means never having to go back to that trailer, and it means a life of forgetting my dad. I want to be so big he can't touch me. I want to move my mom somewhere else and get her all set up so she's not tempted to fall back into old habits.

Above all, I've just wanted some semblance of peace.

That's what I'm focused on.

A hundred things rise to the surface to say to Kenna, but they stay inside, like I've chained each and every sentence up. It's like I'm walking around with a muzzle on my face, constantly battling those inner thoughts to keep quiet.

Don't rock the boat.

To be silent is to be safe.

Fireflies blip in and out in front of houses we walk past, and there's a slight chill in the air. Next to me, Kenna wraps her arms around herself, so I shrug off my zippered sweatshirt and offer it to her.

"I'm fine," she says, but I don't take her word for it. I let her walk in front of me before I place it around her shoulders. She eyes me when I move back alongside her.

My sweatshirt dwarfs her. All I can see of the Bulldog logo is the side of its face before it gets lost in the extra folds.

"Am I changing your mind about football players?" My own, sure voice startles me.

"Are you trying to?"

I shrug. "Maybe I don't give a fuck about the rest of the team. Maybe I'm just trying to change your mind about me."

She eyes me. "It might be working."

Stopping in front of her place, she rests her hand on the white picket fence. I jam my hands in my pockets and try to come up with something else to say to keep her out here longer.

"Are you ready for your first game?" she asks.

There's nothing I'm more sure of than football. "Always."

"I hope I'm not interfering with your own workout schedule."

"You're not trying to back out of our deal, are you?" I attempt to tease, but it comes out all wrong. My voice is hard because I don't want her to back out. I like spending time with her.

"Ah, yes, football practice." She looks down at the toe of her shoe digging into the sidewalk.

I take a step closer to her, drawing her attention

back up. I wait until our gazes are locked to say, "I have a confession to make. I don't care whether you come to practice or not."

Her forehead wrinkles. "But—"

"Yeah, Coach will be mad, but he's been mad before. I hate what happened to you. It wasn't right. I don't exactly agree with what Coach wants you to do."

I watch her take my words in. Eventually, she lifts her chin. "So, now you're trying to get out of our pact? A deal's a deal, West Brooks."

A genuine smile crosses my face. "Will you come to my game?" I ask, my heart in my throat. It feels like I just threw myself off a cliff. I used to get this way when I asked my father to come.

"I don't know," she says.

My stomach drops a little. "You don't have to."

She shakes her head. "I have a meet the same day. It's away, and I think I'm still allowed to travel with them. I don't know if I'll get back in time. Or if, you know, if I really want to."

It's like she's kicked me in the balls. I guess straight up saying no is better than the false promises my father always gave me.

"It's nothing against you," she says quickly. "Or Aidan, or some of the other guys. It's just—" She tugs on the sleeves of my hoodie. "Fuck. Listen, things are really fucked right now, West. My mom doesn't even know I won't be diving. You're you...but you're a football player, and this..." She gestures toward her face.

What a cruel joke it would be if I found the one girl who could get me to open up, but she can't stand to look at me because of what I represent to her. To her, football is everything that's wrong. And not just with this town, but with society today. At least, that's what her parents said every chance they could get.

"You don't have to," I tell her again, my mind and my mouth already closing back up. I can feel the velvet curtains being pulled across my fake bravado. End of act.

"It's not about you," she says.

I stare back at her, but I don't say anything because there's nothing much to say. I *am* football. It's what I know. It's what I do. It's what I'm obsessed with.

Football changed my life.

And now the one thing about me that makes sense —the one thing about me I actually love—might be the one thing that turns her off from me.

"See you tomorrow," I tell her before I spin around and walk away.

I hear her call out, "Your hoodie!"

But the moment I put it around her, I knew I never wanted it back. Even if this doesn't go anywhere, she'll have a little piece of me.

CHAPTER ELEVEN

Kenna

WEST BROOKS SMELLS FUCKING AMAZING.

I bury my head in the side of his sweatshirt for the hundredth time. Sure, it's more like a blanket on me, but his scent...*damn*. They shouldn't make guys who smell this good. Especially guys with bodies and personalities like West Brooks because he's making me rethink everything.

Like, everything.

I pull open the door to the trampoline party place and take a deep breath, trying to calm the nerves skittering in my stomach. Sydney wants me to officially ask West to her Lip Sync Contest as my date. I told her it was unnecessary since he's probably already coming with Aidan, but then she gave me a look. He might be coming, however he's not coming *with me*. If I ask him,

112

it means I want him there. She also gave me shit for not having a naked West Brooks in my room when she got home last night. Like I'm going to just jump into bed with him because he stuck up for me in front of that small-minded jersey chaser.

That was before I smelled him, though...

"Hey." His voice surrounds me like a warm hug. I turn, finding him standing from a bench and putting away his phone.

"I didn't think you were here yet," I tell him. "I didn't see your car."

"The Charger? That's Aidan's."

"Oh." I take a step back and peer out the front door. There are two other cars in the lot besides mine. A huge truck and a super small electric half car that looks like the truck could bulldoze it over.

"I'm guessing you didn't get out of the clown car?"

His cheeks turn a shade of red I haven't seen on him before. He runs his hands through his hair. "Not exactly. Um, the local car dealer noticed I didn't have a car, and they said they'd give me one to use for the rest of the year. You know, NIL and all that."

My brows shoot up. "Wow. Like a sponsorship deal? They gave you a truck? That truck?"

He nods quickly. Local businesses are always giving the football players things, and now that they can legally, it's only gotten better for them. "That's... amazing, West. Congratulations."

A smile flickers over his face. He lets out a breath. "I'm pretty stoked about it. I hate always borrowing Aidan's car, and there's no way I could afford one on my own."

I eye him. I guess I don't really know much about West, other than the campus worships him. On the outside, it seems like he has everything.

I shrug. "My parents bought me mine. I guess I'm lucky."

"My mom's car is a piece of shit. You can hear it blocks away, and she has to crawl to the passenger seat to get out of it because the driver's side is stuck in the locked position."

"I guess not something you wanted to bring to campus."

His tight jaw smooths, and he eventually smiles. "Not really."

He didn't mention his father, and I'm itching to ask, but I keep to myself. If he didn't mention him, there's probably a reason why.

"Alright, well..." West motions toward the wide-open space. I don't know how he did it, but arranged a deal with the owner that he would open up an hour early so I could come in and practice my tumbling. Luckily, I've been feeling super strong because of all the lifting I've been doing.

"Right," I say, looking out over everything. "I'll do a little warm-up, but I want to work on my twists today."

He claps his hands in front of him like a coach. "Let's do it."

As he follows me out to the trampoline, it feels like my back is on fire. He hasn't said anything about me walking in wearing his sweatshirt. I told myself I would try to give it back, but I'm getting used to having it. Maybe I don't want to return it.

I unzip it, letting it fall apart and then pull it down to toss it on the ground next to their biggest trampoline. I lower my sweats, too, until I'm in a sports bra and shorts. Baggy clothing isn't a good idea when you're doing twists.

The trampoline depresses after me, and I turn to find West following me out into the middle. I start to jump, and he joins in. His jumps get bigger and bigger, and I giggle when he hits just before me, sending me flying into the air. My arms flail at my sides, butterflies erupting all over.

This guy's got me feeling like a kid again.

"I wish football had fun exercises like this," West muses.

There's something different about him today. He's a little less reserved.

"I thought you loved running into things?"

"I do," he says with a mischievous smile. "But this feels like summer."

"Summer?"

He shrugs. "I was friends with a kid once who had

one of these in his backyard, and I used to only go over there in the summer."

"I had one, too," I tell him, jumping higher. "I'd stay out on it for hours. My parents were talking about putting me into gymnastics, but then the summer Olympics came on. These girls on TV were doing all these twists and tucks into a pool, and I was hooked. I wanted to dive ever since."

"It must have been a hard sport to get into. Football is everywhere, but my high school didn't even have a pool."

"Mine did, but they didn't have a dive team, only a swim team. I had to join a club. My parents drove me an hour and a half each way three times a week."

His brows raise. "That's commitment."

I try to time my jumps to get there right before West. I miss a couple of times, but on the third, I slam as hard as I can a half second sooner than he lands, and he soars into the air like a rocket. He throws his head back, a laugh escaping his throat at the very top. It's so loud and carefree that it takes me by surprise.

I hadn't heard West Brooks laugh yet.

He lands and immediately falls to his knees. "That was evil."

"I thought you wanted to be a kid again," I tease. "Have you ever tried a forward flip?"

"When I was five."

"Let's do it."

He shakes his head. "You need to train."

I stop jumping and cross my arms over my chest. "I'll train once you land a front flip."

"Another bargain?" he asks, lifting his brow.

I hold my hand out. He eyes it, and my heart thrums in my chest, waiting for him to shake on it. When he finally does, I have to bite my lip at the instant connection I feel with him, my whole hand practically getting lost in his palm. "You have to teach me, though," he says, squeezing.

I almost lose my breath. My tongue feels as if it gets stuck on the roof of my mouth. "I can do that. I think you'll be a quick study."

"Yeah?"

"I mean, you're West Brooks. You can do anything."

His gaze zeroes in on me, and I'd give anything to hear his inner thoughts. He stares at me for a beat too long, and when he lets go, he stays in contact with my fingers until the very last moment.

I have to look away to get my bearings.

Sydney's right, I've got it bad. West Brooks isn't just growing on me, he feels like an inevitability.

My stomach squeezes.

Stepping into the middle of the trampoline, he awaits instruction. I run through the important parts while starting to bounce. "Jump until you have enough height. Wait until you're at the apex of the jump and then tuck, throwing yourself forward. The trick is to open up at the right time. Too late, and you'll face-plant. Too early, and you'll end up on your back." Then I demonstrate it for him.

He shakes his head when I finish. "I can't believe you're making me do this."

"You've already committed," I tell him. "No take backs."

"Thankfully Coach isn't here." He starts with tiny jumps, getting higher and higher each time. His expression turns serious next, his lips thinning as he throws himself forward just at the apex, like I said.

The first one, he lands on his butt.

The second, he overcorrects and goes right to his hands and knees.

I giggle, and he glares at me. "Keep laughing. This is the one."

"I already know it," I tell him. He is a specimen, for sure. He has such a different physique than divers. I'm not used to seeing someone with so many muscles flip through the air. I have to step out to the side, so I don't start bouncing with him and get in his way.

Just like he said, the third time, he nails it. He lands on his feet and then goes right into another jump before slowing down.

I give him a slow clap. "Excellent job, Mr. Brooks. A+. Do you want your medal now or later?"

"Oh, we're handing out medals now?"

He walks toward me, the excitement from his jump turning into something else. He steps next to me, and the trampoline depresses so that he has to catch me before I fall into him.

"Maybe," I say.

"What if I want something else?"

His strong fingers have a hold of my upper arms, and even on this unsteady apparatus, it feels like he has roots like concrete. I lick my lips. "What do you want?"

He peers down, taking me in. I specifically wore this outfit to show off my new features. Little pops of muscles in my shoulders, thighs, and biceps. I think he notices. Actually, he definitely notices as evidenced by his slow perusal.

"I want you to go out with me."

I let out a slow breath. That wasn't what I was expecting. I thought maybe he'd say he wanted me in his bed or on my knees. Maybe that's just where my brain is at, but I really didn't think the hero on campus would ask a girl for a date—especially me. Not when he has girls throwing themselves at him. "Do you go out with girls often?"

"Never," he says, chest expanding. "But there's a first time for everything."

A first time for everything... Now, I'm freaking out. "What does West Brooks think of as a date?"

He chuckles. "I hadn't gotten that far. My only goal was to ask you first, then figure it out."

The peaks of his cheeks turn pink. God, my knees are Jell-O, and it's not from the warm-up. "I will..." I agree. "But I want you to do something for me, too."

His smile widens. "More pacts?"

I shake my head. "No, I—" I take a deep breath, nerves shuttling through me like a runner on wobbly feet. Here's my chance. "Sydney's Lip Sync Contest is tomorrow, and I wanted to know if you would come...with me."

There. It's out.

I have to stop myself from closing my eyes.

He doesn't waste a bit of time. "Yes."

I giggle nervously. His fingers press into my skin until I meet his gaze again. Shit. His green eyes are bright, expecting.

If you'd asked me at the beginning of the year, I would've said my main objective was to stay away from as many football players as I could, but here I am, practically in one's embrace, and there's not really any other place I want to be.

It's scary.

And fucking exciting.

My parents would die.

My heart starts to pound as I stare at him. A crazy rhythm that doesn't seem to want to slow.

Eventually, he reminds me what we're there for. "You should get back to work."

"Yeah, twists," I remind myself. I'm working on

twists today. "Coach watched me dive a few times last practice, and she wants to see improvement in my twists."

He pulls away. "If that's what Coach thinks."

I rub my arms, trying to bring the same feeling back into them that West leaves. Excitement. Surprise. Expectation and inevitability. "Just need to shake off the rust."

He steps off the trampoline, taking a seat on the outside safety area. I go through my normal routine, starting with smaller flips, then one twist. Then a flip and a twist together and building from there.

The truth is, I was happy Coach actually took notice of me last practice. Unfortunately, my water entry was terrible with a splash like I belly flopped, but the fact that she's paying attention to me is a good thing. It means she hasn't written me off yet.

It can only go up from here.

I'm so engrossed in my movements that I don't break until the young guy at the counter calls out, "Ten minutes!"

My head whips toward him, and I find West still sitting, watching with his arms wrapped around his legs. My cheeks heat. "That went by fast."

"You look good," he says, getting to his feet. "I mean, I don't know the nuances to look for, but you looked strong."

"They felt good," I agree, walking off beside him.

He hands me a water, and I attempt to twist the cap when I find out he's already done so for me. Warmth explodes in my belly. "Thanks."

He shrugs before reaching down and grabbing his sweatshirt and my sweats as we make our way to the front. As soon as we step outside, he wraps his sweatshirt around me again, and I can't help but smile. I was hoping he wouldn't take it back.

"So, tomorrow?" he asks.

"Tomorrow," I confirm, butterflies swarming everywhere. I can't believe I'm going to the Lip Sync Contest with West Brooks.

"I'll pick you up in my nice, new truck."

Out in the parking lot, his vehicle stands out. It's shiny black, and I wouldn't be surprised if it's lifted. It looks like a beast. "It suits you," I say. When we get closer, I laugh. "Seriously?"

On the side in a green decal, *Hulk* is written out along with West's number. 53.

He shrugs. "They really wanted my sponsorship."

I shake my head. *I guess so.*

He looks unsure for a moment. "Is it too much?"

"Nah. It's perfect."

CHAPTER TWELVE

West

"DUDE," Aidan grins.

I shut the dorm door behind me, nerves churning as I walk back into our shared room. "What?"

He raises his brows at me. "I didn't even know you owned a shirt without a Bulldog on it."

I lift my hand to flip him off, which only makes him smile wider. He knows how nervous I am. He's been teasing me all fucking day, and it only got worse at practice.

Tonight, I'm going to the Lip Sync Contest with Kenna. Tomorrow is our season opener.

He stands and pats my arm. "Good choice. That gray really brings out your eyes."

"Get off my dick."

He howls. "You couldn't handle me."

I shake my head. "You meeting me there or what?"

"Yes, but if you think I'm playing your wingman all night so that it's only me and McKenna talking, you're crazy. I'll just straight up walk away."

"I talk to her," I protest. He gives me a look. "She invited me, you know?"

I must be doing something right...

"Not sure how you pulled that one off."

"My delightful personality," I deadpan.

"Keep telling yourself that."

I grab my wallet and keys off the bed and spin toward him again. "Don't bring those stupid jersey chasers around Kenna."

He gives me a mock salute. "I wasn't happy about it either. Coach loved your idea, by the way."

I grin. Hopefully, it all pans out and Kenna isn't mad. It's time to show everyone that the football team isn't just a bunch of obsessed jocks prowling campus in blue and white.

I pull open the door, and Aidan yells, "Go get 'em, Tiger!"

"See you soon, asshole."

I have to run the gauntlet to get out of the dorm. It's Friday night, so everyone is out and about, making plans to party. I get invited to two keggers and a tipsy girl wraps her arms around me and invites me back to her place. After carefully extracting myself, I tell her no thank you and hightail it to my truck.

The day they handed over the keys, I sat it in for an hour just staring. My parents never had a vehicle this cool. Hell, they barely even had a working vehicle. It's a dream come true to own a truck like this.

Everything is happening like I wanted. Football is saving me. Not only did the dealership give me this car, but it came with a generous stipend, too. Enough to last me the entire year and then some. Coach said a couple of other businesses have reached out that he hasn't gotten a chance to get back to yet. Even the trampoline place gave me extra hours for Kenna to practice as long as I agreed to do a commercial with them. Plus, a local brewhouse that wants to work with me has been blowing up my phone. I just have to figure out if it's right for my brand.

I didn't even know I had a brand.

The truck thrums to life underneath me, and I make the short drive to Kenna's apartment. Earlier, she tried to tell me that she'd just meet me there, but I wasn't having that. This is a date. She's not walking anywhere.

With a stomach full of nerves, I park on the street and walk up her front steps.

I press the doorbell and stand back. When I do, it suddenly hits me: I've never actually been on a date before. Not a date-date. I've hung out. I've been someone's boyfriend and hook-up buddy, but dating? Nope. I hope it's not—

The door swings open, and Kenna stands there, gazing up at me with her beautiful brown eyes flecked with gold. Form-fitting jeans hug her body while a simple black top with sleeves past her elbow gives the slightest hint of cleavage. For a moment, I can't talk. She's stunning. Her hair is down, the majority of it hanging over one shoulder and somewhat hiding her scar.

"Hi," she says. "I would've walked."

"I know. Maybe I wanted an excuse to drive my truck."

"Ha," she exclaims, smiling. "Why am I not surprised?" Turning, she starts back into the house. "I just have to grab a sweater."

I walk in after her, shutting the door behind me. The house is cute. To my right, I peer inside an open door and instantly recognize it as Kenna's bedroom. It's just so *her*. She has a gray and yellow comforter on her bed and a small white desk along one wall, but what really drew me in is the almost full-length poster of a man in a pair of Speedos, water dripping from his torso.

Is this the kind of guy Kenna likes? I know it's a poster, but I would crush this dude. Despite the six-pack he's sporting, he's...tiny. Fit but trim.

"West?" she calls out.

"In here."

She turns the corner, her expression lightening

when she sees me. "Oh, you found my poster. That's David Boudia. He swam for Purdue and was in the '08, '12, and '16 Olympics." She reaches out, her fingers touching the edges of the full-color print. She beams when she looks at it.

"Is that something you want? To go to the Olympics?"

"Oh God, I would die." She laughs, pressing her palm to her chest. "I don't think I quite have what it takes, but I used to pretend when I was little. McKenna Knowles, gold medalist." She smiles wistfully.

"And does Mr. Speedo have a gold medal?"

"He certainly does," she states, facing me with her hands on her hips. "Are you making fun of David Boudia?"

I raise my hands in surrender. "Never."

She lifts her chin. "He has a medal in every color, actually. Two bronzes." Shrugging, she says, "He's retired now. It was the 2008 Olympics in Beijing that made me want to be a diver."

"And let me guess, you think he's hot?"

"Of course. It's David Boudia," she shrugs, like that's supposed to mean something to me.

"Aren't most girls obsessed with rock bands or celebrities or—"

"David *is* a celebrity," she interjects. "In the right circles..."

Oh, the right circles. I give her poster a look. "I'm not sure about his choice of swimming apparel."

"The Speedo? It's for freedom of movement. It's what the guys wear."

I could give a shit about that, but I've been dying to see what Kenna wears when she dives. I'm sure it's something sensible rather than what I'd like to see her in. "Whatever you say."

She tugs on my arm. "Come on. If you can't respect David, you're not allowed in my room."

I chuckle as I bring my phone out, sending a quick text to the team to tell them to find Speedos for tomorrow and to not ask any questions.

After I fire it off, I pocket my phone and hold my arm out to Kenna. She wraps her arm around mine, and we walk outside after she locks the door. Where we touch, my skin fires like it's a packet of Pop Rocks.

I help her into the truck, and she looks around at everything. The leather. The blue-lit entertainment console. "I'm impressed."

My heart soars. I close her door and run around to the other side. "Look," I tell her, then push the button on the truck for it to start. My dad had a car once that he had to jam a screwdriver into the ignition in order for it to start, so this feels like a crazy luxury.

"Sweet," she says. "Push-button start."

"The works," I tell her. "Remote start, heated seats, blind-spot monitoring, leather…"

When she doesn't answer, I peer toward her and find her smiling. "You're going to do great in that commercial. Just keep this same excitement."

My face heats. "Thanks. I told them I might suck at it, but I'd try my best."

It's in my nature to be quiet, but before I left, I already thought of a few things to say so Aidan or anyone else wouldn't have to save me during my date. So, as I pull away from the curb, I ask, "Did Sydney pick out a song?"

"She did, but she didn't tell me because she wants it to be a surprise."

"I hope she does well."

Kenna sighs. "Me too. I'm not too worried. Sydney's...extra. I just hope she's not disappointed if she doesn't get to perform at homecoming."

"Oh right. I forget about that every year. It's not like I get to see it."

"I've never been."

I sneak a peek at her. "You've never been to homecoming?"

"Not the football game, no."

"Wow, you really are a football hater."

"I don't know," she smiles, "it might be growing on me."

My fingers flex on the wheel. I tell myself not to peek over at her, since I probably have the dopiest look on my face. I hope this means she'll come to one of my games, even if it is only homecoming. I might be awkward in real life, but I shine on the field.

"Are you nervous about your game tomorrow? Season opener and all that."

"Yeah." I won't lie. The start of the season always heightens my nerves. If she hadn't asked me out tonight, I probably would've stayed in my room and went over the playbook. "I like to start out the season with a win. Set the tone."

"But it's not all up to you."

"Exactly," I tell her. If it was all up to me, I'd be less nervous.

She shifts in her seat. "Maybe you can text me, let me know how it goes."

"You too. About your dive meet, I mean."

She shrugs, turning away to stare out the window. "I'm not even diving unless something tragic happens, but I'll be there to cheer everyone on. Coach says she's going to try to get me an exhibition spot to see where the judges score me."

"Really? You didn't say anything." Excitement buzzes through me, but she doesn't seem as enthused by the prospect.

"She just told me today. It's not a guarantee. The other team has to have an exhibition, too."

"Kenna..."

She peers toward me. "Hmm?"

"Why are you not freaking out?"

"Oh, I'm freaking out," she admits. "But I'm also not trying to freak out about something that might not happen. You know? I've had disappointment after disappointment, and I don't want to get my hopes up. I shouldn't have even said anything."

I want to tell her she's wrong. Thinking negatively isn't what she needs right now, but I know if I say it, she might take it the wrong way.

"I wish I could be there," I tell her, keeping a smile to myself.

We're definitely going to need those Speedos.

"It probably won't happen. Plus, it's an away meet and a pain in the ass to get to and..." She drolls on, and every single obstacle she spouts makes my stomach clench harder.

Her coach better get her a damn exhibition spot. She *needs* this.

When I pull into the lot and park, she clears her throat. "Thanks for helping me train, by the way. I probably wouldn't even be getting this spot if it weren't for your help."

I reach out and squeeze her biceps through her shirt. "Getting there."

"Yeah, my micro muscles are coming through. So...," she moves her sweatshirt out of the way and hands me a bright pink pom-pom. I lift my gaze to hers, and she laughs. "Sydney's request. I have one for Aidan and me, too. To cheer her on."

"You serious?"

"Unless you want to face Sydney's wrath..."

I take it from her and give it a little shake. The glittery-pink plastic tassels fall over my hand.

"It totally suits you."

"I prefer Bulldog-blue."

"Me too, but this is Sydney's color."

I hold my other hand out. "Let me break the news to Aidan."

She snickers, handing me the other pom-pom. "As you wish... And please tell me you know where that quote is from; otherwise, I'm not sure I can be seen with you in public."

"*The Princess Bride*, obviously," I snark. "Give me a hard one next time."

She lifts a brow at me, clearly impressed. "Okay, okay. We're good for today," she says, opening her car door and sliding out.

One thing I know for sure is that I'll keep trying to make sure we're good. No matter what.

CHAPTER THIRTEEN

Kenna

THE HIGHLIGHT of my year might be watching West and Aidan shake their hot-pink pom-poms to Sydney lip-syncing a Lady Gaga medley. She strutted out in a matching wig and an iridescent skirt that had the audience going wild.

If she isn't chosen to headline homecoming, the damn thing is fixed.

There are plenty of jersey chasers, including the one who asked me about my scar, who are going out for it, too. Skimpy outfits and sexy dancing, but they're not really polished. Not like Sydney.

When she comes out from behind the stage, I open my arms wide. "Girrrrl!"

She squeals. "Oh my God, that was so much fun!" She leaps into my embrace and hugs me tight.

"You killed it!" I tell her, strands of her wig getting caught on my lips. She smells like berry bubblegum.

Another excited screech empties from her mouth while she peels away. Immediately, she side-eyes the stage, though. "Have you checked out the competition?"

"What competition?"

Her lips curve into a smile, and she nods slowly. "Exactly what I wanted to hear."

"Great job, Syd," Aidan speaks up from behind her. He has a gorgeous smirk on his face, and his eyes are practically twinkling as he ogles her.

She turns toward him, placing her hands on her hips. He swishes his pom-poms, and they eye each other while his grin widens. The air between them crackles. Something will most definitely go down between these two. They both have that carefree spirit, but it makes me nervous for Sydney. Aidan is the quarterback of the football team. I've already expressed my reservations to her, but she dismissed it, saying, "If you get to have your hottie football player, I do, too."

West places his arm around my back, startling me from my thoughts. He leans over and whispers, "I think we might have to make ourselves scarce tonight."

My heart thumps wildly. His touch, his voice... God. It's a lethal weapon. Every nerve ending is firing in my body, especially the ones between my legs. Being this close to him makes all those feelings more adamant.

"You think so?" I ask, leaning closer because I just can't help myself.

His arm around me tightens. "I've seen that look on Aidan's face before."

"He won't hurt her, though, will he?" I bite my lip, worry trying to edge through.

West pulls away, face tense. "Hell no. He's one of the best guys I know. If he's just looking for a hookup, he'll tell her. If he wants more, he'll tell her that, too."

His stare makes me weak in the knees.

"Do you...do that?" I ask, suddenly needing to know. I don't want to get hurt either.

He's silent for a long time, jaw tensing and relaxing in increments. Over the last few weeks, I feel like I've gotten a good read on him. He's calculated. He mulls his thoughts over, and I suspect he's doing so now.

I just don't know what the outcome will be.

My mom always said good things come to those who wait, and she's right.

When West Brooks, star fucking player for the Warner Bulldogs, finally answers, I almost cream my panties. "If you're wondering what I want from you, it's everything. I want to date you. I want you in my bed. I want you at my games in my jersey." His chest rises like he's attempting to calm himself.

I need some of that, too, because I'm firing on

all cylinders. He makes me feel like I'm staring down at the pool from the highest platform. In that moment, right before it becomes routine, my body is doused with adrenaline and my mind tells me that this is nuts. I'm surely going to hurt myself.

But here with West, I think the jump might be worth the risk.

"I...I like that," I tell him, peering up to meet his intense green eyes.

His widen for a split second, but then his fingers tense around me again. He moves closer. We're inches away, his hot breath fanning over my lips like the perfect precursor to a kiss. I close my eyes—

Aidan claps West on the back, making him lurch toward me until our noses bump. "What are we going to do next?" he asks with the worst timing in the fucking world.

I chuckle, leaning forward until I rest my head on West's shoulder.

"I'm going to kill him," he whispers.

"Get in line," I mumble. My hands clench into fists, and I straighten them out to relieve the tension. This close. This fucking close to feeling West Brooks's lips. To kissing him.

Another act starts up on the stage, pounding out a Lizzo tune.

"Well, I'm staying here to eyeball the competition,"

Sydney says. Under her pink glitter eyeshadow, her eyes keep sliding to the stage.

Aidan throws his arm around her, looking chummy. "I'll stay with you. You two?" he asks, turning his head over his shoulder to look at us.

I'm having fun here, but I'm torn. West is making a move. If we leave, will it be different? If we stay, will we continue this? Now that he's talking more, I want to get to know him better.

I peer up to see where he's at, but I get nothing. In front of us, Aidan pulls out his phone, dropping his hand away from Sydney. He frowns, then starts typing. "Cade needs a ride," he calls out to West.

"We'll get him," he says immediately. Then he turns to me. "If that's okay with you?"

I shrug. "Yeah, sure."

Aidan doesn't even look up from his screen. "I'll tell him to look for the Hulkmobile."

"Stop calling it that, dick."

Aidan smirks before pocketing his phone, giving his friend a wink that says he knows he's a dick but he doesn't care.

West turns toward me. "You sure you don't care?"

"No, I'm good. It'll give us time to talk."

He gives me a dry smile. "Great. Something I'm really good at."

"You weren't doing too bad a little while ago," I remind him. I mean, if he keeps talking about me in his bed in that voice, I don't know how much longer I'll be able to hold out.

He reaches for my hand and grasps it. Leading me through the crowd is easy as everyone parts for him, shouldering one another to get out of his way. I just have to stay in his shadow until we make it to the edge of the crowd.

When we get outside, I say, "You come in handy, West Brooks." He gives me a curious look. "Everyone moves out of your way."

He tilts his head like he never thought of that before. "It's kind of nice, isn't it?"

It certainly is. He helps me in his truck and then strides to the other side. I watch him move, his body a perfect composition of muscle and agility.

"Where are we going, anyway?" I ask when he starts the truck.

West pulls out his phone, checking his messages. "He's at a Sigma Phi party. He's going through some shit."

Cade Farmer? He acts like he's God's gift. He's supposed to have graduated already, but he decided to stay an extra year because he had a year of eligibility after being red-shirted.

Crazy how I know all of this information about the football team and I don't even go looking for it. It's all everyone talks about.

"You guys are like a well-oiled machine," I offer,

nodding toward his phone where the screen is still on the text Aidan sent him with Sigma Phi's address.

"Never leave a teammate behind," West says, and I can't tell if there's any animosity there. Maybe he's just tired. Or worried about the game tomorrow.

He navigates the streets of Warner, and while stopped at a stop sign, he asks, "So, *The Princess Bride*? Is that your favorite movie?"

"Huh?"

"*The Princess Bride*. You tried to trip me up with the quote?"

"Oh." I grin. "No, not my favorite movie. I don't know if I have one. I guess I have different categories of movies. I would include *The Princess Bride* in the nostalgic one, along with *The Goonies* and *Harry Potter*. Then there are just newer films that I enjoy, but I don't know if I would ever call them my favorite movies. You?"

He chuckles. "I have a way less wordy answer."

"Shocking," I mock with a slight roll of my eyes.

"*Varsity Blues*," he says. "Oh, and *Rudy*. I can't forget *Rudy*."

"Football movies. Of course."

He shrugs. "I guess I'm a simple guy. Favorite hype band?" he asks, and I sit back. I like this game we're playing. Even though I might have guessed he would've picked a football movie, it also says a lot about him. West Brooks is anything but simple. He's just focused.

But hype band. I can't tell him. Like, I physically can't. He'll laugh.

I shake my head.

"What?" he asks.

"You'll tease me."

His mouth splits into a grin that is bigger than any I've seen on him yet. "You have to tell me now."

"Is yours embarrassing?" I ask.

"You'll never know unless I hear yours."

"Ugh." I've been keeping this my dirty little secret. I wince, squeezing my eyes closed. "5SOS."

He doesn't say anything, so I peek at him. He turns to the road and then back at me. "5SOS?"

"Five Seconds of Summer? Come on," I groan. It would be even worse if he'd never heard of them.

He bursts out laughing. "I know who they are. I just wanted to hear you own it."

I push his upper arm, except it feels like a steel wall beneath my palm. "Told you it was embarrassing."

"I get it, you like boy bands."

"Whoa. I wouldn't call them a boy band. They're punk."

"They're a punk boy band."

"Agree to disagree," I say, flipping my hair over my shoulder. "What's on your Hype playlist?"

"Eminem, Imagine Dragons, Panic! at the Disco..."

"So, if I see you bopping your head on the sideline before a game, it's to those songs?"

"Probably 'High Hopes' by Panic! or 'Thunder' by Imagine Dragons."

I nibble on my lower lip. Those songs are all about chasing dreams, wanting a bigger, better life. I drop my head back on the headrest and stare at West as he shifts uncomfortably. It makes me feel powerful that he's opening up to me. That I've somehow begun to scratch the surface of this campus superstar.

He's not throwing me lines. This is the real him.

"I like those songs, too," I finally say. "So, what was West Brooks like as a kid?"

His fingers flex on the steering wheel before he turns right, and for a minute, I think he's stopping the car just to tell me, but when the bass hits me from the house party, I realize we're at Sigma Phi already.

He places the car in Park and wipes his palms on his jeans. "Saved by my drunk friend on that one," he says, looking unsure of himself. "I'll be right back."

I sit up straighter. "You want me to come with?"

"I'll just be a second." He jumps out, closing his door behind him, and I watch as he jogs up the front walk. Partygoers call his name, clapping him on the back.

For someone who doesn't like the spotlight off the field, he tends to get a lot of it. I wonder if that's what makes him so introspective.

If he keeps going the way he is, he's only going to get bigger and bigger.

My car door swings open, and I turn in my seat, heart thumping. I didn't see West come back out.

A girl blinks up at me, her eyes are glazed. She's clearly drunk. "I thought this was the Hulk's truck?" She steps back, wobbling on her feet. She blinks again, staring at the back side panel where West's nickname is written out.

"It is," I tell her, stomach squeezing.

"Oh." She stumbles forward, catching herself on the door and the side of the truck. "What are you doing in here, then?"

"Um, riding with him?"

"But I don't know you," she slurs.

"I don't know you either." It's a lie. I recognize her from always being around one of the football players.

"Do you go here?" she asks.

"Yeah."

Behind her, West comes out with a drunk Cade who keeps shrugging off West's attempt to help him walk.

"Dude, we got a game tomorrow," West implores.

"I'll be fine."

Once she hears their voices, the girl turns. "There you are."

West's jaw hardens as he peers between me and

her. Cade has a completely different reaction, though. "Hey, baby. You're looking good."

"You said that to me already."

He shrugs, catching his balance. "I guess I really mean it."

When he gets to the truck, he finally sees me. Cade lifts his brows. "It's warrior woman! Hey, warrior woman."

"Um, hey." My stomach does a flip. I don't know why he's calling me that. Is he picking on me?

"Get your ass in the truck, Cade."

"Ooh, I'm coming," the girl coos.

"Sure," Cade says, at the same time, West says, "No."

"Aw, come on," Cade calls out good-naturedly.

West hovers at the side of the truck as Cade opens the back door. He gets in, and the girl tries to follow, but West pulls her back. "Listen, we got a game tomorrow. You don't want to be the reason why we single-handedly lose the first game of the season, do you?" He talks to her like he's reasoning with a child.

"You didn't used to go celibate the day before a game." She grins.

I turn in my seat. Jealousy hits me like a battering ram, but I squash it. It's not like I thought West was a virgin or anything.

He closes Cade's door, and somehow, he evades the girl while getting in the truck. I stare straight ahead.

Cade's laughing in the back. "I'm glad you guys finally got together. Maybe Hulk won't be so mopey now."

"I'm not mopey."

"You're mopey."

I listen to Cade's drunk banter for a while until the truck stops again. When I peer around, I realize we're outside my place. West is already out of the car before I can say anything, and then he's opening my door, helping me out.

"Give it to her!" Cade yells out as I step down.

"Sorry," West says after sending Cade a hard look. "He's worse than I thought. I need him back in his room to sober up, get him good for tomorrow." He quiets my fears at being dropped off early in a moment. It was an abrupt end to our date, but Cade is really out of it. "Also, I don't know what that girl said to you, if anything, but..."

"She didn't say anything," I tell him. "She was just drunk."

He takes my hands, rubbing his thumbs up and down the bones at my wrists. "I wanted to hang out with you longer. I'm sorry it got all messed up."

"I am, too. Don't think you're getting away with not answering that last question."

He gives me a half-hearted smile, and with just that one small movement, my stomach tenses.

"Kiss her already!" I hear from the truck.

West sighs, dropping his head. "I really hate all my teammates today. Every single one."

I push up to my tiptoes and give him a quick kiss on the cheek, my lips pressing against a fair bit of stubble. I stay there for a beat too long before settling back on my feet.

West stands there, stunned, blinking his green eyes at me.

"Good luck tomorrow, West Brooks." I back away, breaking our connection. His hands fall to his sides, and mine keep buzzing from the contact. "I'll be thinking about you."

Then I leave him on the sidewalk as I retreat into the house. When I get inside, I lean against the closed door, my hand over my pounding heart.

A quiet West is a sight to be seen, but a West who talks? A West who picks up his drunk teammate the night before a game? I shiver, goosebumps running up and down my arms.

He's something else.

CHAPTER FOURTEEN

West

"GET READY, BOYS," Coach calls out from the front of the bus.

A few of the guys groan, but Aidan steps out and saunters down the aisle in a pair of Speedos like he belongs on a Calvin Klein runway. "I might wear these all the damn time. Look out, ladies."

Catcalls ring through the bus, which only makes him strut more.

I first broached the idea about showing up at Kenna's meet with Coach, and he loved it. Athletes supporting athletes. Some real school pride. I have to give it to the guys, they took to it, too. Some of them, I'm sure, are only interested in checking out the girls in their swimsuits, but others, like Aidan, totally get what we're actually trying to do.

Warner football gets all the props on campus, but the swim and dive team are really good. After practicing with Kenna the last couple weeks, I can say for sure that they put just as much into their sport as we do. I don't know how well attended these meets are, but it can't hurt to show support—and show Kenna that football players aren't all bad. We don't just care about ourselves.

I peer down, squinting at my complete lack of clothing.

Damn. These Speedos are tiny.

Suddenly, I'm having second thoughts. These things aren't made for someone with my build, but all around me, the other guys are getting into it. They're painting each other's chest, spelling out Bulldogs in royal blue.

"I'm the *D*," Cade calls. "For obvious reasons." He smirks down at his crotch, welcoming the banter that comes next.

For the love of God...

I thought he'd have a harder time this morning, but Cade's a pro. If you didn't know he'd drank himself into oblivion last night, you wouldn't be able to tell from the way he's acting today. He's his usual fun self.

Good. We need him at his best during the game.

The bus starts to slow, and I gaze out the window as it crawls to a stop outside of a steel building. Huge silver metal beams form triangles in front, making an entrance that sticks out geometrically.

Coach stands and turns toward us, demanding our attention. He calls out in that way that only Coach can, his eyes steely and hard. "Listen up. We're here to support our Bulldog teammates. You will cheer your asses off because we want everyone to know that Warner football supports others. *Warner football* takes pride in our school. *Warner football*," he takes a deep breath, letting the tension build, "fucking cares. If I hear of any shenanigans in there, I will pull you from the game so fast your head will still be spinning after the fourth quarter. Do you understand?"

"Yes, sir."

"Do you understand?" he yells again, punctuating each word.

"Yes, sir!" comes the rallying cry as my teammates wake the fuck up. Coach has that way about him, making people perk up and pay attention. He *commands* their focus.

"Be back on the bus by three p.m. sharp. If you're late, we're leaving your ass, and you'll be suspended for two games, including homecoming."

"Yes, sir!" we all call out again. No one dares grumble because none of us will be tempting Coach like that. As a junior, the last thing I would want to do is miss homecoming.

Nerves skate through my stomach like two

growling bulldogs going at it. I hope no one fucks this up for us. Coach has already scouted to see if there are any other Warner sporting events happening during our other away games for the rest of the year. I was lucky when I realized that Kenna's meet was only fifteen minutes out of the way of the route we were taking to get to our game against Zephyr tonight. It was the perfect setup.

I hope... Shit. I hope Kenna actually likes that we're doing this. I'm bursting to see her dive at a competition. She said she might not get to, and even if she does, it will be an exhibition, but she needs this win. She needs it for herself, and she needs to show her coach that she can do this.

Either way, I'll be there to support her. We'll all be there.

"I need an O," Mitchell calls out.

"Me," I volunteer, making my way to his spot on the bus.

One of the second-string rookies peers up at me as I pass and then down at his own chest. "I suddenly feel less manly."

I smirk. "One day, you'll grow up, too, little man."

Aidan cups the back of the guy's head in a placating gesture. "Just not today."

Mitchell shakes his head while painting a blue *O* over my chest and abs. The guys start filing off the bus, and I'm so nervous that it's difficult to get my legs to start moving. It feels like I'm about to show up at my own game. The thrill of competition. The drive to be great. It's all there, brewing inside me, except it's all for someone else. It's...strange, this feeling. Foreign.

One of my teammates starts to clap, two slow ones, then three fast. We erupt in a cheer of "Let's go, Bulldogs!" as we file off the bus and into the modern aquatic center.

Immediately, the setting is different than I'm used to, even if the feelings are the same. Luckily, the diving competition is scheduled to go first, and if everything starts on time, we'll be able to just catch Kenna take an exhibition dive before we have to get back on the bus. That is, *if* she gets to dive.

Clap, clap, clap-clap-clap.

"Let's go, Bulldogs!"

Spectators take out their phones. We climb the bleachers to a spot at the top. I'm behind Cade, who doesn't mind strutting for all the recordings going on. I can only imagine the gigantic grin on his face.

My head, though, is on a swivel.

Where's Kenna? Is she out here yet? What will she do when she sees us? Me?

A sophomore on the row of bleachers in front of me complains, "Aw man, they don't wear bikinis?"

"No, dickhead," I shoot back. "Do we play football in bikinis? We play in what's best for our sport."

He holds his hands up. "Alright, alright."

Shit. Maybe Kenna and her parents are right about us. Just a bunch of dumb oafs focused on sex and—

A slight figure comes running out of the mouth of a doorway that leads to the pool, eyes wide. She stops with her hands on the doorframe, peering up at the stands.

It's Kenna.

Clap, clap, clap-clap-clap.

"Let's go, Bulldogs!"

My heart does a flip inside its cage. She scans my clapping, chanting teammates, and I'm hoping the whole time that she's searching for one football player in particular—me.

I'm glad I see her first. It gives me a moment to take her in without being spied. A royal-blue one-piece hugs her body, the Bulldog logo inconspicuously hidden near the top right. A pair of Bulldog shorts rounds out her dive attire while a black towel is fisted tight in her hands as she grips the door casing. Still, she searches.

I raise my hand at the same time her gaze shoots to mine, and then I point at her. Like I'm claiming her.

You.

You're the one I'm here for.

For a moment, nothing happens. Then, a smile peels her lips apart, and my stomach turns over in one tsunami-size flop.

I'm head over heels for this girl. There's no denying it.

She shakes her head, biting her lip. Her stare scans down my front, and I'm acutely aware I'm wearing only one-tenth of what she's used to seeing me in. Just the tiny, tight Speedo cinched against my hips. Some of the guys have their Bulldog zip-ups hanging loose over their shoulders, but I'm the O. I'm not covering up, and I'm certainly glad I didn't when Kenna continues to rake her gaze down me. I told her I'd look better in a Speedo than her crush. I'm going to make her want to replace that huge poster with one of me.

Turning, she nods back inside to what I imagine is the away team's locker room, and then she jogs off without looking back. A second later, our chant dies off as the announcer interrupts, explaining what we're about to see. They introduce the judges. Some sit pool-side, while others are seated at roped-off areas in the bleachers at varying heights. My research tells me that each judge is looking for something different. Take off, entry, flips and twists.

Back down at the pool, the first diver ascends the platform, and it hits me what an individual sport this is. If I screw up, I get backup from my team—hopefully. These athletes don't have that. Even if you're diving in synchronized pairs, it's still all on the individual. Plus, what they're being judged on only lasts a few seconds.

The pressure. Jesus. We have a whole four quarters to turn things around if we need to.

One by one, the divers go up.

We cheer for the 'dogs. We sit politely for the other team. The one time I sat in on one of Kenna's practices —I had to promise her coach I'd behave myself—it was so early in the season that there wasn't much technical diving going on. Now, it's cool to see the actual end product and what those moves on the trampoline actually end up looking like.

My competitive nature picks little nuances in the different dives. The best scores go to the divers who enter the water at a near perpendicular angle with little splash.

One girl dives in, and it looks like reverse suction. "Shit, that was nice," Aidan says, remarking on the same thing I saw. A few drops spring up from the pool and fall back in again. The diver swims underneath the surface before popping up poolside. She has a C on her swimsuit, bearing the colors from the opposing team.

My knee starts jumping up and down. I hope Kenna gets to dive. I want her to feel all the encouragement from my teammates—and me.

Mostly me.

After forty minutes of diving, the score is close. I spot Kenna at the side of the pool where her coach has pulled her aside. I wring my hands together, watching.

She nods at something her coach says and then turns, walking toward the end of the pool...and the platform.

My stomach squeezes. Gazing up, Kenna locks eyes with me and smiles before disappearing behind the large, white structure.

What does that mean? Is she on? Is she going to dive?

I slowly get to my feet. The announcer says, "Next up, an exhibition dive from Warner University platform diver McKenna Knowles." He continues on, giving her career stats and accolades.

When I see her next, she's at the top of the platform. Her hair is in a single ponytail, pulled back and dripping wet. She takes a deep breath near the back of the platform and then walks slowly to the edge.

Oh, shit. The platform suddenly looks higher, more dangerous.

Is she really going to dive from that?

"Dude, that's Kenna," Aidan states.

"Oh, yeah." Cade puts his fingers in his mouth and gives a piercing whistle.

I hit him to shut him up. She needs to concentrate. However, it doesn't look like what he's done has even fazed her. Kenna's in the zone.

She turns her back, her heels hovering over the edge. Nothing below her now but air and pool. I've seen a handful of girls do this, but worry still grips me.

I can't breathe as she bounces on her toes and then leaps.

Shit, shit, shit...

She's so close to the platform. Why is she so close?

It feels like forever while she twists in the air before entering the water. Near perpendicular with a tiny splash.

I jump up and down, nerves whooshing out of me.

It was a fantastic dive.

The whole team erupts into applause, and I celebrate with them.

"Dude." Cade leans over, smiling. I look at him to find that I've grabbed his wrist while watching her dive. He starts chuckling. "You got it bad, man."

I do. I've got it bad.

I shove him away playfully and clap, cheering with the rest of the guys. It might be me, but it sounds like she got the loudest applause. She pops up from the pool with a big smile before diving below again, swimming to the end.

Dragging herself up and out of the water, she turns and waves, her gaze connecting with mine.

A shockwave rockets through my body. It's only a nanosecond, a brief blip, but I feel it all the way to my toes.

Turning, she stares up at the scoreboard and waits for her marks to come up. Though they don't count toward the meet, she lands in the higher middle.

"Fuck yes," I say under my breath, relief and exhilaration ripping through me.

Kenna bounces up and down on her toes before walking over to her coach, who puts an arm around her and squeezes her into her side. She beams. Other teammates approach her, too, and I watch from the stands, wondering which one of them is her former synchro partner who abandoned her. She didn't deserve that. What happened was out of her control.

Eventually, I lose sight of Kenna. She was the last dive, so her other teammates swarm around her while walking back to the locker room.

The dudes are up next, and we stay for a few until Coach claps his hands twice to tell us we need to get going. I'd recognized a lot of the divers from around campus. I can't say I know their names but, who knows, this might change that.

Scanning the side of the pool, I search for Kenna, but it doesn't look like any of the women divers have returned poolside. Their coach is probably debriefing after the meet. I'd love to tell her goodbye, so I wait until I'm the last one, still staring at the locker room door, hoping she'll emerge. When she doesn't emerge, I have to leave or face Coach's wrath.

I'll just text her.

The sun shines down as I walk outside. The wide, metal beams leave strange angular shadows on the sidewalk. Next to the curb, the bus waits, engine cranked.

"West!" a female voice calls.

I turn to find Kenna jogging out of the exit. She has a Bulldog hoodie and pants set on, her hair still wet. She stops a few feet in front of me, her stare roaming toward the players lining up to get on the bus, then back to me.

"You came," she finally says. Her gaze drops. "And you wore a Speedo."

There she goes, biting her lip again.

"I wanted to see you dive."

"But you didn't even know I was going to, and you got the entire football team to wear Speedos," she remarks, gesturing toward my teammates.

I chuckle. "I think a few of them really enjoyed it, actually."

"Well, what did you think?" She raises to her toes and then back, waiting for my answer.

"I think..." I step toward her, taking her in. "I think you're a fucking warrior, Kenna, and you looked absolutely amazing."

Coach calls from the bus, "Let's go, Brooks. I will leave my star fullback. Don't think I won't."

I close my eyes briefly, then open them to tell her I have to go. Before I can get a word out, she grabs my head, tugging me down to kiss me. It's a sweet kiss, urgent. Lips upon lips.

A promise of something more.

Too soon, she pulls back, leaving me rattled and

shaken. I hadn't expected her to do that—not in front of the guys or Coach or, hell, even the bus driver.

"That's the second time I've kissed you," she says, grinning. "I expect the next to come from you."

With that, she walks away, leaving me standing there, stunned.

"Brooks!" Coach calls out again, this time with a little more urgency, and I turn on my heel and jog toward the bus, my lips still buzzing.

That was one hell of a kiss...

But it wasn't enough.

I want more.

CHAPTER FIFTEEN

Kenna

MY STOMACH CATAPULTS like I'm standing in front of a stadium full of people. I'm an electric wire, buzzing and snapping as I watch the bus from under the triangle-shaped awning. The team razzes West while he makes his way down the aisle. I can't hear what they're saying, but I can read West's lips. "Shut up. Shut up."

When he sits, he scoots to the window to find me. For a moment, I don't know what to do.

Should I act like I haven't been watching him? We're past that, I'm sure.

I'm also sure I've never seen anyone fill out a Speedo like West Brooks. The man is a walking, talking—okay, not-so-talkative—sin. Ripped, tight abs.

A huge chest. And I looked lower. I *definitely* looked lower. It was unavoidable. Literally.

We lock gazes, and he lifts his hand just as the bus pulls away, pressing his palm against the window.

Never in a million years did I expect him to come to my meet. Or bring the whole team. Or get them to all cheer like that. Like we're one of them.

I take out my cell phone to text Sydney.

> Me: Emergency. Can you take me to the football game? The whole team showed up at our meet.

> Sydney: No fucking way!

> Me: In Speedos.

> Sydney: Holy Mary, mother of God. Aidan in a Speedo??

> Me: I wasn't looking at him.

> Sydney: Of course you weren't, you dirty ho.

> Sydney: I'm getting in the car now.

> Sydney: Wait, I need to put deodorant on and freshen up, then I'm getting in the car. Will Aidan still be in his Speedo?

I shake my head, smiling. I'm practically giddy—a feeling I haven't felt in a long time.

A body steps next to me. Up ahead, the bus takes a right out of the lot and disappears.

"So, you're dating West Brooks now?"

My jaw snaps shut. I turn my head to find Laney standing off my left shoulder. Maybe she doesn't mean it, but there was a hint of judgment in her tone. "I'm sorry, did you want something?"

Her shoulders deflate. "It wasn't my idea, you know. To partner me with someone else. I don't know what you thought would happen, though."

"But it was your idea not to tell me about it or ask how I was doing. We've been friends for years, Laney. You know, you haven't even talked to me since my last surgery, and even then, it was like it was a chore for you. I expected more."

When she doesn't say anything, I peek over at her to find her staring at my scar. I take in a deep breath. For a whole hour or two there, I almost forgot I had one. I'm not going to let it define me anymore, though. If anything, I'm going to let it fuel me.

"I needed more," I tell her, and this raw honesty makes my stomach twist. I should've come out with it before, but now is as good a time as any. "I was recovering from two surgeries and dealing with helicopter parents and praying every night that I wasn't going to look like Quasimodo for the rest of my life. Even when I thought it should have been you texting, *I* was texting. And regardless of what I should've assumed would happen with you as a synchro partner, it would have been a hell of a lot easier to hear the news from you."

She swallows hard. "I..."

It hits me then that I don't really care. Any excuse she has to give won't make any of it better. Maybe the incident actually did me a favor. It showed me who deserves to be in my life.

Laney just stands there quietly, staring at me with round eyes.

Like West said, I'm a fucking warrior now. With his help.

And NoOne's.

NoOne told me my scar was like war paint.

Maybe they're onto something. I realize I haven't thought about NoOne in a while. The truth is, I haven't needed him.

And I don't need Laney either. I spin, leaving her there to go find Coach, so I can tell her I won't be on the bus back to school. I have something important to do—like drooling over West Brooks in a royal-blue jersey.

"Good job today, Kenna," Coach says when I walk up to her at the side of the pool. "I wasn't sure what to expect, but you...did well. We should talk Monday before practice. Come a little early."

Rabid butterflies that have just escaped from certain death erupt in my stomach. My score was a solid one. Real solid. It must have shocked her. "Sure thing, Coach. I'll be there."

"And, um..." She looks away briefly, catching one of our male divers as he leaps from the platform. As soon as he splashes in, she looks back at me. "Are we to thank you for the cheering section today?"

A smile peels my lips apart. "I think so."

"I liked it," she says. "I'm sure it was a nice morale boost for everyone."

"I liked it, too," I muse, remembering the moment I locked eyes with West. It was his face that drew me in first. His focused, sincere gaze, but then it was difficult not to appreciate the bigger picture. He's hot enough to eat off of.

Or maybe I'm just hungry.

My phone vibrates, and I take it out to find a text from Sydney.

Be there in 20.

I hope that's enough time to make it to his game. I pull up the football schedule and Google Map the directions to the opposing team's field. Luckily, it's not too far away.

I sit on the sidelines with the rest of my teammates as we watch the guys dive.

After ten minutes, the officials switch the pool over for the swimming portion of the meet, and I take the opportunity to grab my bag and wait out on the curb for Sydney.

When she gets there, we haul ass to the game. After needling me for details about what the football players looked like in their Speedos, I find a couple of videos on Insta—one on the Warner Athletics page— and hold the phone up while she drives. Her eyes widen. "I think West might make any girl extremely happy, so you should probably jump on that."

I avoid that topic because I haven't been able to think straight about it since he left.

While I contemplate my life choices, Sydney talks happily about winning the Lip Sync Contest for homecoming. She met with the halftime team today and went over different possibilities with them, so she's on fire with excitement. I'm on fire for a different reason, but Sydney's a nice distraction while I sit here with my stomach squeezing from nerves.

As we get closer, cars line the street in the unfamiliar town. "Should I park back here?" Sydney asks, scooching up the driver's seat like it'll make her see better.

"I guess." I peer around, but it looks like street parking only gets worse as it nears the school's parking lot. All the spaces are probably gone.

"Man, this is crazy." She quickly pulls to the side behind another car. We're three blocks from the university. Up ahead, groups of people are walking that way in purple and yellow. When I open my door, two college-aged dudes run past in matching golden shirts. Whistles are going off. Loud cow bells. The *pop* of noisy fireworks.

If only diving got this much attention...

I push that thought out of my head as Sydney meets me on the sidewalk, and we make our way with the crowd. A small kid sits atop his dad's shoulders, his brother asking a bunch of questions.

"How cool is it that Warner comes to play us for our season opener?"

"How many yards do you think Brooks will get?"

"Do you think we're going to win? I kind of hope Warner wins, but I also kind of hope we win. I don't know."

He gets easily distracted with jumping over a crack, and Sydney jabs me with her elbow. "He just talked about your boyfriend."

"He's not my boyfriend," I retort, my stomach doing that flip thing again. I swear that's all it's done since I saw him sitting in the stands. It's the moment of free fall that makes me take notice. Like being scared and exhilarated at the same time. And it happens every time I think about West.

"You're totally blushing," Sydney says. "If you get with West, get a good word in with Aidan for me, would ya?"

I peer over at her, and she's smiling from ear to ear.

"I just have some research I need to do." She lowers her voice. "Think along the vein of how good football players are in bed. You know, stamina, muscles, pleasure points."

"Oh. My. God." I laugh. Sometimes, I can't believe the things that come out of her mouth.

"You're definitely embarrassed now."

"It's the redness from my scar," I tell her, but she knows I'm full of shit. My mind has wandered to West in bed, and I can't shake it. He's a specimen of athletic ability. I'm sure—

"There it is!" the kid ahead of us yells.

I snap back to reality and glance up at the stadium that comes into view. It's pretty big, but not as big as the one Warner boasts. It's completely open and looks more like my high school's football field, except the stands are packed. Mostly blue and white shirts dot the crowd, but on the side closest to us, there are more yellow and purple.

A fast-talking announcer spits out plays with the speed of a chatterbox on crack. "We're missing it!" The kid echoes my thoughts, and his parents exchange a look and pick up the pace.

We're right behind them when they get to the ticket booths. We're not the only ones either. A massive crowd still moves toward the stands with us. We get in the shortest line available, and when we finally get to the front, the attendant says, "You can

166

still get a ticket, but it's probably standing room only."

She glances up at us and then down at the Bulldog insignia on my jacket. "Wait, are you Warner University students?"

"Yes, ma'am," Sydney and I say at the same time.

"You get discounted tickets, then, and I'm sure there are still seats in the student section. I'll just need your student IDs."

I blow out a breath of relief. Sydney and I both hand over our IDs, and I pay for her ticket since she used her gas to bring us here. We scurry toward the entrance with our tickets, and an usher points us in the right direction. Now that we're close, the field is bigger than I originally thought. It's still not as nice as Warner's facilities, but it's nice for a smaller school.

Sydney grabs my hand as the crowd thickens. We end up in the away team student section and have to squeeze past a group of people hovering over someone. I recognize Reid Parker in the middle of it, our former QB. He's straining his neck to watch the game around the people who have gathered next to him. His forehead is pinched in annoyance, but the girl holding on to his hand is hiding a smile.

"Hey, that's—"

"Yep," I say to Sydney, eager to move around so I can watch.

"I had a class with him my freshman year. He was

nice. I thought it was cute how he always walked his girlfriend to every single class. Every single class. Can you imagine, Kenna?"

I remember that, too. Reid was the talk of the university when I first got here, but he was down-to-earth. "He got drafted, right? Wonder why he's here?"

A guy who's sitting a couple of seats over from him speaks up. "He's got a break. I was talking to him before the game." He peers at Sydney and me. "You guys need a place to sit?"

He scoots down, forcing everyone else to sit closer together, and there's just enough room for Sydney and I to sit on the edge of the row. "Thanks," I tell him as we take the offered space. I was beginning to worry that we weren't going to get a spot.

Once seated, I look ahead and see that we're just behind the team. I scour the sidelines and don't see West right away.

The other team punts and our offense jogs onto the field.

"There he is," I say, pointing him out, unable to help myself.

Sydney cranes her neck. "Looking good in those uniforms. Still think I would prefer the Speedos, but..." She lifts her shoulders.

"Beggars can't be choosers?"

She zeroes her gaze in on me. "Please. West is practically begging to get into your pants. You don't have to choose at all."

Flip-flop.

I hold my stomach, trying to calm it down. No matter how many times I try to talk myself out of it, I keep coming back to the same reality—the same one Sydney just said.

West Brooks *likes* me.

Holy shit.

Our offense isn't on the field for very long. Aidan throws two complete passes while Sydney screams her head off for him. Then, on the third play, he hands it off to West, and I get to see the Hulk in action. He plows through the smaller defensive players, and they bounce off him like ping-pong balls.

They don't even stand a chance.

When he runs it into the end zone, I find myself standing and cheering just like everyone else. My heart slams; my pulse skyrockets. I jump up and down on the tips of my toes.

No wonder everyone likes football. This is fun. It's exciting. A bit more primal than diving. The loudest crowd I ever heard at a meet was today when the football team brought their energy.

I'm still clapping and cheering when Sydney lets out a whistle that nearly pierces my eardrum. "Aidan, West!"

I gasp, pulling at her shirt. "What are you doing?"

She's not listening to me. She's waving down at the field. I hesitate to look over, but she hits me with her elbow. When I scour the field, there are Aidan and West, walking back from the end zone. West has stopped moving, his gaze locked onto mine, and an electric current passes between us. He has his helmet in his hand, and his knuckles turn white as he grips it.

My body trembles at the shocked expression on his face.

Did he not want me to come?

No, that can't be it. He's just surprised.

One of his teammates runs into him from behind, slapping him on the shoulder, and that's what finally gets him moving again.

He jogs to the sidelines. A teenager in a white polo shirt offers him some water, and he takes it, gulping it down. After handing it back, he beckons the kid to follow him as he rummages through a bag on the sideline, pulling out a royal-blue jersey.

He turns to look at me, and I finally peer away. I can't watch him like a stalker.

I try to concentrate on the game. The other team is okay. Next to me, the guy who gave up his end seats for us is explaining to a girl on the other side of him that the team we're playing isn't even in the same division as us, but they're local, so we start out our season here.

He sounds like he knows what he's talking about,

and I get lost in his explanations until a voice says, "McKenna Knowles?"

I glance up to find the water boy that was just down with West staring at me.

Sydney bumps me with her shoulder. "Yeah, that's her."

"Here," he says, offering me the jersey in his palms. On top, there's a note:

Kenna,
I'll kiss you next, but I want to
make sure we're on the same page.
Wear my jersey?

SYDNEY SQUEALS and claps her hands. "Wear my jersey?" She cups her hand around my ear and whispers, "That's footballer talk for he wants to fuck you."

I can't even laugh at her. I'm just stunned.

Is that what he's asking? It definitely seems like he's asking for something more.

"How do you know?" I ask.

Sydney starts pointing out all the players' girlfriends. First, there's Briar Page. She's still smiling, sitting next to Reid as they watch the game together, both of them wearing the same jersey. Then there are a few other girls, too. All girlfriends. Not jersey chasers. Not fuck buddies. Not casual flings.

I peer around the water boy to find West, his green eyes focused on me in earnest, sweat lining his temples.

Please? he mouths.

If I had willpower to refuse his offer, I don't anymore.

I take the jersey and fold the note to put in my joggers. Unzipping my jacket, I take it off and while I'm standing there watching West, I tug his jersey on.

The crowd erupts around me, but all I see is the sparkle in West's eyes. My chest constricts. A lot of feelings flow through me as I ball up my jacket and hold it on my lap.

His jersey makes me pull my shoulders back. The material dwarfs me, of course, but I don't care. I peek down to find his number across my chest.

West Brooks's—possible—girlfriend, and I am here for it.

CHAPTER SIXTEEN

West

NO ONE— Fuck, no one has ever come to see me play football before. Not anyone that mattered. I watch Kenna pull the jersey on, and my stomach twists. I hope she knows what she just did because there's no going back now.

Kenna Knowles is mine.

Fucking mine.

The first game of the season goes by in a blur, and it takes every ounce of effort to pay attention to what's happening on the field. Our opponent is a gimme. At least it is today.

Nothing can stop me today. I am the damn Hulk.

It's the best season opener I've had in ages, and as the game clock counts down, I only have one thing on my mind.

Kissing my girl.

My gaze skips up the stands as I run back in after another Bulldog touchdown to find Kenna smiling and clapping, her focus on me. The running back who ran it in claps me on the shoulder. "You're on fire today, Big Man!" He leans back, letting out an animalistic growl, his head pointed toward the sky.

We're all feeling it.

I love football on days like this. The grass is green. The breeze cools the sweat on my neck, and the water I gulp down tastes like it came fresh out of the purest stream in the world. I am alive. Like a live wire, the electricity is palpable just underneath my skin.

The game clock zeroes out in the fourth quarter, and Aidan chest bumps his center. He had a great game. If anyone was wondering if he wouldn't live up to Parker's play, he just showed them. Lining up, we march out onto the field to shake hands with the other players and then there's more celebrating.

Goosebumps cover my skin from head to toe as I scour the stands for Kenna. She's all I want to see right now. I'll celebrate with my teammates back in the locker room, but I need her. I slow my steps, chest heaving. If she went home, I might die.

I scan the crowd for the third time when I finally spot her with Sydney. She's hanging on to the chain-link fence, pressed up on her tiptoes to find me. Our stares collide, and my feet start working, picking up the pace.

I stop in front of her, shoulders moving with my deep breaths. If this were a movie, it would be the part where the guy finally tells the girl he loves her. Or that he wants to be with her, and it would be this huge shock, but for the life of me, I can't form words other than, "You came."

A slow smile spreads her lips apart. "I didn't know what I was missing."

My heart pumps so fast that the beat of my blood moving through my body and Kenna are the only things I can focus on. They're both larger than life.

Sydney chuckles. "Are you guys just going to stare at each other or..."

Her teasing words spring me into action. I drop my helmet and reach for Kenna. She just stands there. Her stare settles on my lips, but I'm not kissing her for the first time with a fence in my way. I reach under her arms, lifting her in the air.

"West," she protests, but she speaks around a short giggle as I easily maneuver her over the fence before settling her on her feet. "What are you—"

I clasp the back of her head, my fingers working through her long hair that's had time to dry now. Tugging, I make her look at me. Her lips part as she takes me in. Her eyes don't waver, but a breath builds in her chest that she doesn't have time to let out before my mouth is on hers. Soft at first, exploring, testing, but my resolve to take this slow breaks. I tilt my head, pulling her closer and pressing past the seam of her plush lips.

A low moan escapes her throat, which only spurs me on. My other hand comes up to touch the side of her face, my fingertips feathering along her jaw, tracing the outline of her scar while I devour her with my mouth.

She pastes her body against mine, and I curse my bulky pads. I want to feel her, all of her. I hitch her leg up, maneuvering her closer until another satisfied groan sounds. Pulling back, she teases the wet hair at the back of my neck, but I can't stand to be away from her. I press my forehead to hers. "If I'd known you could kiss like that, I would've let you take the reins the first time."

I swallow, a grin coming to my face. "I liked your kisses."

Her shoulders shake with a laugh as she leans further into me, like she's trying to hide herself. "I don't know what I'm going to do with you, West Brooks."

"I have some ideas."

She bites her lip, moving her gaze to mine. "Me too."

For the love of God, I hope we're on the same goddamn page. I step away, fingering the material of my jersey that's currently hugging her body. She's rolled up the bottom, but it's starting to come undone with the way we were wrapped around each other. The sight of her wearing my number makes my breath hitch. If this is the feeling I was missing out on when no one else supported me, it was well worth the fucking wait. I'll take all the disappointments from before to have this one moment.

"I need to go," I finally tell her, reluctantly. The last blue jersey is already halfway toward the locker rooms. Coach will be wanting me.

"I know."

Squeezing her hand, I linger a little longer, "I have to ride the bus home."

"Okay."

"But can I see you tonight? I'll text you."

"Yeah...yes." She shakes her head at herself. She's so damn cute, but if I don't go now, I won't.

I grip her hand one last time and lead her toward the gate in the fence. She frowns when I undo the latch. "You mean I could've just come in the easy way?"

"That was the easy way."

A blush starts up her neck and settles in her cheeks. "If you say so."

"Tonight," I tell her as I close the gate behind her.

"Yeah," she says, still not walking away. I'm one

hundred percent certain we look like fools right now, but I can't stop myself.

"Okay." I back up, still hesitant to leave, but in the back of my head, I don't want to face Coach's fury either. I give her one last smirk before turning away.

"Oh, West," she calls out.

I peer over my shoulder to find her gripping the hem of my jersey.

"Do you want this?"

I run back toward her and realize I was about to leave my helmet out there, too. I'm flustered, but there's one thing I won't have happen. I grip the fence and stare her down. "Don't you dare take that off."

My words make her blush red again. "Ever?"

"Ever."

"Is this some sort of claiming?" she asks, tilting her head at me with a bemused expression.

"If I say yes, will you still wear it?"

"Probably."

"Then yes."

She chuckles, and I really have to go now. Coach is probably already cooking up some torture in his head for my absence. I run over to my helmet to pick it off the ground and then jog backward. "Tonight."

Sydney rolls her eyes as she approaches Kenna and practically peels her away from the gate. "I can already tell this is going to be sickening."

Kenna leans into her, and I make myself turn and

jog toward the locker room. People are still waiting at the fence, and I run by, high-fiving them.

I barely hear their congratulations. I feel like I can do anything at the moment. This excitement is so pure and raw. It was like the first time I took the field at peewee, except more acute.

"Hey!" a voice yells.

The sharp tone snaps my head up. My legs falter. The last figure standing, waiting to see me...

It can't be...

I squint, my insides squeezing. The sweat tracks over my eyes, and I have to wipe at them to peer up again while I slow my stride.

To my right, a little kid yells, "Hulk! Great game!"

I don't even know if I acknowledge him because I can barely breathe.

His hair is longer than before, at least around his ears. Last time I saw him, he was balding at the top, but he's wearing a cap now. He tugs the bill up, settling it back over his head, and I have to grab the fence as my father returns my stare. The whites of his eyes are cream-colored. Just a little off. Even his skin tone is ashen. The corner of his mouth wrenches up, his "smile" more fearsome than any other smile I've witnessed.

It's by sheer nature that I still step forward. One leg in front of the other. It's not that hard, but when the rest of me is shutting down, I'm surprised I'm still moving at all.

"Hey, son."

I'm nearly to him now. My breaths have shallowed. There's a twist in my gut, and those eyes, those fucking eyes, make me feel small again.

I slow, stopping in front of him. My body is at war. Part of me wants to walk away, the other part of me is scared of the repercussions, like that day I accidentally got Play-Doh stuck in the rug. I knew if I didn't sit there and listen to his lecture, I'd get it worse.

"Stupid kid. Stupid. Is this how you act? Is this what you do to the nice things we buy you?"

I look around and spot the beer cans strewn over the counter and the fake-wood cabinets that were coming off their hinges in the kitchen. I didn't see any nice things, but I certainly didn't mean to get the Play-Doh in the carpet either.

I knew I needed to answer him. Tuning him out never worked. His voice would just get sharper. His words more cutting. He'd force me to talk until I hated the sound of my own voice. So meek. So small.

"No, Dad."

The answer I gave didn't matter. It took me years to figure that out because even saying what he wanted me to say wouldn't stop his anger-fueled words.

"You're not going to say hi to your old man?"

A diamond stud—most likely fake—glints in his

ear. The yellowing of his teeth near the gum borders on brown decay. Remorse hits me in the gut at the sight of his clear deterioration. He's had a hard life.

I shake the pity off though. Those are just the thoughts of a child who was trying to find any excuse as to why his father was a dick.

He's a dick because he is one. Period. Life didn't make him that way. Everyone has choices they can make every day to better themselves and their surroundings. People like him who don't veer off their center and make excuses for their actions sicken me.

I lick my lips, my mouth going dry. A rattling breath escapes my lungs, and then I remember I'm in my football jersey. My suit of armor. I puff out my chest, but it doesn't last long. All the bravado dies on my tongue when I attempt to talk.

"Coach is waiting for me."

My jaw snaps shut. *I don't owe this fucker any explanation.*

"I've been calling you for a month."

"I've been busy."

"Too busy for your father? That's a fucking joke."

That pitch. That sharp edge of a razor that cuts right through me and has for so many years.

Panic starts to set in.

I never dreamed he would show up here. I thought he'd get bored with trying to get a hold of me and then he'd give up because I'm not that important to him, anyway.

Standing there, not speaking, is making it worse. My father sighs, and it's the sound that brings a lot of worries back. The precursor to the vile words he'd sling at me.

I press my lips together. I'm frozen. I'm so, so small. I can't even remember what the feeling was like to see Kenna in my jersey or to know that someone had actually come to my game to watch me.

Well, I guess two someones did. If he even saw the game.

"Brooks!" an assistant coach yells from the open locker room. "Get your ass in here!"

I jump. His words suddenly spur me into motion, and I wrap my hand around my helmet even tighter and start to jog past my father, giving him a wide berth.

"Jesus fucking Christ. Really? Really?" he yells, making a scene. All those people who'd waited for me are watching this play out. The longer I jog, the more I want to retreat inside a suit of armor.

But my jersey isn't even enough for this.

Of course he would show up to my game and make it all about him.

"Pick up a fucking phone, West!" he screams, his words still hitting me like bullets flying through the air. "Or don't you know how to work one? I taught you better than that!" There's a long pause, and then a grumble. There's always a low grumble, his retreating war cry. "Dumb piece of shit."

I can see him now, shaking his head like he can't believe I'm his. I'll always be a disappointment to him. Always.

CHAPTER SEVENTEEN

Kenna

I PICK MY PHONE UP. Nothing from West yet. Damn. How long does it take to get back from a game? Maybe the bus stopped off so the players could get something to eat. Or maybe their coach is long-winded.

It just seems like he should've been back an hour ago.

Unless...

Unless nothing, I scold myself. West Brooks is totally into me. I felt it in the way he practically tattooed his name on my lips, claiming me.

I stare up at my David Boudia poster, and I have to admit that he's not doing it for me anymore. Don't get me wrong, there's nothing unbecoming about him, but there's everything so, so right with West in a Speedo.

He probably gave all the grandmothers in the stands a minor heart attack.

I know I shouldn't, but I pick up the phone again. When there's nothing there, I check the volume to make sure it's turned up. "Not in the Same Way" by 5SOS wraps around me as the lyrics punctuate out of my Bluetooth speakers. I quickly skip the song. "Lover of Mine" comes on next, and the slow melody makes me antsy.

Jesus. What's wrong with me?

I start my Going Out playlist, which also masquerades as my Feeling Good playlist. I have some Lizzo on there, some T Swift, and Panic! at the Disco.

My phone *pings*, and I snatch it up to find a group message with some of my dive teammates. They're all meeting at Molly's. The device vibrates in my hand as more people confirm that they're going. Molly's is a cool little sports bar. They have greasy food, good tunes, and it's within walking distance from the campus and my house.

My leg bounces up and down. The teammate in me feels like she should go, but I would rather hang out with West. I want to explore what this is between us.

It's not wrong if I message him first, right? Totally not. Maybe I could tell him I'm going to hang out with my teammates until he gets back into town. Yeah. That sounds good. Not stalkerish or over-the-top, just letting him know what I'm doing. A sly voice inside me also says that it shows I'm not sitting around waiting for his text either, even though I so totally am. He, however, doesn't need to know that.

I'm a strong, independent woman. Hell, I'm a warrior woman. Yes? Yes.

I pull up West on the school's app and start typing. **Hey, I got invited to go out with my teammates, so...**

I backspace out of that and try again.

My teammates want to hang out at Molly's. I'll be there when you get back in town.

I stare down at the message, toying with my lip in a nervous habit that I haven't been able to break. West's number emblazoned across my chest catches my eye. Yes, I haven't taken his jersey off yet, and it's a good reminder that he made the first move. He may be West Brooks, but he wants this.

Okay, okay...

I delete the second message and start again.

> McKennaK: My teammates want to hang out at Molly's. Let me know when you get back into town.

There. Good. Done...and sent.

Standing, I peel off West's jersey and lay it on my comforter. *Brooks* runs from shoulder to shoulder. I haven't paid that much attention, but I don't think I've seen anyone else wearing his jersey before.

I change into a respectable outfit, just a plain shirt and jeans, and then run a brush through my hair. Peering at myself in the mirror, my eyes snap over to my scar, but I don't feel the self-loathing I used to. It's just a part of me now. It kind of looks a little smaller, actually. I twist my head from side to side, then I put a bit of powder across my face and call it done.

When I step back, my phone *pings,* and I pull it out while I shout for Sydney, before remembering that she went to see her parents when we got back. Guilt trip from her mother.

> NoOne: I had a shit day.

I tilt my head. NoOne hasn't contacted me in a while. I search back up our message thread and see that the last time we talked, he called me a badass for my scar. My mind has only been on West since.

> McKennaK: I'm sorry. Want to talk about it?

I finish the message and then grab my card and ID and shove them in my back pocket. My dive jacket goes on last, and I leave the front open as I lock up the house and head down the sidewalk.

NoOne: It's my dad. We don't get along, and he just embarrassed the shit out of me.

McKennaK: He came to campus? That sucks. Are you okay?

I alternate between typing out the message and watching where I'm going. NoOne was there for me when no one else could penetrate my walls. I don't know who he is, and I might be obsessed with West Brooks right now, but NoOne's my friend.

NoOne: Not exactly.

I'm not sure which question he's answering.

McKennaK: What did he do?

NoOne: Belittled me. He makes me feel small. You ever wonder if your parents really wanted you?

I stop in my tracks, staring down at the screen. I've never felt that way. My parents are more the hover type. Annoying, kind of, but I guess the opposite of that isn't great either.

McKennaK: That's terrible. I'm so sorry.

I huff out a breath and stare up at the darkening sky. The first few stars are out and the sight of them always reminds me of camping with my parents. Of feeling like I'm a small piece in the grand scheme of things. But what if stars look at us and think *wow. They're so tiny, yet bright.*

Sure, some of us sparkle more than others. Some shine with megawatt smiles in front of adoring fans, but NoOne, he was my bright spot for a while. He doesn't deserve to be feeling this way.

> **McKennaK:** That's fucked up, actually, and any parent who doesn't want their kids is shitty. End of story. I don't know you very well, but I know you deserve better than that.

> **NoOne:** Kenna…

I stare down at my screen, my feet still firmly rooted to the sidewalk. That's the first time NoOne has used my real name.

> **NoOne:** Turn around.

My breath hitches in my chest, and I feel like I'm going to puke as I slowly turn.

Shit. Holy shit.

"West?"

He walks toward me, his university football jacket hugging his wide shoulders. I watch him as he pockets his phone, determined footsteps moving my way. The entire time, he keeps his gaze locked on mine.

"Don't be mad," he says.

"You're—" My mouth suddenly feels dry. All the way to the back of my throat is like a scorched desert. "*You're* NoOne?"

He nods slowly before stopping in front of me and jamming his hands into his pockets. Like usual, he dwarfs me. His presence is second to none, and I think back to the words he just wrote me. His dad makes him feel small. *Impossible.* Not West Brooks. Not the fucking golden boy on campus.

Plus, I was at his game. I didn't see his father.

I don't say any of those things, though, because my mind snags on what him being NoOne means. "You've been talking to me this entire time? Since right after I got hurt?" My scar tingles, and I reach up to touch it.

West grabs my hand before I can. "I didn't think you would talk to me if I wrote you as me." He shuffles his feet. "I wanted to tell you." Grimacing, he looks away. "Actually, that's a damn lie. I kind of liked being able to talk to you while not being me."

"While not being someone I hated?"

"Not just that." His face starts to close off. "You're mad, aren't you?"

He peers at me again with those shadowed green eyes, and I don't even know what to say. I check in with myself. I'm more in shock. Not really mad at all, I guess. In fact, once I got to know West, there were some things that rang similar, like the badass warrior comments. I just— He should've—

Shit. This is not about me right now. I squeeze his hand. "Your dad?"

He drops his head, gaze lowering to the sidewalk between us. "I've been walking around your neighborhood since we got back into town. I didn't know how to tell you. I—" He blows out a breath. "I've got daddy issues." He cracks a smile, but I know he doesn't feel it. He curses, his voice barely above a whisper. "No one likes to think that people like me have issues like everyone else."

My stomach squeezes. God, how many times have I thought that he's had the perfect life? That he's the golden boy while I was stuck in hospital rooms?

"It was easier to tell you as that stupid name I made up. I wanted you to know, I just didn't know how to say that I wasn't sure I'd be good company, even though I made you promise like five times that we'd hang out tonight. Please don't be mad."

He's a far cry from the West Brooks I saw out on the field today, and this version of him gets under my skin even more. I tug on his hand and walk him back to my place.

Silence lingers between us as I shut the front door and head into the kitchen to get him a glass of water. I'm just procrastinating. I don't know what to say to him. Soft, careful footsteps sound behind me as I reach for a cup, and I immediately feel his warmth. Before I can turn, he closes his arms around me, wrapping tight around my midsection while he buries his head in the crook of my neck.

Heat engulfs me. West Brooks is like a teddy bear. A giant teddy bear that has an erratic heartbeat. I can practically feel it through his large chest, *thump-thumping* away.

"I hate the way he makes me feel," he says so softly that I'm not sure I heard him right.

I turn in his arms, keeping us attached as I lean against the countertop, and he follows me, pressing his hips into mine. "What did he say?"

He flinches. "He's been trying to get a hold of me, but I didn't know because I don't have his number. My mom told me he called her upset that I hadn't been picking up his calls, so I guess that unknown number was him."

I take all this in, my mind working through what he's not saying. I can't imagine a relationship with my dad where I didn't have his number.

"He was mad?" I guess.

West scowls. Behind me, his hands turn to fists. "That fucker hasn't even come to any of my games, and then he shows up to scold me like I'm five years old."

Reaching up, I run my fingers through the hair above his ears. His lids flutter closed. When he speaks again, it's much softer. "I've been trying to get him to one of my games for... Well, forever." His Adam's apple bobs with a large swallow. "That's why I couldn't believe I saw you there today. No one ever comes to see me."

"You're West Brooks," I tease. "Everyone is there to see you."

"No one I care about. Until now."

He locks gazes with me, and the world tilts a little. Like the universe has to accommodate for the fact that West Brooks is staring at someone the way he's staring at me.

I want to promise him the world. That I'll keep going to his games because no one deserves to feel like he has, but fear runs through me, so I bite my lip instead. I don't know what to do with all these feelings trampling around inside me, running over every muted thought I've ever had.

My heart leaps around inside me. "Your dad sounds like a jackass, and he doesn't deserve you."

His chest brushes mine, our lips mere inches away from one another. On the one hand, his dad problems are a serious talk, but he's turned it into these life-altering words about us. I don't know what to dwell on first. Is this what being into someone like this is like?

My thoughts aren't my own. They're all jumbled and scrambled, like a game of Scrabble, and I'm just trying to come up with any words that are coherent enough to speak.

West has other ideas, though. After searching me with his gaze, he lowers his lips to mine. A soft embrace; a press of one piece of anatomy to another that turns into something more when it's between us. I don't think God invented kissing. I think we did.

A shockwave rolls through me at the connection, the same I'd always felt around him but didn't want to admit it.

His mouth barely moves, but its imprint is on me forever.

He pulls back far too soon. "I think I'll have that water now."

Taking a step back, he gives me even more space, and I have to carefully school my features so I don't self-combust here on the spot.

I don't think this man knows what he's capable of.

CHAPTER EIGHTEEN

West

I RUN a hand down my face, peeking at her out of the corner of my eye. Talking is usually difficult for me. No guy likes to open up. At least, that's what I used to think.

I'd been battling the rising fear inside me. What I imagined when I was outside Kenna's apartment doesn't happen, though. She doesn't run. She doesn't tell me I'm not worth it.

She actually listens. She goes from hugging her legs to herself to stretching out over her bed, her head propped up in her hands. I lie next to her, acutely aware that I take up most of the single bed. The proximity makes it easier. Outside, the stars can easily be seen through the blanket of darkness, like light at the end of a tunnel, and in Kenna's bedroom, I feel the same. Like she's my light.

"Sorry," I say, hiding my face.

She lifts her hand to grab my own, pulling it away. "Don't be."

She doesn't let it go, holding on to it between us on the bed, her fingers pressing into mine. A ghost of a smile appears on her lips.

"I think your past... Don't get me wrong, it's awful," she says, peering up at me. "But it's given you a hell of a lot of reasons to be who you are now. I know I don't know everything about stupid football." She rolls her eyes for good measure, and I grin. "But I do know you're going places. West—" She shakes her head, her eyes filled with unshed tears, and my heart breaks a little. "You're like the perfect comeback story. Everything you just told me about how you grew up, and everyone says you're a shoo in for the NFL. Holy shit."

My stomach squeezes. I still have a long way to get to the NFL, but it's been my goal. I've already been scouted, but nothing is certain. Life is funny. I could get injured. I could—

"Woah," she says, pinching my fingers. "You just went someplace bad."

I take a deep breath. "What if I don't do it? What if—"

She blinks. "West, that's crazy talk. I only hear things from around campus, but I'm pretty sure I've heard your name and the NFL in the same sentence since we were freshmen. Couldn't you have gone into the draft last year? And this is me not knowing anything. What if I were to Google you right now?"

My heart leaps in my chest. "Don't. Please."

She bites her lip, giving me a sultry, playful gaze. "Oh, I'm doing it now."

Pulling just enough away to reach onto her desk to grab her phone, she returns with a sly smile. She taps away on the screen, then uses her thumb to scroll. I wish I could say I hadn't Googled myself before but that would be an outright lie.

"Ha," she says, as if she's just found a missing clue. "Let's see, Sports Illustrated has ranked you the number one player that could've gone to the draft last year but didn't." She peers up at me, expression guarded. "Why didn't you go into the draft?"

I shrug, stomach clenching. "I wanted a degree."

"That's it?"

My mind swirls. "Yeah."

She watches me a little longer before she focuses back on the screen. "Let's see, draft prospect rankings: number three." Her eyes pop out of her head. "West, number three?"

"Those rankings change all the time." Actually, I'm a little chuffed. I was four before the game earlier. Not that I look...a lot. I look a normal amount.

"I don't know. Maybe you're too cool to hang out with me."

She's joking, but it lands like a lead weight inside me. "None of that stuff means anything."

"Are you kidding? It means everything. West, you're going to do it. You're going to show your dad and your mom, and—"

I lean over, pressing my lips to hers. From the decision to the moment our lips touch was merely a second, but it was still too long. She's surprised at first, stilling, but I keep my lips on hers, cupping her cheek in my hand. No one that mattered has ever believed in me, and I'm filled with the need to show her what that means.

She's like a delicate fine art painting, and the things I want to do to her are rough and uncultured.

I'm at war with myself. The need to have her is pulsing through me. My hands start to shake with the effort to hold back when she groans.

"Fuck," I growl, that rubber band of restraint straining. I move my hand from her face to her hip, kneading it before pulling her to me. Her yielding body molds to mine. Tentatively, she raises her knee, so I can get closer. Oh so fucking close. Her breasts are pressed against my chest, her lips forming over mine again and again.

I dive my tongue inside her mouth, and she

responds by hitching her knee higher up my hip until my cock meets her soft flesh. Her fingers curl around my shirt, scraping the skin of my pecs underneath. "West."

Her lips move over my own as I gulp in air. Our gazes meet, and all it does is make me hungry for more.

I start the kiss again, plunging into her mouth and palming her ass, urging her against me.

My cock is rock solid in my jeans. The stupid zipper keeps dragging across me, but to hear the little noises coming from her throat, I wouldn't stop for anything. "You feel so fucking good," I groan.

She drops her head to my shoulder, her hips rocking into my cock. "This is so embarrassing, but I might come from this."

Fuck being embarrassed. "Like this?" I ask, moving with her finally.

A restrained cry catches in her throat. "West."

I'm addicted now. I want my name on her lips forever.

She shifts, circling her clit over my dick. I get lost in the moment before remembering I can't come in my jeans. That's a rookie move.

I urge her over me, faster, tighter. She grinds out in frustration, and I lower my hands to her jeans. "May I?"

She nods, her face flush.

I undo the button and then slowly lower her zipper, watching her face. She's searching mine, her chest rubbing across my pecs while I lower her jeans enough to press into her nub, then swirl over her clit.

"Oh," she sighs, leaning her head back into the pillow as I take control. Her fingers flex into my skin.

I love the way her body yields to me, softening under my touch. The way she just lies back, as if she knows I'm going to take care of her. "Does this feel good, baby?"

She nods again, and I pick up on as many subtle cues as I can before I find her perfect speed and pressure. My thumb gets wetter and wetter. Before too long, she grabs my forearm and slides down to my wrist, her hips working against me before she throws her head back and lets out a silent scream.

Gulping air, her spent body molds to the bed, her jeans undone and open. Her hair fanned out over the pillowcase. She still has hold of my wrist, and her thumb traces the sensitive skin on the underside.

She giggles nervously, and it only endears me more. "I didn't mean to do that," she says.

"Me neither, but I couldn't help myself."

She props herself back up on her hand to stare at me. "I guess neither of us could."

I have a feeling I might use that excuse a lot.

I touched your ass. I just couldn't help myself.

I slid inside you. I just couldn't help myself.

I stared at you, again and again. I just couldn't help myself.

"So, the football jersey?" she asks after a little while.

My gaze moves behind her to my jersey folded neatly over her desk chair. "Yeah?" My heart nearly skips. I remember what it felt like to see her put that on for the first time.

"Does it mean what Sydney thinks it means?"

My lips curl. "What does Sydney think it means?"

Kenna looks away then, her feet fidgeting against one another.

I watch for a moment, in awe that I could make someone feel like this. I'm used to fan talk. To jersey chasers telling me how amazing I am, even though I'm sure they don't understand a single thing about what it takes to get to where I am, and they sure as hell don't know where I've come from.

Yet, here's Kenna, anxious and nervous. I can't even bring myself to make her say it. "If Sydney says it means that you're mine, she's right."

"Yours?" Her brows pull together.

"Officially."

"So, for the record, I agreed to date you before I knew what you could do to me with your pants on."

A laugh escapes my throat. Can she be any more

perfect? "I think you'll like what I can do to you with my pants off, too."

She locks gazes with me. "I'm looking forward to it," she says with a grin. "But really, I wanted to make sure we were on the same page."

"Were you thinking the same?"

Her smile widens. "I wouldn't have put your jersey on if I wasn't thinking you were at least saying that you liked me better than any of the other girls here."

"I like you way more than any of the other girls here."

"Excellent. We're on the same page again." She tilts her head. "Hmm."

"What?"

"I'm trying to decide if my parents will like you despite being a football player."

Shit. I hadn't thought of that.

She pushes my shoulder. "Don't look scared. You won me over."

"Maybe we don't have to tell them."

She rolls her eyes. "Oh yeah. Mom, Dad, this is West. He's six-foot-something. I know he's built like a football player with all the muscles and the wide shoulders of a football player, but obviously, he's not a football player. He's the furthest thing from a football player. He's—"

"A normal guy."

"You, West Brooks, are anything but normal."

I grip her hip, squeezing it a little. I'm not used to getting compliments from people I care about. "Maybe we'll tell them I play soccer instead."

She shakes her head.

"Baseball?"

The look on her face says *yeah, right.* "With these guns?" she asks, poking my biceps. "No, we'll tell them exactly who you are."

"Now that's scary."

She chuckles. "As soon as we say your name, I'm pretty sure they'll know, anyway. *Everyone* knows West Brooks."

"No, everyone only *thinks* they know West Brooks," I tell her, rolling to my back.

She scoots closer, laying her head in the crook of my shoulder. "Who else knows about your mom and dad?" she asks.

"Just you and Aidan."

She nods into my chest, then moves her hand to my torso. Her breath evens out, and I only know she's awake because she rubs her fingers across my skin every once in a while.

"Can I stay?" I ask. She's so content here, I don't want to leave. Plus, I'm comfortable. It feels nice to be connected to someone like this.

"I'd like to see you try to go."

"I don't know," I tell her, glaring at her swimming poster. "I don't usually let other guys watch me while I sleep. Especially ones in Speedos. They really cut into you, you know."

She giggles into my side. "I think he might have to go, too. He was looking at me accusingly when, well..."

"When you were coming all over my finger?"

Instantly, the air is charged again with a heaviness that has my heart racing.

She takes a deep breath. "Yes."

I've had my choice of girls since I've been at Warner, but none have made me feel like this. Like if I don't have them, I would think about it for the rest of my life. Like one touch could soothe everything and the loss of it would ruin me. "Well, we can't have that." I measure my breaths before I get too excited. "Because I plan on making you do that a lot."

"It's okay," she says finally. "I think having a real-life half-naked man in my room might be more fun."

"Just any half-naked man? Good to know."

She lifts her head to stare down at me. "I think you know what I mean, West."

I know what she means, but I want her to say it. I want to see the confirmation in her eyes that I wasn't toppling over without taking her with me.

I've never told anyone about the real me, and that simultaneously exhilarates and scares the shit out of me. Kenna knows me more than anyone else in the whole world, which means she holds all the power.

Powerful people do terrible things.

But staring down at her while her lids are closed and there's such a peaceful expression on her face, I can't imagine she would be anything like my father.

She's perfect.

CHAPTER NINETEEN

Kenna

SYDNEY DROPS down in the chair across from me, blowing out a breath. "I don't know what's worse, you not realizing you were in love with West Brooks...or you realizing you're in love with West Brooks."

"Shh," I hiss, staring around the library to see if anyone's heard her. Everyone's already been talking about how West gave me his jersey at their first game. The jersey chasers have been sending me dirty looks for a few days.

Sydney rolls her eyes. "Oh, everyone knows. You can't keep that goofy smile off your face. Although, seeing him in that tiny little swimsuit, I can understand why."

I give her another look. She's well aware we haven't slept together yet. She only asks every time West and I get a spare moment together. "I don't have a goofy smile," I tell her, even though I totally do. My face always hurts at the corners of my mouth now.

Completely ignoring me, Sydney asks, "Where is he anyway?"

"Practice. They're preparing for homecoming."

At that, my friend deflates. I've been noticing the dark circles under her eyes, and when she's not in class, she's in rehearsal for the halftime show. Lighting, sound, costumes. It's coming off like she's performing at the Super Bowl, for crying out loud. "Speaking of, I have another long one tonight."

"Just think about how awesome it'll feel when you nail this."

She flashes her eyes at me and grins. "You know it."

"I might be out late, too." I stare down at my textbook and pretend to turn the page, like I've been sitting here studying and not thinking about going out with West tonight.

"Oh, that's right. Your official date night. Not like the one where I caught him in your bed super early in the morning."

I ram my book into her hand and then smile wide at the girl passing by talking into her phone. Hopefully, she's not pretending she didn't hear my former friend and roommate's last words.

"I never knew your mouth was this big."

Sydney laughs, throwing her head back. "I need

something to get excited about that doesn't involve the current stressor in my life. Let me live vicariously through you, Kenna. Take pictures of that dick. I—"

"Whoa," a male voice says, chuckling. I glance up to find Aidan approaching our table. My heart leaps, and my face heats. West isn't following him, though. He places his arm on the back of Sydney's chair. "Who's sending who dick pics?"

Sydney immediately straightens and plasters a sexy smile on her face. "I'm just wondering when West and Kenna are going to seal the deal."

Aidan stares down at her, his expression charged. "I've been wondering the same."

Sydney claims nothing has happened between the two of them, but I'm not so sure. The air around them fills with tension. Of course, they're both super busy right now—Sydney with her halftime show, and Aidan doing his QB thing. This coming weekend is a big one for both of them.

They stare at one another for a while longer until he turns to me. "I forgot, West is waiting for you down in the truck, Kenna. Something about a special date night."

My body thrums. I've been looking forward to this all day, but West hasn't told me anything about what we're doing. He wanted it to be special, so he's planned the whole thing from start to finish.

I gather my books and shove them in my backpack. Sydney smirks. "Be safe. Make good choices."

Aidan chuckles alongside her. "Aren't they cute?" He touches his heart in a mocking gesture. "My babies are growing up."

I stand, tossing the backpack over my shoulder. "Aidan?"

"Hmm?"

I grin back at him. "Fuck off."

The laugh that pours out of him earns him a scowl from the librarian, so I decide to scoot out of there before we get one of her infamous lectures. She runs this place like an army barracks.

My insides twist in excitement as I hurry toward the exit. Through the glass door, I spot West in his truck, drumming his fingers on the steering wheel. He's freshly showered, his hair still a bit damp, and he's staring down at his phone.

My footsteps skirt over the slate ground out front, and then I'm at the curb. I open the passenger door, drawing his attention. He grins at me, and I take it in. His face completely opens up. He went from being guarded one hundred percent of the time we were together to this right here in front of me.

"Hi," I state, my voice coming out dry and fast. He makes to get out of the truck to help me up into the cab, but I wave him off. "I got this."

Before he can answer, his phone rings, cutting

through the electricity in the cab like a razor. He checks the screen and then ignores the call. The word *Mom* blips off the screen, and then he turns his phone completely off. She's been calling him a lot lately, but he hasn't said much about it.

I get myself in the seat, and he frowns. "I was going to help."

"I don't need it."

"Maybe I just wanted an excuse to touch your ass."

"In that case," I tell him, pretending that I'm going to back out of the truck, earning a laugh. Before I get all the way out, I heave myself up and shut the door. "Are you going to tell me where we're going now?"

"Not now." There's an unguarded expression in his eyes as he pulls away from the curb. He starts off, deftly maneuvering his huge truck down the streets of Warner. I decide not to try to guess where we're going. Being surprised is fun.

"Are you guys ready for Saturday?"

"Always." He reaches over and places his hand on my knee, his huge palm engulfing it. An inevitable warmth starts, quickly followed by the rapid beating of my heart. I couldn't have been more wrong about West. He's caring. Sure, he's intense about football, but he's not aloof like I thought he was. He just doesn't do a lot of talking to people he doesn't know, which I know is brought on by his father.

Luckily, he hasn't tried to contact West again since the game.

"Are you nervous?"

He shrugs. "I'm more nervous about the commercial spots I've promised everyone after homecoming."

"They wouldn't have asked you if they didn't already love you."

His grip on me tightens, and he peers over to catch my gaze momentarily before focusing back on the road. He got weird last time we talked about it, but I have a feeling he'll be doing a lot more commercial spots in the future. When the NFL comes calling, he'll be a big deal. I can feel it in my gut.

It's all so...exciting, and knowing more about where West came from, I'm pulling for him even harder. He deserves this.

He makes me want to try harder.

Outside, the trees rustle in the wind. The sky is growing orange while the sun sets. Oddly enough, West has driven me outside of town—not that I'm trying to guess where we're going. I just don't know where the heck we are.

After a few more minutes, he pulls over onto the side of the road. I peer around, searching up the road and down it. I turn a sly gaze to him. "I don't—"

"Just wait. I hope you don't mind walking in the woods."

I lift my brows, but he doesn't get a chance to see it.

He's up and out of the truck, walking around in front while I'm still trying to get my bearings. The door on my right opens, and he stands there, offering his hand, the eager expression on his face telling me to trust him.

My pulse jumps.

I hop down, landing in gravel, and he leads me to the back of the truck where he takes out a small cooler. Now I'm really intrigued.

He keeps pulling me around to the driver's side of the car, and we step off into the woods where there's a slight opening to a trail that leads up and curves around. "Where are we going?" I ask, half laughing.

"Someplace cool."

I bite my lip. The forest is quiet except for the wind through the trees and our footsteps as we climb. He helps me over fallen trees and points out rocks so I don't trip. After ten minutes, he dips under a wooden rail, and I follow. Here, the trail is marked with tiny gray stones that lead the way.

Ahead, through a break in the trees, I spot green brush, and at almost the exact same time, the trickling of water filters through.

West peers over his shoulder at me with a wide grin. He picks up the pace, stopping only when the view opens up. In front of us is a rocky, squared-out area filled with water overlooking a river flowing some twenty feet below.

He places the cooler down on a flat black rock that

serves as one of the corners of the little pool. "This is a natural hot spring," he says. "See the steam?"

My mouth drops. In the air, there's an almost transparent cloud of white making its way up to the now orange-pink sky.

"It's part of the state park system. They're closed right now, but I heard about that path."

I squeeze his hand. It's quite possibly the most beautiful view I've ever seen. The spring is crystal clear. Large, flat rocks line the bottom, and then more rocks were set around the outside to force the square shape.

"Do you like it?"

I blink up at him, a smile forming on my face. "Do I like it?" He raises his brows, expectant, and I find I can't joke with him. "I love it."

The breath *whooshes* out of his chest. He reaches out for my other hand, and then he faces me. "I brought some food in the cooler. Drinks."

"On the eating plan, I'm guessing."

"Most of it," he says with a smirk, "but there might be a few extra things in there."

I peer around. "I gotta say, Hulk, I think you nailed the first date thing."

"Yeah?"

I nod, stretching up on my toes to give him a kiss. He pulls me in close, capturing my lips and holding me there, his large body framing me in. I feel myself being swept away, and it's scary and exhilarating at the same time. He deepens the kiss briefly before stepping back.

In one swoop of his hands, he has his shirt off and is tossing it on the ground, his bare chest flexing with the movement. Then, his fingers curve under the waistband of his shorts. My throat closes up momentarily, until he pushes down his athletic shorts, showing off a pair of boxer briefs clinging to his thigh muscles. I've seen him in less than that, but there's something so sexy about him right now.

"Now you."

He takes another step back to give me room. My stomach squeezes when his eyes roam up and down my body. "I see what you're doing here," I tease, nerves getting the best of me. I hesitate.

"We can't dip in the springs in our clothes." He shrugs, his lashes fanning down over his cheeks. "But you don't have to," he says quickly. "Whatever you're comfortable with."

How can I say no to that? I reach down, flirting with the hem of my shirt and then yanking it up. I don't even remember what bra I put on this morning, but I'm hoping whatever it is, it actually matches my panties. I peer down to see emerald and heave a sigh of relief. I know damn well I have a matching set, so I undo the clasp on my capris and work them down my hips before stepping out of them.

My workout routine has made me a little more

confident. Plus, it isn't as if he hasn't seen me in workout pants that have suctioned to my body or, hell, even in my dive suit, which doesn't leave much to the imagination.

West Brooks stares at me, our gazes colliding in a crash of heat that swamps over me. My heart feels like it's beating right out of my chest when he holds out his hand once more to help me down into the spring.

The next level of rocks is actually a bench. "Careful," he says softly as I dip my toes into the warm water and land on the solid surface.

I smile up at him. "Wow. It's actually really heated."

"The water is eighty degrees all year round."

"You're kidding."

I step even farther in to stand at the bottom. The water only comes up to my knees, and that's the exact height of the bench, the warm water just barely skimming over the surface.

I walk toward the edge, peering out over the river. The rush of water is louder now. It trickles and flows, curving its way downstream.

West comes up behind me, wrapping his arms around my torso. I set my hands on top of his and lean back. "I'm glad you like it," he whispers.

We stay that way for a little while, watching as the sky turns a deeper pink.

Eventually, West breaks away and lowers to his

knees. I follow after him, sinking into the heated water. It laps against my navel as I sit back on my calves, moving my arms out to trace the water. "Seems like this would come in handy after a hard workout."

"Definitely," he muses. "But I don't want to talk about football right now."

I meet his gaze. My question dies on my lips as we connect, the charged air around us intensifying with the heat from the spring. He moves closer.

Like two forces drawn to one another as if by cosmic design, he grabs my hips, pulling me toward him until I'm pressed against his hard length.

Me and West, we're inevitable. Like sunshine after a rainstorm. Like a clear sky after a fire. We're here. Exactly where we were always meant to be.

CHAPTER TWENTY

West

I DIDN'T BRING her up here to seduce her, but from the moment she was framed in front of me, staring out over the swift-moving river below, the heated spring teasing the skin of her knees, my body wants nothing else.

Possess her.

Care for her.

Love her.

Those thoughts blink in and out like the countdown to game time, each one passing after the other, bringing with it excitement and expectation. Her hips fit snug against mine, the thin fabric between us leaving nothing to the imagination. In her eyes, I see the mirror image of my own.

"I want you, but tell me to back down, and I will," I

offer, the words flying from my mouth because if I don't say them now, I'm so overtaken I might not ever say them.

She's more than I expected. To have someone that sees me, really sees me, makes my heart race. To have someone I can really talk to... There aren't words.

"Right here?" she asks. Her tongue swipes across her lips, and I watch it with fascination.

I tuck her hair behind her ear, letting my fingertips play over her scar, and she closes her eyes as I memorize every nuance of her face. Once again, I find myself lost for words, and only urge out, "Here."

I trail my finger down her spine, placing pressure against her lower back. Without thinking, I knead my hand there, using the motion to move her into me in a sultry rhythm.

"Not fair," she says, lids fluttering. "You know what you do to me."

My skin buzzes. "I have no idea what I do to you, but I know what you do to me." I don't think I've ever been so hard in my fucking life. These rhythmic teases aren't helping, but I can't get enough. "You own me, Kenna. If you want me."

She glances up, her lips slightly parted. The expression on her face is complete vulnerability and wonder. It reminds me of when I made her come on her bed, only making the urge worse.

She places a kiss on my shoulder, working her way

across my body to the base of my neck. A groan pours out of my mouth, and I dip my head to catch her lips, waiting until she kisses the stubble on my chin, then the corner of my mouth. I want to feel all of her. Our lips finally meet, and it's a sweet kiss at first. Control is something I'm very good at, but I'm close to breaking.

I don't want to break her, though.

She licks at the seam of my mouth, and I open for her, finally deepening the kiss while I hitch my hips into her.

Her body shudders for a moment before working against me again. The same rhythm I set before, she takes over. I hoist her up in my arms, and she wraps her legs as best she can around my large frame. "I got you," I tell her, my lips moving over hers. She runs a hand up my neck, tangling her fingers in my hair. She yanks a little, pulling me forward so she can return my deep kiss.

We breathe each other in, staying locked in an embrace until it feels like I'm going to explode. I don't want to push her, but I can't keep grinding against her without losing myself. With another long moan, I extricate myself, stand, and lead her to the side of the spring. "Do you trust me?"

Her lips are full, marked by my own. She gives me a nod, and I guide her to a seated position on the rock ledge. Staring down at her, I'm in awe. She feels like a treasure, something precious I need to take care of.

Her chest heaves when I lower to my knees, spreading her legs around either side of me. I inch my hands up her thighs and wrap them around the waist of her panties. I lift my brows, staring at her for approval, and she gives me the slightest nod.

My dick jumps. We're both all too excited to taste her. To listen to her moan.

Silhouetted around her, the sky has turned dusky, a pink glow clinging to the horizon. It washes her in soft shades as I reveal her hip bones, then the V of her legs, the panties finally giving way to her naked form when I pull them off and set them next to her.

Her cheeks have reddened, but I give her a small smile in reassurance, then slip my hands under her ass so she can rest on me. Her legs automatically open, widening as I move closer. I kiss a trail up her thigh, and she leans back on her arms, watching. Waiting.

"West," she murmurs, moving her legs farther apart. A quiver runs up her legs, and I squeeze her ass, moving her up to place more kisses on her folds, her pretty, pink skin soft and yielding. I trace my tongue across her core, catching some of her juices, and a strangled cry flees her mouth.

"West," she says more urgently.

"Tell me."

She fists her hands. "Oh God. Please more."

I like the sound of that. *Please. More.* Those words

thump in my brain while I give her exactly what she and I both want.

More.

I flick my tongue across her clit, and she lifts into me as if begging. "More here?" I ask, sitting back to look at her. I'm mesmerized by the shape of her. The taste of her. By her.

"Yes," she breathes.

Pressing my lips to her pussy, my tongue circles her clit in slow movements, the outside world fading away. I focus on her breathing, the involuntary movements of her hips when I hit the right spot, the drip of her juices on my tongue and lips.

I've given oral before, but this is a different experience. It's not about the end game, the climax before the whistle-stopping play. I'm savoring it like the high of winning. Every pant from her is a clap on my back. Every time she whispers my name, it echoes around me like a chant.

Suddenly, her thighs close against my head. "Oh God."

I surge forward, gripping her to me, relishing the last remaining moments before her body gives in to pleasure. She cries out, her hips straining toward me when she hits the precipice. Glancing up, I take in her forehead knitted in pleasure, her mouth open, her chest heaving.

Then she looks at me, taking a deep breath while

she lowers her hips back into my hands, and it feels like I've been served a decadent moment in life. A time-stopper. The kind of moment that will sit with me forever.

The shy smile she gives me afterward sends my heart thrumming.

"You're, um...good at that," she says between breaths.

My cock strains. I'm not the best with words on a good day, but right now, I can't get my mind and my mouth to work together. I just stare, my gaze still taking her in. The thrum of her pulse at her neck, her breasts pushing into her bra, the way her legs have settled over the rocks as she lifts herself up.

I back away, and she follows after, lifting onto her feet. Her slight frame moves into mine, her neck hinged all the way back to peer into my eyes. The comfort I find there relieves all the pressure I feel to do the right thing, to say the right thing.

My hands find her bare ass and squeeze.

"I want to see you," she says, her voice transformed into a throaty whisper. I'm soaked from the waist down, but if I wasn't, I'd have the telltale signs of precum darkening my briefs.

Stepping back, she feathers her fingertips down my stomach to press against my hip bones. She traces the deep V cut that I've honed over the years. Women have worshipped me there, but this is an entirely different experience. My muscles jump under her touch, as if they can't stand to stay still in her presence.

My cock is the worst offender. Blood pumps from balls to hilt, the desire overwhelming as she works my boxer briefs around the head of my dick and down. She sucks in a tiny breath, almost soundless, but I'm so attuned to her, I feel and hear everything.

Gripping my base, I try to relieve some of the pressure, but all I get is a jolt through me, a need. I stroke my length, unable to help myself.

"West," she breathes.

Her saying my name is like the first call of the game. I speed up my strokes, watching her stare down at me. She wraps her hand over mine, slowing my movements to a steady, nut-busting pace. "Did you bring a condom?"

I swallow, the dry thickness in my throat too much. All I can do is nod.

"In your shorts?" she asks.

I nod again, and she reaches up on her tiptoes to kiss me before backing away and retreating to the side of the small pool. She finds the foil there.

"Are you sure?" I manage to ask as she approaches me.

The tips of her cheeks turn pink when she smiles. Her hand finds mine again, helping me guide my fist up and down my cock. With her other hand, she passes over the condom, and I use my teeth to rip it open.

Rolling it over my length is the easy part. From then on, my mind blanks out.

I grip her hips, yanking her up my torso until she settles around my waist. My cock slides across her stomach while I peel away the cup of her bra and nudge her tit into my mouth. I flick my tongue over her nipple, making goosebumps sprout across her skin. Her nub hardens against my tongue as I lave it with kisses, sucking it into my mouth and listening to her breathe out in heavy, pleasureful sighs.

She creates space between us, fisting my cock and angling it toward her center. I nudge her there, my dick sliding into yielding flesh.

"West, I need you inside me."

I rock into her, using the head of my cock to work over her clit. I need her as ready as possible to accept me. The last thing I want to do is hurt her.

"Please," she begs.

"I need you wet, baby."

"I'm fucking dripping," she grinds out.

Fuck. She tips her hips in just a way that I slide in. Only the tip at first, and then I drive inside her in short strokes.

Her eyes widen with each inch she takes. "Fuck, West..."

"I know. Almost there."

She hasn't taken nearly half of me yet, and as much as I want to drive my dick home, I can't.

It's the best torture.

Kenna rocks with me, meeting me stroke for stroke. The last inch, she pushes forward. Her head flies back, her fingertips digging into my shoulders, and I feel her shudder around me. "West!"

I hold her steady, letting her do what she needs to grind out more pleasure. When she settles her head against my neck, I realize I've been holding my breath, and I let it out in a *whoosh*.

"I..." she breathes.

"I just... Oh," she moans. "You hit just the right spot."

I start to move again, slowly at first, then lengthening my strokes. "This one?" I ask, sliding in to the hilt.

A cry flies from her lips, her pussy squeezing me so tight it's almost unbearable. "Mm-hmm," she groans. Her hands find purchase on my shoulders, and she pushes away to look at me. We're even right now, forehead to forehead, lips to lips. Her breasts against my chest. "Does it feel good?" Uncertainty flutters her eyes closed as she circles her hips, my cock at her mercy.

My heart pounds. "It feels fucking amazing."

"Show me," she urges.

I don't want to hurt her, but her eyes are so pleading.

She reaches around her back, unclasping her bra

and dropping it in the water so her bare tits are squished against me. "Take me."

All restraint leaves. I brace her ass with my hands and drive inside her until she's practically bouncing on my cock. Guttural moans escape my throat, and in her smile, I see the uncertainty fade away.

The water splashes up to my knees as I stay steady, and for a moment, I thank my training so I can take her like this. She's completely malleable in my hands, dependent on me.

Sweat slides down my spine in rolling drops. Despite the slight chill in the air as we lose daylight, my body is a furnace. Pleasure climbs higher and higher as well as the volume of the tiny cries escaping Kenna's mouth. It's the only reaction to something I've done that I want to hear for the rest of my life.

Suddenly, her knees clamp around either side of me, her body locking up.

"Yes!" she cries, and my dick answers. As soon as she starts to spasm, cum shoots from my tip. I bury myself inside her, and we cling to one another, our bodies finding that immeasurable pleasure at the same time.

My cock empties, and I groan into her neck. She shifts her head, nudging me so our lips meet. We kiss around quick breaths, our tongues twisting and colliding.

As our heartbeats return to normal, she breaks

contact, pressing soft kisses up my jaw until she teases my earlobe. "Holy shit, West Brooks."

I smile. My sentiments exactly.

Kenna and I have come together like fire and ice. I've melted her, showing her the real me until we both burn brightly, but none brighter than when we're connected like this.

CHAPTER TWENTY-ONE

Kenna

I SQUEEZE past the door into my room, closing it quietly behind me while I stare at West's large form in my bed. We brought the picnic back to my place last night. We ate cheese, crackers, M&Ms, and Goldfish with only the light of a candle I got on clearance. The smell of fall wafted around us as we told secrets with our mouths full, fell into one another's arms again and again, and then finally slept side by side.

I can't remember the last time I felt this full.

West shifts in bed, staring up at me while I wait by the door. He blinks, his gaze searching the room. "What time is it?"

"You still got time," I tell him, finally moving over to the bed.

He sits up, running his hands through his hair and

shirking the covers away. Rummaging through the bag, he pulls out his phone and holds down the power button.

"When is your first class?" I ask.

"Ten, but I have a football meeting at nine."

"Oh," I tease, voice dropping. I widen my eyes in shock, but I can't hold back my sly smile. His gaze shoots to mine, and my lips tug higher. "Just kidding."

"That wasn't very funny."

"It depends on if you're you. Or me."

He shakes his head, his stare taking me in. "I'll be making you pay for that later."

I'm about to tell him that I'll probably like whatever punishment he'll come up with when his phone starts going crazy. Vibrations and short tones sound off one after the other. We both peer down at it. "Mr. Popular."

His forehead wrinkles. Shoulders bunching, he scrolls through some texts and stills. Then he scrolls some more. I see him click on a link, and it cuts to a news anchor talking in front of a desk. In the background, a screen is playing, showing the Hamilton football players dressed in their jerseys with no pads. My heart immediately races. This is about the feud. About homecoming. All I see are a bunch of jocks jumping up and down until the raw camera footage pans some more, and I spot a scruffy guy standing there, staring intently into the lens.

West shoots off the bed, his fists clenching his phone. For a moment, I think he's squeezing it so hard it rings, but it's just a call coming in. Before I can even ask what's going on, West growls and then answers the call. "Coach."

I can't hear what his coach is saying, but West starts to pace. All the tension in his muscular frame that had loosened yesterday is back. He doesn't talk into the phone. He doesn't even look at me. After about thirty seconds, he hangs up without even saying goodbye.

"What is going on?" I finally ask, standing on my feet. I don't give a shit about football theatrics, but I do care about West. I don't understand his reaction.

His jaw ticks. He's so angry, it's as if he takes up all the space in the room. "My dad."

"Your...dad? What about him?"

A frustrated groan rips from his mouth, and he circles around the room before grabbing his bag and almost tearing my bedroom door off the hinges on his way outside. He's already to his truck when I decide to follow after, hugging myself. There's a chill in the morning air, and I'm only wearing a T-shirt and capris. I start to shake, little trembles that's as much from the cutting breeze as it is from nerves.

I've never seen West like this before. His family is a touchy subject that he's discussed with me, but from what I know, he doesn't have anything to do with his dad and little even to do with his mom.

The phone in his hand goes off again, and he throws it into the interior of his Hulk truck then climbs behind the wheel. He cranks the engine, closes the door, and puts it in gear before looking up.

Our gazes connect, and I feel the same familiarity ricochet through me. I hold myself tighter, my feet stuck to the ground as if the sidewalk were quicksand.

This is not how I imagined this morning going down.

I woke up so at peace. So happy.

As soon as West sees me, he climbs back out of his truck, leaving it idling in the driveway, then strides toward me. His long, tree-trunk legs eat up the space between us until he's standing like a giant in front of me. Carefully taking my chin, he angles my face to meet his anguished green eyes. "I'm so sorry, Kenna. I have to go. I'll text you as soon as I can."

He drops his stare to my lips, and just as quickly, his mouth is on mine. My lids flutter closed. His kiss is urgent, but it's still soft and reassuring. It's everything I know West Brooks to be. My hands unravel, and I push up to my tiptoes to return his kiss.

Too soon, he steps away. "I'll text you. I promise," he states, then gets back into his truck, and reverses out of the driveway.

Soon, his black truck turns the corner and is out of sight.

I don't know what the hell just happened.

I replay everything in my head, wondering if I should've pushed for answers or made sure he was okay before letting him drive off. He was obviously distracted and angry.

Fucking Hamilton.

His dad, too, whatever that's about.

Turning, I head back inside to find Sydney peering down the hallway at me, wearing a concerned expression. "Is he okay?"

I close the door, shrugging. "I guess. I don't even know what's going on."

"Oh, Kenna. It's bad." She grimaces, looking slightly uncomfortable. "At least, the media is going nuts with it."

"Going nuts about what?"

"West's dad. He's hooked up with Hamilton and is talking major shit about West."

My first inclination is to laugh—from the sheer ridiculousness of it, but also how seriously people take this homecoming game. I'm surprised Hamilton has been quiet up until now.

"His dad is on TV and everything."

I bite my lip. West mentioned he had issues with him, but from what he's told me, he hasn't spoken to his dad since he basically escaped to Warner, aside from him showing up at the game. What's his deal now? Why would he do this?

As I stand there and take all the information in, Sydney walks up to me. "Where did West go, hon?"

I shrug. "To see his coach, I think. He didn't say much. He just got mad and left."

She breathes in deep. "I'm sure Coach Thompson will know what to do. He'll squash this before any big media gets it. How freaking low is it to bring someone's personal life into a sport?"

"What are they saying?" In my head, I can't imagine anyone having anything negative to say about West. I don't even like football players, and he's managed to get me to not just like him but fall for him.

She links her elbow through mine and guides me into her room. A TV sits on her desk in the corner. Sydney hates doing work at a desk. She's either on her bed or the floor or the hot-pink beanbag chair she has. If my room is an ode to diving and 5SOS, Sydney's room is an ode to bubblegum pink. The hot-pink pompoms we bought to cheer her on for her homecoming set sit just to the side. On the screen, a local news station is on, the same video playing again and again over the reporter's left shoulder. The headline reads "Warner Stud a...Dud?"

I gasp. "What the..."

"It's hard to watch." Sydney grimaces, staring at the video of Hamilton players lined up with West's dad. They keep egging him on to say more and more about West. And all of it sounds awful.

"This isn't news," I grumble, rolling my eyes. "This is West's dad being a dick. Why are they even giving this airtime?"

"If it bleeds, it leads, and we all know West is the golden boy right now."

"They're just trying to get everyone to pay more attention to the game," I seethe, gesturing wildly at the TV. "West's real fans will understand this is bullshit." Bullying tactics, feuds, and rivalries. "Can't they just play the game and shut up? West is going to wipe the floor with them."

"He'll certainly have a lot of fodder to take these guys out."

"Turn it off," I tell her, disgusted. I'm sure his coach is concerned for West, but these news reporters are making this a big deal when it really isn't. "If no one pays attention to it, it'll cut Hamilton off at the knees."

"You think?" Sydney asks, frown lines etched into her usually placid face.

"I'm sure of it. If no one cares, they'll stop playing it."

"I hope you're right. For West's sake. I can't imagine having my parents on TV telling everyone what a fuckup I am."

My stomach seizes. West is going to take this hard,

even though he shouldn't. His father doesn't deserve him, that much is obvious.

But the rest of this nonsense? It'll all blow over in a day. A half a day, even. No one on campus is going to actually believe any of this.

"I wonder what Warner will do to retaliate?"

My shoulders stiffen. *Retaliate.* That's exactly what Hamilton did when I got caught in the crossfire. They retaliated to something Warner did, and at this state in the rivalry, they probably don't even know who started it first.

"Hopefully nothing," I murmur as I walk from the room. My head is a jumbled mess of thoughts. I grab my phone to see if West has texted yet, and he hasn't. Not surprising since he only left a few minutes ago, but I'm worried about him.

The anger I understand, but this will most likely hit him someplace deeper, too. Even with a strained relationship, don't we all want our parents' approval? I can't imagine if my parents had taken the opposite side when I'd been injured. What if they were on the news talking shit about me instead of going on the offense and ridiculing the actions of others?

I take a seat on my bed and stare up at David Boudia. He can't help me with this, though. He's an inanimate object. Sure, one I've gained strength from countless times, but this isn't diving related and staring at him isn't giving me as much pleasure as it used to.

Getting to my feet, I stretch up on my toes and unpin him from the wall. I roll the poster up, put a hair tie around him, and stick him in the closet.

Sydney sticks her head in, her gaze immediately going to the bare wall. She turns toward me. "Let me guess, it weirded West out?"

"Well, he certainly wasn't intimidated by him." I laugh. "But I think he said David was looking at him accusingly."

Sydney lifts her brows. "He was probably trying to get a peek at that massive dick," she singsongs. "Is it too soon to ask—"

"Yes," I interrupt, my cheeks heating at the reminder of our time together last night. How sad that our moment of bliss lasted less than twenty-four hours. I almost asked him if he wanted to ditch classes altogether today, but that's my neediness talking. There was no way he was going to skip practice, and now this.

"You're so selfish," she teases.

"Get your own dick." I grab my bag and meet her at the door. It's class time for both of us, so we need to get going. "How about Aidan? Or one of your other admirers? I'm sure once you kill it during halftime, you'll have guys lined up."

"Aidan's nice, but he's kind of young, you know? I'll be like a cougar or something. Plus, I'm graduating at the end of the year."

I turn toward her, puzzled. "But if it's just a fling?" I shrug, watching to see her response.

"Right," she says, smiling. It looks a little forced.

A little like she might regret it if it was just a fling.

Me too, girl. Me too.

CHAPTER TWENTY-TWO

West

MY MIND WHIRS. Everything I saw this morning turns over and over in my head on a highlight reel of things your family should never do. We might as well sign ourselves up for most fucked-up household on the planet.

I go through the motions at practice, anger pulsating through me at every turn. I always knew my father was a jackass, but this is a new low.

Coach's words from before practice stay perched on my shoulder like the heaviest barbell that I can't quite seem to lift off the ground.

It might go national, son. If ESPN picks it up...

"West? The fuck?"

Below me, a rookie glares up at me from his back,

sweat glistening on his brow. He tugs his helmet back into place.

Shit. I'd really barreled into him, practically blacking out. I heave myself off him and hold my hand out to help him up. He slaps it out of the way and gets up himself, rearranging his bright-yellow pinny. Apparently being on the opposite team is not the side to be on today.

"Brooks!" Coach calls.

I suck in a calculated breath, resting my hands on my hips. I'm soaked through with sweat, but I can't even remember what we've done today. I've been checked out.

After taking another calming breath, I pull my helmet off and peer Coach's way. He signals for me, so I jog toward the sidelines. He grabs my shoulder pads and gives me a quick shake. "Do not let this get to your head."

I nod, looking away, catching a few of my teammates sneaking glances at me. Hardly any of them have come up to me, aside from Aidan who sat with me in the locker room while I bitched up a storm.

Among the many messages and notifications I got, one of them was from my mother. *This is what happens when you ignore him, West. You know this.*

She blamed me.

Me.

Not the fucking backstabbing prick who's running his mouth about me.

"I told you he was calling you."

And because I didn't answer, that meant he had to go make a fool of me? It's bad enough that Hamilton would stoop this low, but what he did is even lower. I have no use for the man. He's a scum-eating bastard.

"Do you hear me?" Coach asks. The concern in his eyes is unnerving.

I nod, even though I haven't heard a single word he's said.

"Good." He claps me on the back. "Now, get out there and try not to kill my second and third strings. Save that anger for the game."

Screw waiting for the game.

Logically, I know the best response I can come back with is to play my ass off on Saturday and completely obliterate Hamilton. But the petty parts of me—the parts that want sweet revenge—want to tear my father apart, and I want to do something as equally shitty to Hamilton as they've done to me.

Before I get back on the field, I find the rookie. "Sorry, man. My head's not in the best space right now."

Clearly calmed down, he says, "It's cool, dude."

It's not, though. I can't let my teammates see how much this has gotten to me. I'm supposed to be one of the pillars on the team. If I let this get to me, everything else could crumble. Like a domino effect, we can say goodbye to our goal of a winning season.

With only a few minutes left of practice, I keep my head in the game as much as possible. It's a relief, though, when Coach blows the final whistle. We're two days away from one of the most important games of the season, and I shouldn't be feeling like this. I need to get grounded and stay focused.

I stop by the sidelines and squeeze water into my mouth and over my head. The cold feels like a reset button on my brain.

The only thing on my mind right now is getting in touch with Kenna. I haven't spoken to her all day, completely going back on my word to text her when I could. Not really the impression I wanted to leave her with after the amazing evening we had yesterday.

I think about forgoing a shower and showing up at her place as I am, but when I finally peel all my pads off in the locker room, that's the last thing I want to do. Instead, I take the quickest shower and am out of there before nearly everyone else. I grab my duffel, swinging it over my shoulder and making my way through the snappy remarks my teammates fling at each other while they're in varying degrees of getting cleaned up.

They look at me as I pass, some of them with sympathy, some with confusion. I get it. I didn't know whether I should even address what was being said, but Coach advised to leave it for the time being, and we would reassess it after twenty-four hours. Probably to see if there was going to be any more smear campaigns.

"Where are you going, big guy?" Aidan asks, jogging to catch up with me.

"Kenna," I mutter, like she's the answer for everything.

"You want company?"

"To see my girlfriend?" I side-eye him.

He lifts his brows but doesn't comment. "I was just wondering if you wanted to get out. We could go to Scoops? Or Richie's?" He leans in close. "It might be good for you to be out around town looking undisturbed, you know?"

Indecision crashes into me. "I don't know. I completely blew Kenna off all day. Dick move."

"Dick move," he agrees. "But..."

I turn over his suggestion in my head. It probably is a good idea. If people see me out walking around, they're not going to view what the news is playing as a big deal, right?

As soon as I think it, my stomach twists. All this is doing is giving me the kind of attention I don't want. I just want my football skills to speak for me. I'm too young and too unimportant to have a scandal yet.

Well, I guess that's the silver lining. I'm not even important yet. This is going to blow right over, just like

Coach said. "Sure," I tell Aidan. "Richie's it is. I'm starving. I've barely eaten anything all day."

"Cool, I'll call Syd. She can arrange it."

I'm too tired to argue with him that I should text Kenna myself. Who knows if she'll even want to go to Richie's, but Aidan immediately scrolls through his contacts and is on the phone with Kenna's roommate before I can make up my mind.

It takes all of ten seconds for them to make the arrangements, and fifteen minutes later, Aidan and I are seated at a booth at Richie's. A true classic American diner, the booths have that plastic feel and are red and white vertical stripes. The servers wear these throwback, flat hats. Songs from the fifties and sixties play from a real-life jukebox. But best of all, Richie's consistently wins best hamburger of the year for this county since the early 2000s. They display the plaques proudly at the entry.

The bell rings to signal someone has walked in, and I glance up from the menu that's lined in classic cars to find Kenna moving toward us. I elbow another football player who's leaning over our table to talk about the game, and when he glances behind him, he gracefully bows out, telling us he'll catch up later.

I scoot to the end of the booth and stand. A piece of me feels like the events of today have canceled out all the traction Kenna and I have gained recently. Immediately, though, she reaches for me, and I put my arms around her. She wraps strong arms around my waist, burying her head in my chest.

Words sit heavy on my tongue, but I don't say them. I should be apologizing. I should be telling her everything that has gone down, but I don't even know if she's seen the news yet or heard from anyone else. I completely skipped school today and just went to the meeting before class and our late afternoon practice. The rest of the day, when I wasn't talking to Coach, I sat in my room and replayed my mother's voicemails as well as all of the news outlet headlines that bore my name.

Basically, I wallowed in my own misery, and I didn't want to bring Kenna into that mess.

When Kenna and I finally let go of each other, Sydney says, "So, how are things going?" She pins a concerned gaze on me as she scoots into the booth.

I shrug. My mouth just feels stuck. The words are there, but they don't plan on coming out anytime soon. I sit and move to the wall. Kenna follows and then places her hand on my thigh, giving me an encouraging squeeze.

Aidan sees me struggling and speaks up. "Practice was great. My arm's ready. I'm about to hand Hamilton their ass on Saturday." He holds his hand out in front of him, stretching it across the table while he twists it this way and that. His muscles ripple.

I bet he did have a good practice, but it wasn't on my account.

Sydney and Aidan start talking, so Kenna leans into me. She doesn't say anything, she's just there. Her shampoo smells flowery, and I breathe in the scent, telling myself to forget about everything else and only focus on her right now. I can't do anything about what's going on outside of what I can control. And I've never been able to control my father, and I sure as hell don't want anything to do with Hamilton.

"Your hair smells nice," I tell her.

She tips her head up, a ghost of a smile crossing her face. "I had to get the chlorine smell out of it from practice."

"Any news on Friday's meet?"

"Another exhibition dive. But Coach says if I get another high score, it's possible they'll have a spot for me."

The biggest smile I haven't felt since I saw Kenna walking into her room this morning fills my face. "Really?"

She nods.

"I knew you could do it."

She peers down at the table. "And I finally got the courage to tell my mom that I almost got kicked off the team."

"Yeah?"

"She didn't take it...great," she hesitates. "But it

wasn't as bad as I was imagining. She knows I got the okay from the doctor, but I think she's still in worry mode, you know?"

I nod quietly. At least Kenna has someone to care for her like that. Stick up for her about something important. Her family did exactly what they should have.

Not mine, though. Of course not mine.

"This is what happens when you ignore him, West. You know this."

I turn away as the waitress approaches with menus, pretending like I'm figuring out what I'm going to eat, even though I get the same thing every time we come here. Why did things have to happen like this? I wish I would've met Kenna when I was in the NFL already. When I was someone important. Right now, I'm still the West Brooks who grew up in a trailer park with parents who fought all the time. I'm no one. Nothing.

And she is obviously on a completely different level than me.

"What are you getting?" Kenna asks.

Turning toward her, I catch her gaze. She scans my face, cute concern lines etching between her eyes. I don't think it's fair to put this baggage on anybody. Especially not her. I can see it now. Another football player ruining her life. It'll be a constant struggle until I'm big enough that he can't touch me.

My stomach rolls. Did I just think that leaving

Kenna was a good idea? She's literally the best thing that's ever happened to me.

"I think we should go," I tell her.

Aidan interrupts, "But we just got here."

Yeah, and suddenly *here* is not where I want to be. I don't want to be anywhere where I think things like that. I mean, that was stupid.

Right?

But looking at her now, I see everything she can be. I see her strength. I see her fuel and motivation. I used to think it was a lot like mine, but I've been fooling myself this entire time.

I'm not strong.

I'm not anything.

I'm still the scared little boy hiding in his closet.

Kenna places her hand on my cheek, making me look at her. "Are you okay, West?"

I close my eyes, and when I open them, a figure walking into Richie's catches my eye.

My muscles lock up.

My mouth goes dry.

Suddenly I am seven years old, singing myself "Happy Birthday" alone on the floor in my room because no one decided to celebrate my special day...again.

CHAPTER TWENTY-THREE

West

THERE HE IS.

He's wearing the same shirt from the first football game of the season. It doesn't look like he's shaved either, and his hair looks scragglier, more unkempt. I didn't pay attention to what he looked like on TV, and I'm trying to remember if he looked this bad when his mouth was running or if I missed it completely.

After him, big dudes follow, and my fists clench around the menu. Hamilton players. Dad walks straight for our table, but the players find their own spot across the room. The tension mounts and the dining area quiets.

Kenna shifts and looks up at what my attention is on. The table full of my teammates behind us quiets, too. They all saw Hamilton's social media post. There's no denying that this is my dad.

My heart seizes. I feel my body crumbling in on itself. Sure, I'm bigger than him now, but I know what will always be more monstrous than I can ever be: his anger.

I want to shield Kenna, but it's too late. My father stops at our table, leaning on the edge. Behind him, the Hamilton players aren't hiding the fact that they're recording this exchange.

What did Coach say? Hopefully, this will blow over. Hopefully, ESPN won't pick it up.

"West." My father nods.

Mute. I should've been mute. Why was I born with the ability to talk if I can't ever use my voice to be heard when I need it?

As always, my wingman holds his hand out. "Mr. Brooks, I'm Aidan. West's roommate and QB." He sends a daring glare to the other side of the room. Behind me, I feel my other teammates shift. If this goes wrong, we have the potential for something really bad to happen. Coach would murder us if we fought them before the game on Saturday, but it's happened in the past when things got too hot.

And right now, I'm boiling.

My father shakes Aidan's hand but keeps his attention on me. "You still never answered my calls, so I had to take other measures to get your attention. You did see me on TV, didn't you?"

He's too close to Kenna—way too close, and it's got me on edge. My dad wasn't usually physically violent, but I don't know this person in front of me. Once upon a time, he just made us small in our own house, but now he's expanding. He's like a ticking time bomb, and I don't want him to take her with him.

Aidan whispers something into Sydney's ear, and she brightens right up, placing a fake smile on her face. "Kenna, let's let these guys talk, and we'll go pick out a song at the jukebox."

My dad's gaze finally moves around the table for more than a split second. He ogles Sydney first, who's currently scooting across the bench to get out of her seat. His stare focuses on a place it shouldn't.

"There's some pretty girls here," his rough voice says, the hint of alcohol on his breath. Or maybe my brain is trying to come up with any excuse to why he would be doing this now. This man couldn't have cared less about me before...unless it was to yell at me existing. "Maybe that's why you can't ever answer my calls."

Kenna attempts to stand, which draws his attention. He stares her up and down. "You... Are you, uh —" His stare falls on her scar, and he recoils like a jackass. Kenna grips the table so hard her knuckles turn white. He sneers, peering at me. "Is this your...girlfriend? What about this other one here? Her face isn't fucked up."

I shoot to my feet, the table groaning as it skids across the checkered floor, nearly pinning Sydney to the bench. My teammates are up and out of their seats in the next second, as are Hamilton's. Aidan edges in front of my father, but it isn't to save him.

It's to save me.

"Leave. I got this," he grunts.

My nostrils flare. I breathe in deep, my shoulders rising and falling with the effort.

My father chuckles. "She most definitely is your girlfriend, then. I'm sure even you can do better."

"I got this," Aidan growls, cutting me off at the knees as my gaze slices to my father. Pleasure simmers in his eyes. Aidan yanks my hand, forcing me out of the booth and into Kenna. He starts instructing the team to stay calm.

I wrap my fingers around Kenna's wrist and focus on putting one foot in front of the other while I lead her toward the exit.

"Is she getting all your NIL money, then?"

Step...

"You'd think you'd want to share the wealth with someone who raised you," he yells.

So, this is what this is about?

Step...

"Then again, maybe you can use it to fix her face."

His laughter sucker punches me, and I stumble.

Kenna grabs onto my wrist with her other hand, and together, we walk outside while Aidan's voice rings out through the entire diner. I can't even focus on what he's saying, but he's handling it like usual, I'm sure. Charm. Humor. He has everything I don't.

Right now, all I have is rage.

The snap of the frigid air whips across my face. Light footsteps chase after us, and when I whirl, I spot Sydney coming up behind us. Kenna wiggles out of my grasp just in time for Sydney to throw her arms around her.

Kenna starts crying. Her shoulders heave, and it feels like the more agonizing her sobs become, the angrier I get.

How dare he?

How fucking dare he?

I pace back and forth, talking myself in and out of going back in there to punch his face in.

"Shh," Sydney quiets her. "The guy's obviously an asshole, and he only said those things because he wanted West to retaliate."

West should retaliate. West should kill him. That would solve all our problems.

Cade slips out the front door. He takes in Sydney and Kenna huddled together, but he makes a beeline for me. "Brother, we're getting you out of here. Keys?" When I don't move, he scans the parking lot, then moves toward me. "I'm not getting touchy-feely." He reaches a hand into my pocket to grab the keys to my truck. "This way."

I fall in after him. I'm good at taking orders. Run this play, not that one. I can understand the thought process behind getting me and Kenna out of here. It's smart. Strategic. Take me out of the equation and everything in there will calm down.

Sydney guides Kenna the same way. Her car is parked next to my truck, and for the first time since I got it, I don't take any pleasure seeing my name splashed across the side.

"In the passenger seat," Cade orders, pointing toward the cab. He peers at the girls. "Are you coming with us?"

Sydney moves away to look at Kenna.

"I want to go home," Kenna whimpers. "Please."

Her whole body shakes, tears streaming down her face stained red from embarrassment. I don't think I'll ever be able to get this image of her out of my head.

He just did to her what he always did to me. He made her feel small. Worthless. He made her dim her light.

Before I step into the truck, I grab Kenna's cheeks and make her look at me. I finally find my voice through it all. "That man is an ignorant narcissist. But you, Kenna... You're beautiful inside and out. The words of small-minded people don't affect us. Do you understand? They do not affect us."

I hold her gaze until she nods. Tears still build in her eyes and threaten to spill down her face, but at least she's focused on me now.

This girl... Damn. Her strength never ceases to amaze me. She is more beautiful than the most traditionally perfect human. "I love you," I whisper.

She sucks in a breath, biting her tear-moistened lip.

At that moment, the bell above the door sounds, signaling someone is either coming or going.

"In. Now," Cade orders.

I squeeze her cheeks gently and then turn, getting in the truck. Sydney helps Kenna into the other car, and when Cade starts to back out, I tell him to stop. "Make sure Kenna gets out of here safely."

Cade taps his fingers on the gear shift, and as soon as Sydney maneuvers her car out of the parking lot, Cade is right behind her. Except, they turn right. And we turn left.

I hope that's not a sign of what's to come.

I want to go the same way Kenna does, but I don't know if she'll ever forgive me for this new round of public humiliation. Or if I even deserve her.

CHAPTER TWENTY-FOUR

Kenna

SYDNEY and I had fallen asleep on the couch watching the new rom-com on Netflix. I wake to the credits and stretch. My whole body is exhausted. Crying always does that to me. It's like spending too much time in the sun, it wears me out from the inside.

I let out a breath. It's been hours, and even though we put the movie on to take our minds off what happened, it didn't work until I fell asleep. Now, everything comes rushing back to me.

West's father is a dick. I play my fingers over my scar. Oddly enough, being with West has made me forget almost completely that it's there. Now, I've been thrown back to hating what happened to me all over again. I'll always have this reality check when I glance in the mirror.

I pull my feet off Sydney's lap carefully and reach over to turn the TV off. The clock on the wall reads one a.m. Yawning, I place the blanket over Sydney, but she stirs. "Hmm, huh?" She blinks sleepily a few times, then looks around the room. "I'm going to bed," she mutters before standing and padding to her room in a dazed state.

She was a great friend tonight.

She bumps into the wall and keeps going, disappearing behind her bedroom door. I lay the blanket back on the couch, grab my phone, and turn the lights off as I head to my room. After shutting my bedroom door behind me, I walk to my bed, thinking about West.

He hadn't said anything all day, and we barely got a few words out to one another before the night went to shit. I'm worried for him. I'm pissed for myself.

Maybe I should've gone with him and Cade, but I was just so embarrassed to be called out for being West Brooks's ugly girlfriend.

My throat closes, and I have to take a few breaths so I don't downward spiral again. I look toward my David Boudia poster, but it's not there. My phone is, however, and it notifies me that I have a message from someone surprising.

NoOne: I'm so fucking sorry. My dad is a piece of shit. Maybe I should've told you more. Maybe I should've warned you that he is the worst type of human just in case you ever came into contact with him. I never know what to do around him. I feel like a little kid all over again. Panic sets in, and I just need to hide. I couldn't even save you.

Sadness creeps up my throat again. I close my eyes briefly before I read the rest of West's messages. I don't know why he's gone back to using NoOne. There has to be a reason, though. I'm no therapist, but I'm guessing it's because he feels more comfortable going incognito.

NoOne: I'll never forgive myself. And I'll understand if you don't either. Everything is going to shit. I'm lost. Maybe I'm too fucking weak for you.

My heart starts to pound, and my stomach twists. I don't like the sound of that. I keep reading through his texts, checking the time he sent them. Midnight.

NoOne: I'm outside your window.

NoOne: I knocked on it, but you aren't there.

NoOne: I just need you.

My gaze flicks to the window. He sent these over an hour ago. I sit on the edge of my bed, wondering what to type.

McKennaK: I'm here.

I hear a faint *ping* and glance at the window again. *It can't be...*

I put my phone down on my bed and walk toward the glass. It's pitch black outside, except for the streetlight that's in front of the house, but it doesn't illuminate this side of the yard.

Blinking, I strain my eyes. If I'm not mistaken, there's a shadow on the grass that's darker than the other areas. I unlock my window and open it, the wood groaning in protest as I push it up. All of a sudden, the black mass shifts.

"West?" I hiss.

A head peeks up. The hint of light coming from my bedroom washes him in a soft glow. It is him. I lift the screen, too, shoving it open as much as possible. I stand there in the tiny shorts and top I changed into after Sydney and I got home earlier, and the crisp, middle-of-the-night air pours in, sending a chill through me.

He gets to his feet, hunching over so he can peer in through the opening. Dark shadows taint his handsome face, and his worry lines are pulled taut. Pieces of dead leaves cling to him.

"You stayed outside my room?"

He lifts his shoulders in a hopeless shrug. "I didn't know what else to do."

"Knock on the door?" I offer.

He casts his gaze down. "I wasn't sure if you'd want to see me."

I pause for a few seconds, taking him in. He's so uncertain. So quiet. As NoOne, he's always said everything he wanted to say, but maybe as West he feels incapable of having the same liberties. "Get in here," I tell him softly.

He places two hands on the sill, then heaves himself through the opening, which is barely big enough to fit his body. He uses the wall as leverage to gracefully pull his leg through and stand to his full height. I step back to watch him, then cross my arms over my chest.

He takes one peek at me and then turns around to close both the screen and glass of the window, stopping the flow of chilly air. Then, he flicks the lock back into place and tugs the shade down. He stays there with his back turned for a few seconds before slowly turning around.

"I—" His mouth moves a fraction, but nothing comes out. Then, in a whoosh, "I can't tell you how sorry I am."

I step up to him, my heart hurting for how lost he looks. "It's not your fault."

"You were so upset," he says, eyes glazing over.

"I was embarrassed...and hurt," I force out. I close my eyes, remembering. Everyone was looking at me. Some glanced away again almost immediately, but there were others who were gawking. "Regardless, it wasn't you."

He scowls. "I don't know. Maybe I'm just destined to be no one."

I reach for him. He'll never be no one. Not to me.

I grip his bicep, then move my hand up his shoulder. By the time I get to his neck, cupping the corded muscles there, he peers at me. That instant our gazes connect, I feel it. A connection so tight that it pulls us together time and time again. "Do you love me?" I ask. He nods, his green-eyed gaze piercing mine. "Show me."

No sooner do the words leave my mouth than West takes them to heart. The hurt, the uncertainty, disappears in a blip and his lips are on mine. Searching, softening, finding me there, waiting with everything I have.

In earnest, he shows me. He delves his tongue into my mouth, soothing all the torn edges of our story that occurred today. I wrap my arms around him, and he aligns our bodies, gripping my hips with a fierce protection. It's as if everything he wishes he did earlier comes out now.

His body is a shield. A comfort.

His fingers flex into me, releasing and squeezing

my flesh in a rhythm of what I suppose is need and trying to take his time. Leading me toward the bed, he kisses me senseless. The backs of my knees hit the frame, and I start to fall. He catches me, holding me securely as he lays me until I'm safely on the bed.

Standing back, he towers over me, illuminated by the bedroom light. He takes in my heaving chest and the way my knees have fallen against the sheets. His throat works. Ever silent, he takes his shirt off in that sexy way, tugging the back until he reveals his abs and chest and then the shirt disappears somewhere behind him.

He teases his fingers up the outside of my thighs, his rough fingertips leaving goosebumps in their wake. When he gets as high as my waistband, he pulls at it, forcing me to close my knees so he can work my bottoms down. He takes my panties with it, sparing me of them both with one movement.

Immediately, he zeroes in on my clit, rubbing the pad of his thumb across my sensitive nub. He cocks his head, watching me as my mouth parts on a moan. Framed by my knees, I can see what this is doing to him, the tent in his pants getting more prominent.

"Take off your shirt so I don't have to stop touching you," he orders.

I lick my lips, biting my bottom one a little before I raise up to my elbows. Still basking in the pleasure he's giving me, I reach behind to unclasp my bra. My breasts fall heavy against me while I yank the hem of my tank up, grabbing my bra with it and pulling both garments over my head.

His gaze locks onto my chest. I lie back, gripping the sheets in my fists while he rubs his thumb in my juices and starts stroking my pussy, teasing my entrance with short thrusts of his finger. "Do you want my tongue or my cock?"

His gruff voice makes me moan. He's really going to make me choose? What if I want both? What if I want everything?

He slips his thumb inside, working it in and out of me. I gasp for breath, leaving me no time to answer.

"Too late," he groans. "I've already decided."

He uncurls one of my fists and places it on my folds. I've never played with myself in front of someone before, but it comes naturally as he peels off his pants and boxers and starts stroking his length.

I tease my nub in short circles, making my hips come off the bed in pleasure.

"Let me see you insert your finger."

Groaning, my toes curl. I rub myself in circles, getting closer and closer to my entrance. I slip the tip of my finger inside, my hips lifting up to meet me. My lids flutter closed, and I open them in time to find him using his precum to coat his cock, making it easier to stroke himself. I rim my entry, then push inside as far as I can go. "Oh..."

"I used to fantasize about you," he breathes. "Pump my cock with images of you in my head."

His words embolden me. I've never thought of myself as a sex symbol, even before my accident.

"I wanted you so bad." His strokes quicken.

"Now you have me," I tell him, matching with his rhythm.

He moves his hips into his fist, his eyes closing briefly before he grips his base and bends over. He pulls out a condom from his pocket and rips it open with his teeth. I watch him unroll it down his length, still touching myself, plunging my finger in and out faster.

He grips my knees, angling his body so that his cock nudges my fingers. I remove them, and he strokes my folds next, sliding up and down, getting closer each time.

The head of his cock slips in, and my body grips it, almost as if holding it there. A pained look crosses his face until he pitches his hips forward, pushing in inch by inch. I lift my hips to help him until he's sheathed inside, hitting that spot that makes me cry out.

"West..."

He shifts, slow at first and then faster. His grasp on my knees tightens while I hold myself upward, awaiting his strokes. The punch of his hips obliterates me. I try to keep as quiet as possible, knowing that Sydney's asleep in the house, but every once in a while,

I can't keep a lone cry from eking out before I clamp my mouth down around it.

Sweat appears on his brow, and then he moves forward, gripping my hips and changing the angle until he hits even deeper. My mouth opens in a silent scream.

I realize West doesn't always need to use his words. He says his feelings in other ways. The way he holds me. The way he fucks me. The way his expression is equal parts soft and shadowy, as if his need is mixed with his care for me.

I reach up to cup his face. "You can let go."

He leans into my hand, his eyes closing.

For a moment, everything remains the same until he takes his restraints off. He falls forward, his hands finding purchase on the bed as he drives me into the mattress. His never-ending strokes intensify everything.

"You feel so fucking good. I want to hear you scream my name. I want your pussy to clench around me. Fuck, Kenna. You're so beautiful." His words are punctuated with every movement of his hips.

My core is an inferno of pleasure, and eruption is imminent.

He traces his fingers down my scar, looking at me so adoringly that something inside my body clicks into place. My pussy clenches, spasming against him.

He focuses on me, and my stomach flips. A pained

expression twists his face until he buries himself inside me with one last stroke, his dick pulsing as he holds himself there. The tendons in his neck strain. He gasps for a breath, and the last of his tension empties.

Lying on his elbows, he meets me face-to-face. Neither of us say a word. We just stare. I breathe in the heady scent around us, using my other senses to soak all this up.

What West and I have is intense and real and scary. And a part of me would wilt if I had to give this up.

CHAPTER TWENTY-FIVE

West

MY EYES DART open at the crashing sound breaking through my sleeping subconscious. I sit up in bed, only to find Sydney staring at me open-mouthed. I yank the sheets around my waist as she peers up at the ceiling. "I, um...oh."

Kenna stirs next to me, and I make sure she's covered, too. Her plump lips that I kissed raw last night press together and release.

"Wasn't expecting that." Sydney chuckles half-heartedly, dribbling her fingers against her thighs.

Kenna jolts to a sitting position now, too, yanking the covers around her front. "Oh, hey. Yeah, sorry. He showed up after you went to bed."

Sydney peeks at me briefly, then back at the ceiling again. "I don't usually barge into Kenna's room.

You can ask her later, but... Have you, uh, seen the news?"

My stomach sinks. Not again. Not *more*. I came over here last night for a reprieve. I wanted to feel like everything was okay, and when we were enjoying each other, nothing could've been wrong. I swear the house could've been burning down around us and I wouldn't have cared.

The morning sun and Sydney's concerned features make for a grim dose of reality.

"What is it?" Kenna asks, gripping the sheets tighter.

"You know, why don't you guys get dressed? Because this is really freaking awkward. Then we'll talk." Sydney doesn't leave time for us to argue. She backs away and shuts the door. On the other side, I hear a huge release of breath.

I can't take much more. I swing my feet to the floor and search my scattered belongings for my phone with a sick stomach. The Hamilton players were recording last night, and I swear if they brought Kenna into this, I'm going to—

My phone falls out of my shorts pocket and slides a little away from me. I pull it toward me with my fingertips, and the mattress behind me dips. Kenna kisses my shoulder as I turn my screen on. Immediately, the air in the room tenses. I have dozens of school app messages, texts, social media messages. I'm even tagged in various social media posts. Maybe I shouldn't have turned the sound off on my phone last night.

Panic starts to claw at me.

This nightmare will never end.

Kenna scoots next to me, lying her head on my bicep. Part of me wants to throw my phone away and forget about it all. Hide in her room all day, pretend the outside world doesn't exist.

But that wouldn't do anything. Football has always been my dream and escape, and it kills me that my father is taking something I love and turning it sour.

I decide to start with the texts first. I click on the screen to find familiar names highlighted. My mom. Coach. Aidan. A few teammates. When I swipe those away, I realize I actually have a few phone calls, too. I prioritize those. Calls are worse than texts, right? If someone calls nowadays, it's a big deal. The first one, I almost don't click on because I don't recognize the number.

I switch hands, bringing my phone up to my ear on the side away from Kenna, and my heart drops. It's Sunny from the dealership that gave me the truck. He wants to talk. He doesn't say as much, but his tone is dire.

My mouth goes dry.

"What is it?" Kenna whispers as I take the phone away from my ear.

"Not good," I tell her. "That was the dealership. They want to talk."

Her fingertips press into my skin. They have a grounding effect that I'm thankful for when I go to the next voicemail. It's from Coach. "Son, we need to talk ASAP. Call me and we'll meet at the school or my house. Your choice."

I stop the recording and hang my head. He sounded even worse than yesterday. At least yesterday he had a bit of optimism.

"Coach," I mutter so Kenna doesn't even have to ask. "He needs to talk with me as soon as possible."

She runs her hand up and down my arm. "I'm sorry, West. Your dad—"

I immediately stand. I can't talk to her about my dad right now. He completely humiliated her. Snatching my jeans up from the ground and pulling them on, I say, "I have to go deal with this shit."

"We don't even know what happened."

I zip up my pants. "I don't want you to worry. I'll deal with anything that has involved you. I promise."

She opens her mouth to say something, but I look away, scooping my shirt off the floor so I can tug it on. My whole body is tense. The need to get out of here is overwhelming. I don't want to be here when Kenna realizes I've brought her into this mess. Her association with me probably put her on the news again.

"We don't know what this is about," Kenna says,

standing. She's wrapped the sheet around her naked form and holds it in front of her chest.

"They were recording yesterday," I growl. I find my sweatshirt on her chair. "What else do you think it is?"

She steps back, her face morphing into anger mixed with pain. "Who?"

"Hamilton. They were recording on their phones. You didn't see it?"

"No, I was too busy getting called ugly," she snaps.

Her words pull me up straight. Forcing my shoulders back, I will myself to calm down. "I'm sorry," I tell her, my voice emotionless. I have to keep it even or I'll erupt, taking out everyone around me. "I'll message you when I know something."

"Like yesterday?" she asks, crossing her arms now. She won't even look at me.

The worst part is, I don't know what to say. Maybe I won't text her. I didn't yesterday. I'm sure I'll feel the same unworthiness and shame as soon as I find out what this new round of media coverage is about.

I wish I could promise her it'll be different today, but I haven't changed since I was a kid, burying all my emotions so deep they never come out.

Reaching out, I squeeze her arm. She peers up at me, unshed tears welling in the corners of her eyes. I lean over to kiss her on the cheek, holding myself there because I wish I was different. I wish I could be the person that relied on her for help, but my past has taught me that's not the right course.

Stepping away, I yank open the door and walk out. Sydney glances up from the couch, but I keep going. I'm out the front door and to the cab of my truck in no time.

My gaze slides to the cool decal, and my stomach squeezes. Now that it's daylight, I can fully see it. Someone's scratched the shit out of the paint right where my name is.

I growl in frustration, throwing my fists down on the hood until I gather myself up and jump into the cab. I don't even bother dialing Coach first. All the players know where his house is, so I head that way. If his car is in the driveway, good. If not, then he's on campus.

My mind is a blur as I drive. When I park on the street, I think about weeding through all the posts I'm tagged in to see what I'm in for, but I don't. Denial, denial, denial. Right now, I'm acting the opposite of how I play football. I don't want to read the other side to plan out my attack. I just want to go back to a few days ago when none of this was a thing.

Coach's car sits in the driveway. I maneuver around it to walk up the front steps. My fist bangs on the door, and I grimace a little. His wife opens it, and she immediately gives me a soft smile. "West, so lovely to see you. He's in his office."

I follow her down the hall, and then we turn left toward their breakfast nook and down another hall where his office is. She knocks and opens at the same time, moving out of the way to reveal me. Coach focuses on me through a pair of glasses before taking them off.

"I'll let you two talk. West, you know if there's anything I can do for you..."

"I know, ma'am."

Coach's wife sees her way out and shuts the door behind her. The man who has coached me and set me up to be a man for several years beckons me forward. "Take a seat and tell me how much you've seen."

I sit in one of the chairs facing him and stare at my lap. "I didn't bother looking."

His chair creaks. "I'm not going to pull punches, Brooks. It's bad. ESPN has been showing the first footage during SportsCenter highlights. They're commenting on your integrity."

My gaze snaps up. "My integrity?"

Coach drums his fingers over the desk in front of him. "Your dad gave an interview to a local TV station last night saying that he's practically homeless, helpless, and penniless, and you've completely abandoned him and rendered him in such a state, blah, blah, blah. He called out your NIL money."

My hands tighten to fists. A black ball of rage blocks my view of the present.

Coach sighs. "Here's what I know: Your father has never bothered to show up to a game, and I've only ever heard you say one thing about him and it was that the topic of him was off-limits, so I'm inclined to think this is all bullshit.

"I know you, Brooks. I know that if your father was worth a shit, you'd give him the shirt off your back. The whole interview was an exaggerated sob story that left me fuming...but other people are eating it up. When the news editor called to ask for my comment yesterday, I told them I didn't have any, but I think the time for being silent has passed." He clears his throat. "The analysts are estimating your draft status will decrease. Anyone can be a great player nowadays. Teams are looking for superstars on and off the field."

My stomach rolls. "What do I do?"

"First things first, you may not owe the public a reply, but a few of your NIL representatives have reached out."

I nod. "The dealership called me."

"I think we should start there."

I shift in my seat, wiping my sweaty palms down my pants. "Was there anything else being shown?"

Coach leans forward, resting his forearms on the desk. "Aidan and Cade messaged me. They said a few Hamilton players showed up at Richie's yesterday and there was some sort of incident. There's some leaked, raw footage that I had to search for but the media isn't picking up yet. I suspect because it makes your father look like a giant douchebag. This wasn't Hamilton footage. I think one of our own players took it. When I find out who, I'm going to have a talk with them about it. If the media does pick it up, I think it could only help your cause."

"Coach..." My knuckles turn white, and I shake my head immediately. "I can't put Kenna through that. He said the most horrible things to her."

He narrows his gaze at me. "Correct me if I'm wrong, was it not because of her parents that I had to have several personal, unpleasant meetings with the dean last year?"

"But they were right," I object.

Coach's lips thin. "I'm not sure I understand you, Brooks."

I gesture with my hands. "Just look at what's going on. Why is what's happening even news? I'm no one. Half the country knows nothing about me, and the other half only knows my stats or that my university was involved in a rivalry prank gone wrong. Are the local news outlets covering the fact that Kenna, despite having two surgeries, has healed and overcome the incident by diving in her team's first meet? No, because that's uplifting news. We can't have that," I deadpan. "We'd rather make fake news about me, who's seen as having everything, and create drama where there isn't any. My father left us a long time ago, and I don't owe him shit. He's a hateful, angry man."

Coach lifts his hands. "I agree with you. The media is great when they're on your side, but they can cause everyone and everything to turn on you. I was merely saying that the other footage is proof of what you've just said. Your father is a hateful, angry man. The way he treated Kenna in the video was reprehensible. Everyone who sees it can't deny it."

"Which is probably why Hamilton hasn't shared their own footage yet."

"Their involvement in this is a different story. I've reached out to their coach, and I'll deal with that aspect myself. We have a game to win tomorrow, and I want everyone's head to be where it's needed to be."

I shrug. "I don't know..."

His brow lifts. "You don't know? Are you telling me you might have a hard time playing in the game tomorrow? That you won't be able to separate the game from your life?"

Coach shakes his head. "Let me tell you something, West, this won't be the only time you'll have to go through this. If you're good enough—and you are—there will be plenty of people wanting to bring you down. They don't care who they drag into it or what they have to say—real or fake. Do you know why? Because it makes people feel better about themselves when they think someone good is just as fucked up as they are. If they can see their own life reflected back in someone who is on a pedestal, they rejoice in their downfall. It's sick, but it is what it is. This is just your first rodeo, but it won't be your last. If you let it impact you negatively now, I'll be seriously worried about your future."

I swallow. I know he's right.

Wishing I was a person with a squeaky-clean past won't do any good when my past made me who I am.

"Let's just start with one thing at a time." He hands me a printout with every single one of my NIL contacts. "You tell them whatever you want to tell them, but I suggest the raw truth. We don't need your future tainted any more than it already is."

With that, I punch in the first phone number, hoping like hell my voice will actually work.

CHAPTER TWENTY-SIX

Kenna

"DON'T you have a meet to get ready for?"

Sydney's question breaks into my never-ending thoughts. I aim the remote toward the TV and pause it. First, I started out with the local news coverage—the original interview West's dad did. Then, Sydney told me that ESPN picked it up, so I've been watching them dissect the interview for hours. Sometimes, they even say the same thing. I've never watched Sports-Center before in my life, but apparently, West Brooks's dad's story is getting a ton of hits all over the country. He's news.

"How long have you been watching this?" she asks, coming up behind me. Leaning back, I catch her sad expression. The headline itself is a punch in the gut. "$3M in NIL Money and Won't Share?!"

It makes him seem like a miser. "All day."

"No morning class?"

"I canceled it."

"No training sesh with West?"

I blow out a breath. "We'd already decided we'd have to pick those up after homecoming. Our schedules got really busy this week."

"And let me guess, he hasn't contacted you today either?"

"He didn't leave on the best terms," I grumble, picking at an imaginary thread on the arm of the sofa. She's well aware, but I guess she figures he'd reach out to me before now. "Plus, he's...busy."

Which I'm sure he is, but I wish I knew what he was busy doing. I could help. Probably...

"You should contact him. He needs you and doesn't know how to admit it. Men are like that. They want to seem all tough, but they're just like us."

"Which is what I thought an hour ago, so I texted him. No response."

"Did you call him?"

I nod.

"Huh."

"Pretty much," I agree. He said he'd contact me, but when shit hit ESPN, I figured I needed to say something. I gesture toward the TV. "They're making it out like he's a privileged asshole who's hoarding all this money."

Sydney moves around the sofa and sits. "Which reminds me...holy shit, did you realize he was making that much money?"

A pit forms in my stomach. I shake my head. It's hard to admit, but I feel betrayed. West comes off like he's this normal guy trying to get by. He said he didn't have any money. He told me when he grew up that his mother's car was a piece of shit. But hell, he has enough money to buy a crap ton of cars!

Three. Million. Dollars.

I knew the start of all these NIL deals for college athletes would change the face of sports. It just goes to show what you can accomplish if you're in a popular sport that you're really, really good at. I've never heard of divers making that much money. Then again, there aren't pro diving meets either. It's college and Olympics. That's it. If you're lucky enough to make it to the Olympics, you'll probably get a sponsorship deal, but we're not talking anything like the money you can make in pro football, basketball, or baseball.

I turn toward her. "I guess I can understand why he never said anything. Seems like a weird way to start a conversation, let alone a relationship. 'Hey, by the way, I'm already pulling in three million, and I haven't even been drafted yet.'"

She takes a sip of her drink. "It's probably not something you want known around campus either. They already have girls who fawn all over them just because they're football players. Add in the money aspect? He wouldn't know who to trust."

I shake my head. "I'm exhausted, and it totally sucks that things were going in a great direction. Now all of this. It feels like a direct hit, sending the two of us right back to the beginning."

"Like when you hated football players and wanted them to all get VDs so their dicks would rot and fall off?"

"Exac—" *Wait, what did she just say? Dicks falling off?* "Maybe not that far."

"I knew it," Sydney states, standing on the couch. She looms over me. "His dick is like a balm to your injured soul."

I pat the couch. "I've never told you this before, but I think you have issues."

She shrugs, plopping back down again. She takes another drink of water and then places it on the coffee table in front of us. "In all seriousness, what are you thinking? I know yesterday was awful, and this is just the beginning. That boy is going places, and that means more people will know his name. More opportunities to be thrown in the spotlight, and I know you get weirded out by your scar."

I rest my head against the couch, staring at the ceiling. "West helped me feel comfortable in my own skin again. But when he didn't stick up for me yesterday, I was hurt. It was all about football. 'Oh, we have to get

West out of here before he blows up and ruins home-coming.' 'Oh, we have to leave because they're recording and if West gives them anything, they'll plaster that video all over the internet. It'll be so bad for the team'," I mock.

She reaches over to grip my hand in hers. "I get that. And on top of that, West doesn't talk very much. He almost looked shell-shocked yesterday. I'm not sure he could've said something even if he wanted to."

Which is a symptom of abuse.

West's personality makes so much more sense now that I've met his father. "I feel for him. I really do."

"I sense a but..."

"But I guess I don't know what I expected to happen when I started to fall for a football player. It's not his fault. He told me how obsessed he is with the game. It's all he's ever wanted. He has all his eggs in the football basket, and I...I don't know how I feel about that."

I take a deep breath, and Sydney squeezes my hand. "I think you should proceed with caution, then. The end of last year was terrible for you. I don't want to see you broken again."

She's not wrong. And the kind of broken that rips out your insides is way worse than this scar on my face.

I let myself wallow for a moment more, and then I push to my feet. I have to get off my ass. I have to be down to the pool to get on the bus for my dive meet tonight.

"Thanks for the talk," I tell Sydney, forcing away all my worries for now. "I've got to get going."

She checks her watch. "Like *now*."

I peer at the time. "Shit!"

The next few minutes are spent in a frenzy as I throw together my dive bag and Sydney drives like a crazy person back to campus just in time for me to make Coach's talk. The whole time, I do my best to keep my mind from drifting to West. He's a big boy. He can handle this on his own, which is apparently exactly what he wants to do.

Coach gives us a rundown of our schedule. When she hands out the roster, I scan it, doing a double take.

I'm on it. As in, diving for points toward the team score.

It's so quiet poolside that all I can hear is the slight trickle of the water running through the filters. When I glance up, the whole team is staring at me.

Coach grins, and I don't know who starts it first, but everyone starts to clap. My face heats. My skin buzzes. I stop myself from maneuvering my hair in front of my scar, a nervous tic I've picked up any time I'm the center of attention.

Eventually, Coach uses her fingers to whistle so the whole team quiets. "I think we all need to take a lesson from Kenna. She's come so far because of hard work and determination. I have to admit, I'm impressed. I thought you were going to need more time, but you've been diving beautifully. You earned this spot."

My chest fills, and I feel like my heart is about to beat right out of its cage. "Thanks, Coach."

"Now, let's go kick some butt!" she yells.

I give the rallying cry along with my whole team. A few of my fellow divers hug me, and nearly all of them tell me congratulations. When I get settled on the bus, my hands shake as I pull my phone out. I know exactly who I want to tell first. No matter what else is true, I wouldn't actually be in this position if West didn't push me.

I press his name in my Contacts list. It rings and rings.

Hanging up, I try again. I really want to tell him personally. It rings and rings again. His voicemail picks up again, I sigh. I have to make a split-second decision, and when the tone sounds in my ear, I just start talking.

"Hey, it's me. I know I already left you a message earlier, but this isn't about that. I'm..." I take a quick breath, suddenly nervous about sharing great news when he's been living in a shitstorm, but the West who helped me get here would be so happy. "I'm diving tonight," I tell him, grinning from ear to ear. "I'm on the roster. Not an exhibition. I'm really diving."

My heart starts to skip a little, and I turn toward the window to lower my voice.

"I just wanted to thank you. You helped me so much. Coach gave this whole speech about hard work and determination, but you fueled that in me. God, I'm so nervous." I chuckle, biting my lip to get myself to stop. "Okay, talk soon. Hope I don't fuck this up! Bye."

My heels bounce up and down against the bus floor as I hang up. A part of me hopes he surprises me again and shows up at the meet, but I know I shouldn't get my hopes up. He has so much going on right now.

Instead, I pull out my headphones and click on my Hype playlist. I've borrowed some of West's, but mine is still filled with 5SOS.

All my life, I've been waiting for moments to come when I catch fire.

I just wish I could share this moment with West.

CHAPTER TWENTY-SEVEN

West

THERE ARE 139 imperfections in the ceiling above my bed.

When I was in the closet as a kid, I used to count the vertical stripes in the ugly brown paneling over and over. It would help drown out the noise of my parents' fighting or the loud, vulgar voices of my father's friends. I hated that closet. It smelled like mildew and cigarette smoke. The smoke would permeate everywhere, like you could never get away from it.

I stole a dryer sheet once and placed it on the floor with me, hoping it would suck up some of the smells. It helped for a little while, but in the end, that ended up smelling, too.

The door to my room opens, and I slide my gaze to

find Aidan walking in. "You aren't answering your phone," he offers, before shutting the door behind him.

"I talked on the phone enough today."

I can still hear the fake sympathy in my reps' voice. Or, who knows, maybe it was real sympathy, but it didn't extend too far because bad publicity is bad publicity. They don't care if it's not true. I actually have to take a stand. If I can figure out a way to discredit my father, I'll be okay. If I can't, some of my NIL partners want to jump ship. I don't "adhere to their brand."

"Listen, the guys are pissed. We're meeting in twenty minutes to talk about retaliation."

Peering over, my stomach squeezes. "Retaliation?"

"Yeah. Hamilton douchebags," Aidan grinds out. "Aren't you mad?"

I heft myself to a seated position, stretching out my limbs and piercing him with a look. "Fucking furious, but not with them. They're just dumb. We'll kick their asses tomorrow. That's the only thing that will put them in their place."

"Then they'll do it to someone else next year, West. This was a personal attack, and we're not taking this shit lightly."

I don't often see Aidan agitated. He has such a gentle, carefree spirit that his uneasiness makes me sit straighter. "This is my father's fault, dude."

"They're playing him."

"And he's letting them," I grind out, my hands turning to fists. "But you're not going to let them play you."

Aidan shakes his head, and I can tell I haven't convinced him yet. He wears a hole in the floor between our two beds. "I hate to see you like this. Look at what's happening."

My muscles tense. I'm in the same downward spiral as I was earlier when a lot of my representatives said they'd love to help but they weren't sure what they could do. They were very apologetic. "So saddened" to hear that I was on ESPN for this reason. "It isn't right," another had said. "However..."

I'm only good for what I can do for them. Other than that, most of them don't care.

In the back of my head, I guess I always thought this might happen. When I rose to the top, my father would be there asking for a handout. It's why I decided that any NIL money I get goes right into a bank account I don't touch. Honestly, I don't know what to do with money. I've never had it. I just want to play football.

None of this is fucking football.

I glance over at Aidan, who's now sitting on his own bed, his leg jumping up and down. "Keep it cool, QB."

He clutches his hands in front of him. "It's hard."

"You're the heartbeat of the team," I remind him. "People will mold to the way you react."

"Right now, I want to find those Hamilton players and kick their asses."

"Which we're not going to do," I tell him softly. "I... appreciate it. But we can't let things get out of hand. Look at what happened to Kenna."

His jaw ticks. He takes a short peek at me and then continues rubbing one hand against the other.

"Plus, if you actually go there to fight, Coach will pull you from tomorrow's game. You and whoever else decides to partake in this nonsense."

"So, what are we going to do?" Aidan asks.

I've been lying here all day, asking myself the same question. My mind at war. My future at odds. "Do you think I should pay him off?"

"What? Who?"

I peer at the floor. "My dad."

Aidan's quiet for a long time. "You want to give him money to go away?"

"It's all he wants. Or so he says."

The tension in the room mounts. It's like the rallying crowd right before kickoff. The screams pitch higher and higher, right up until the kicker connects with the ball.

"Dude, if you do that, it'll never be enough for him. He'll keep coming back when what you give him runs out."

Exactly what I had thought. If I give in now, Dad will realize he has me by the balls. He'll keep doing this little song and dance every time he wants something because he knows I want him to shut up.

This is fucked.

"You worked for that money. Your talent speaks for itself, and correct me if I'm wrong, but none of that had anything to do with your father."

Some could even say it's in spite of my father. There were so many times I could've given up. But I didn't. I persevered, even when I had the shittiest gear or no gear at all. I was constantly telling my coaches I forgot it, or that I lost it. Suddenly, they would show up with second-hand pads or gloves or fucking jockstraps that were either a little too big or small. Nothing ever quite fit right until it was just me and football. Me and the guy standing across from me. Then nothing else seemed to matter.

"Trust me, I don't want to give him a penny."

"Then don't."

The decision clicks into place and feels right. I'd been agonizing all day about what I was going to do, but he doesn't deserve anything, and I'm not going to let him win. To pay him off would've been the easy way out—at least it would've made the problem disappear for tomorrow. But sometimes the easy paths aren't the ones we should choose.

"Okay, I won't. As long as you don't go to Hamilton and act stupid."

He tilts his head. "Dude."

I hold my hands up. "You know it's a stupid move. We need your head right for tomorrow. Go read the playbook or something. Our play will be enough."

Aidan sighs in frustration and throws himself back on the bed. "I hate it when you make sense."

"Tell everyone else not to do anything either."

"Like they'll listen to me."

"You're the goddamn QB. They better listen to you."

Aidan takes out his phone and starts to type. Next to me, mine starts to ring. My stomach squeezes. I've been avoiding it all day. I even changed Coach's ringer so I'd know when to answer it. My mother has been calling since the news broke. She asked if I've really made three million. Luckily, I only listened to her voicemail and didn't have to answer.

The phone rings a couple more times while I stare at it, and Aidan finally peeks up. "You gonna get that?"

"Probably not."

He frowns, then stands until he can see who it is. "It's Kenna. Pick it up."

My heart constricts. The more she's away from me, the better she is. My life is a toxic bomb that's bound to go off, and I don't need to mar her perfection.

"She's probably worried about you."

"I'll text her."

He stares at me doubtfully. "I don't like the look on your face."

"I'm fucked up, okay? My whole life is fucked up. I don't need to bring her into this."

Aidan drops his phone to his side. "You've been pining over this girl for months. Are you telling me that you're going to let your father ruin this, too? I haven't seen you ever look at a girl like you do her."

"Which is why I just can't right now."

It's as if I've built a wall around her. I want to keep her in a sweet, serene cage of oblivion. She doesn't need to step over here. Not that she wants to. She hates football.

"This is stupid," Aidan deadpans. He reaches for my phone, and I finally pop up to my feet to block him. Behind me, the last ring sounds. Aidan and I come face-to-face with each other. "This is a mistake."

"I'm just not ready," I tell him. "There's so much going on, and she doesn't even like football."

"This isn't about football," Aidan snaps. "This is personal."

"Either way..."

He drops his head back, groaning.

Once again, my phone starts to ring. I peek down and see Kenna's name again. She called me earlier, too. I wanted to answer. I really did. I wanted to so badly it hurt, but I'm doing this for her.

While I'm staring longingly at the screen, Aidan snatches it up. He's quick, but I'm bigger. I grab hold of his hand, and we wrestle over the phone for a second. "The fuck," I growl.

Somehow, he eventually gets his thumb on the screen to swipe, and I let go like it's a hot poker. I turn, running my hands through my hair and silently groan into the abyss. Is this what Kenna's tattoo means? Dive into the abyss. That I should do something, even if it's unknown?

"Hey," Aidan says. Then a second later, "No, it's Aidan. But West is right here."

He taps me on the shoulder, and I glare at him, holding my hand out. He places the phone in my palm, and I close my eyes before bringing it to my ear.

"West?"

I swallow, my mouth suddenly dry. She sounds upset. "Yeah?"

She takes in a shaky breath. "Did you... Did the football team... Did they put up the footage from Richie's yesterday?"

"The footage?"

"Is that why you're avoiding me?" Her voice raises. "It's all over Instagram right now. I'm tagged in it, West. It says a football player provided the footage."

"I— I don't..."

The phone makes a noise, and then Kenna comes

back on, even more frantic. "Now I'm getting a call from Channel Eight. They're calling me, West."

I just stand there with my mouth opening and closing, no words coming out. I reach for Aidan's phone, yanking it from his grip before I go to his socials and look it up. Sure enough, the same footage Coach showed me earlier that no one had picked up yet is now being broadcast far and wide. Except, the headlines are friendlier to me now.

"NFL Prospect's Dad Demeans Son's Girlfriend"

"Could We Have Had It All Wrong? Brooks Showing True Character"

The audio starts to play, and the sound has been enhanced. Anyone can clearly hear my dad say all those hateful things to Kenna.

"I'm sorry. I don't—"

"You're sorry? I've been trying to see how you were all day. I've been worried. I called, I texted, and now I see that the football team has released this...this fucking bullshit from yesterday. But I can see why you did. I guess everything will blow over now, huh? Well, that's great. I'm really happy for you."

The phone clicks, and I can't breathe. There's nothing but dead air on the other side of the line.

Aidan scans my face and then his phone in my hand. "Shit..."

"It's, um... I don't think she wants to talk to me now."

"Does she think you did it?"

"Does it matter?" I counter. I release a breath. My heart hurts. I knew this was for the best, but it sucks. It sucks so fucking bad.

I retreat from Aidan and sit back down on my bed. I type and retype a response to Kenna, not even sure what to say. I end up deleting my words over a dozen times. In the end, I end up sending:

> WestB: I'm so sorry. I never wanted you to get hurt. Especially not from anything that has to do with me. I won't contact you anymore. It's for the best.

I feel empty when I hit Send. I don't give excuses, though. I refuse. There's no excuse for what's happened to her twice now, and I feel responsible for both. Sure, I didn't throw the firework into her room, and I didn't say any of those disgusting words to her, but I was involved both times.

It was stupid thinking that I could turn this into something different.

> McKenna: So, that's it, then? No explanations, we're just done?

A fissure opens in my chest. My insides start pulling apart. I have to separate what I feel from what is right. A part of me will always love Kenna, but love isn't enough. Love brings hours upon hours in closets, and then years later, betrayal.

It's better this way.

WestB: I guess so.

And that's the moment I lost the best thing that ever happened to me.

CHAPTER TWENTY-EIGHT

Kenna

CHLORINE BURNS MY NOSTRILS. Drops of pool water hit my back and roll down.

A pang of loneliness smacks me. I'm in the rear of the visitors' locker room, facing a wall of lockers, gripping my phone like I could choke it.

Fucking football players.

I should've known.

He turned his back on me so quick. So fucking quick. The worst part is, I didn't even see it coming. Not with him. But I guess I should've because they're all the same.

It's over.

At least I know now.

His words from yesterday come back to haunt me.

The way he'd cupped my cheeks... He stared at me like I was his everything.

I love you.

Well, he definitely doesn't know what love is.

TWO HOURS LATER...

Sydney clicks her glass with mine. We fought over the soundtrack of my "fuck him" party, but I won since I'm the belle of the ball.

I throw back a shot, setting the empty glass on the coffee table. "I really thought he was different," I say for the umpteenth time.

It doesn't matter how many times I say it, Sydney always answers the same way: "Me too. You sure he hasn't called?"

I check my phone again. "Nothing."

She frowns. "He had me fooled."

"You and me both."

"Aidan's texted me, but I'm not responding in solidarity."

I lift the empty shot class and make her click hers with mine again. I'm not usually a drown-my-sorrows-in-alcohol type of girl, but when Sydney suggested a "fuck him" party, I was all for it.

We turned off the TV and made a pact we wouldn't get on any social media whatsoever and we would talk about nothing but what a dick West Brooks is.

The thing is, I can only think of things to say about what's happened in the last twenty-four to thirty-six hours. It's not like I have a whole laundry list of complaints. Other than selling me out to the media, everything was fine.

Not that selling me out is something I should gloss over.

I throw my head back and groan. "Who does that? Did he think I would be okay with it?"

Sydney nibbles her lip.

I side-eye her when she doesn't respond. She's been hyping me up the whole "fuck him" party, but now she's silent. "What?"

"I don't think he actually sold you out."

"Why? Because Aidan says so?" My words come out childish, but when I'm four or five shots in and nursing a broken heart, I don't feel bad about it.

"Well, he did. I think he's telling the truth, but I don't know why West didn't just say that."

"If he didn't do it, another football player did. It said so on the TV."

"You mean the same TV that so many reporters have been calling you that you had to turn your phone on Accept Calls From Contacts Only?"

"Yep, that one." I fill up her shot glass again, along with my own. Clearly, she's still using logic, and I'm not in that same frame of mind. "Like you said, it doesn't matter. He could've said something. Instead, he's been ignoring me since all this happened. He bailed on me at Richie's. Sure, he came back over to have sex with me and told me he felt bad, but then the very next day, he abandons me again. Again, Sydney! And again, I don't hear from him the whole day, even though I call and text like a good little girlfriend. Still, we're done. He officially said it."

I throw back the shot, letting the liquor burn my throat all the way down.

"I'm shocked. It seemed like he was so into you. He could've fought for you."

"Right?" I burst out. "Ugh."

TWO HOURS AFTER THAT...

"You know he took his sweatshirt back?"

Sydney's such a good friend. She pouts and answers with all the right things. I know I need to wrap this up soon because she has a big day tomorrow, but I can't stop spilling out everything I think.

I nod like I'm answering her. "This morning, before he left. He threw it on and walked off with it. At one point, he said something about wanting me to keep it, but I guess he didn't really mean that."

The alcohol has been put up already. The shot

glasses cleaned. We're both sitting on the couch, staring at a TV that isn't on.

"I even called him today to tell him I was on the dive roster."

She shakes her head. "It would've taken all of two seconds for him to take your call and wish you good luck."

I bite my lip. The alcohol is still making my brain fuzzy, but now I'm getting depressed. "I can't tell if I'm more mad that he did all these things to me or because he didn't let me in when he was going through this."

Sydney reaches over and squeezes my hand, jarring me into the present. I hadn't even realized I'd spoken aloud. It was just a quick thought, a brief acknowledgment of me trying to pinpoint why I'm so hurt and pissed. "He definitely pulled away. He could've handled things a lot better."

"Fuck football players," I mumble for the hundredth time tonight. I get that football is so important to him. It's his future, and he has a lot riding on it, but I wanted to help. That's what people who are together do, right?

Instead, he slinked off on his phone and wouldn't even let me in.

So, every time something big comes up, I'm supposed to accept that he'll go handle it on his own and forget that there's still a whole other part of his life out there, waiting?

Nope.

And it doesn't matter because I guess that's not what he wanted either.

I peek over at Sydney and see her eyes flutter. I'm being a terrible friend. She probably wants to kill me.

After I give her hand a quick squeeze, she peers over at me. "Sorry, what?"

I smile. "I was just telling you that I'm ready to go to sleep now."

"Oh, you sure? I'm here. We can do whatever."

"Yeah, I think I'll just sleep on it," I tell her. "Thanks for being there for me."

"Of course," she says, getting to her feet. She stretches her hands in the air, reaching for the ceiling. She turns to give me a hand up. I take it, vowing that this is the last time I'll say anything about West until her halftime show is over tomorrow. I give her a hug, and she returns it.

"You know, if you don't want to come tomorrow, I'll understand."

I pull away. "Are you kidding me? I'll be there. I might only come for the show, but I've been dying to see it, Sydney. I wouldn't miss it for anything."

She squeezes my hands, then steps away.

"Now, go get your beauty sleep! Big day tomorrow!"

She beams, almost skipping to her room. I shut the lights off and trek the hallway back to my room, making sure the front door is locked before I head inside. The bare space where I used to have my David Boudia poster feels like a chasm of emptiness. I should put it back, but I don't have the energy right now.

Plus, at this point in my grieving, the poster would be a poor substitute for West, physically speaking.

I pull out my pajamas from the closet, and a shirt falls on the floor. I pick it up in the dark, frowning when I don't recognize the fabric.

A pang hits me when I bring it into the light. It's West's jersey. The one he made a big deal about giving me because it meant I was *his*.

"Ugh!" I throw it back in the closet and slam the doors closed.

That's enough of West Brooks tonight.

I should take his stupid jersey back to him and tell him to shove it...

But he'd probably be too busy worrying about the game tomorrow to see me.

Fucking. Football. Players.

CHAPTER TWENTY-NINE

West

NERVES GET TO ME. Mine and Aidan's shared room feels like a tomb of my own making.

The door opens, and Aidan walks through with a towel around his waist. I squeeze the tie I have in my hand. We really don't have to be at the field for another hour and a half, but I'm going early.

"Need assistance?"

"You know it." I hand Aidan my royal-blue tie that matches the Bulldog colors. I've been wearing the same one since I started here and haven't once tied it on my own. Just one of those things fathers teach their sons that I have yet to know how to do.

"I really should teach you how to do this."

"Maybe one day, but it always seems like we're in a hurry." I lift my chin so he can do his thing.

He places it around my head, measuring up both sides. "Are you ready for today?"

"I'll be happy once the first part of the day is over."

He chuckles. "I'm surprised Coach is letting you do this."

So am I. Though, it was sort of his idea. He said the media needed a story, so I'm giving them one. "I think it's because it's not actually interfering with anything. If it did, he'd be pissed."

"Hopefully, this will help everything blow over. You know it won't be right away because you're giving everyone another story, but at least you'll be telling the truth."

My stomach wrenches. I'm not looking forward to airing my family's dirty laundry, but the way I see it, if I do it now, it'll cut my father off at the knees. Plus, maybe I won't have to go through this again.

Aidan finishes, tightening up the knot toward my neck. He grabs my shoulders. "Just be yourself. I'll see you in the locker room so we can teach Hamilton a lesson on the field."

I grin. That's what I wanted to hear. That's the kind of enthusiasm I want for today. "Homecoming, baby."

"Homecoming."

We touch fists, and I am hyped for the game, but my mind keeps wandering to Kenna. I don't mean for it to. I did what I did for a good reason, but she's always there. Plus, I hate the fact that I hurt her. It makes all of this even more shitty.

Twenty minutes later, I'm standing on the edge of the football field. It's empty except for a few workers walking through the stands. There are some tech people up in the box and on the sidelines, but it's crowd free. Just on the other side of these stadium walls, though, the campus is having one hell of a tailgate party. The thump of bass reverberates through the air.

The sun is out and shining.

The breeze has a crisp bite to it.

Everything is shaking up to be the perfect day.

As soon as I'm done with this, I'm turning my phone off and concentrating on the game. If this doesn't appease everyone, I don't know what will, but I'm not going to beat myself down trying to think of something else.

A man and a woman start walking toward me. I recognize them from a local news station. The man is holding on to a camera at his side, and the woman is dressed in a slim skirt with a long-sleeve blouse. "Mr. Brooks?"

I reach out my hand. "Hello. Thanks for coming."

"Well, it's not often the biggest draft candidate requests an interview from little old Channel Eight."

My smile pulls tight. "I just felt like it was the right thing to do to put the record straight."

I swear, the sparkle in this woman's eyes could rival the Hope Diamond.

The man next to her starts fiddling with his equipment as she says, "I prepared a few questions, but I want you to say what you want to get out, so I'll ask you at the end if there's anything you want to add."

Shit just got real.

I've been trying to forget about the fact that I'd have to talk, and even though it doesn't seem like it's that big of a deal in front of these two, I'm hoping I don't choke when the camera is on.

"I'd like to see your questions," I tell her. This was Aidan's idea. He thought it would help me be better prepared.

She cocks her head and smiles. "Great idea." She hands over a small notecard that she has in her hand.

It's all the normal things I expected to be asked. When I hand it back, I say, "Can you ask me something about the homecoming game at the end? I want to bury this and turn it around to football."

"Of course." Her cameraman hands her a pen, and she makes a notation on her card. When she's done, she asks him, "Are we all good? Where do you want me and Mr. Brooks to stand, Sammy?"

The cameraman peers around and then positions us with the upright in the background. Before I know it, he's counting down, and I'm staring at a blinking red light with a camera lens pointed at me. It takes me a second to catch up with the fact that the reporter is already asking me a question after giving a short introduction. "Is it true you wanted this interview, Mr. Brooks?"

I blink. I decide to just look at her. Then I can fool myself into thinking this isn't being recorded and broadcast. "It is. I thought I should set the record straight."

She pulls the microphone back to her, hiding her bright-red lipstick briefly while she asks, "I hear you have some rebuffs from what your father said to our reporter just the other day."

"I do," I answer. I'm quiet for a little while until she urges me with her eyes and keeps the microphone pointed at me. It spurs me on. "Thank you for giving me the opportunity to talk about my past. My father..."

I hesitate. There's no going back now, not that I should, and not that I should even feel bad about this.

"My father isn't a nice man. He was verbally and emotionally abusive my entire life, and he had yet to even come to one of my football games until the first game of this season. I suspect that his whole intention of dragging my name through the mud is that he wanted me to give him some of the money I earned with the new name, image, likeness rules put forth by the NCAA board of directors.

"Prior to this, I hadn't spoken with my father in years. He has not reached out, nor have I. And frankly,

I think it's sad that the first time he did reach out was about money. I suspect that if I was a regular college student, he wouldn't be giving me the time of day, just like he didn't my entire life."

"Can you speak to some of the abuses you say you've suffered?"

I frown at her. This wasn't on her list of questions, and it pisses me off that she went off script. "I won't go into that. It's a private family matter. I'm only coming forward now because he's the one that made it public. I would've been happy to go on with our separate lives."

"So, would it be fair to say that you think your father is attempting to extort you?"

"It was him who brought up the NIL money to your media outlet."

She tsks. "I think it is fair to say that we all saw your father's behavior in the footage with you at a local diner, so this doesn't seem to be too far off."

"About that footage." I turn directly into the camera. "I would like to ask everyone to stop sharing it, please. If you've posted it to your social media, please delete it, and I would appreciate it if news outlets stop running it as well. My father doesn't deserve any more of your time."

"I'm sure your girlfriend was very upset."

My throat works. That wasn't on her notecard either. "I won't be answering any questions about her."

The reporter nods. "How culpable do you find the Hamilton players in all of this?"

I really want to call them out for their shameless, unethical tactics, but I've already decided not to. "I prefer to answer that with my play on the field today."

"Do you have anything else you would like to add, Mr. Brooks?"

I shake my head. "No, ma'am. I just want to say I appreciate you coming down to the Warner University football field today to get the true story. I'm not exactly happy about sharing private details of my personal life, but I won't stand by and watch something I know to be wrong. In the future, I hope that people can see through lies instead of blowing something up that didn't even need to be news. I want football to be my story, and how I act on the field is how I act in real life. I'm fiercely protective. I'm determined. I'm aggressive, but respectful."

The reporter smiles. "And how do you see the game going down today?"

"I'm calling the W for Warner University."

The reporter rattles off when her viewers can catch the game and then we both smile at the camera like puppets being told what to do.

Afterward, she takes a big breath. "Okay." She lowers the microphone and reaches her hand out. "Thanks for the interview. It'll run right before the game."

I squeeze her hand. "Thank you."

Now that that's done, I only have one more win to focus on.

"Just curious," the reporter starts as she lets go of my hand, "why didn't you want to answer questions about your girlfriend?"

The word hits me like a ton of bricks. I have the sudden yearn to talk with Kenna. Now that all this should be over, I want to hash it out with her. I want to run to her and tell her everything that's been going on in my head.

But I can't do that. She's better off without me.

"No comment," I mutter, then I walk toward the locker room so I can get my head on straight.

I've already lost Kenna. I don't need to lose another thing I love.

CHAPTER THIRTY

Kenna

THE HOUSE HAS BEEN quiet for an hour after Sydney left in a tornado of frantic energy. Again, she told me I didn't need to come, but I wouldn't do that to her. Her show is important, and just because it happens to be smack-dab in the middle of something I'd rather not watch, that's no excuse.

Ride or die and all that.

Since I have a moment to myself, I decide to pull out my textbooks and look over any assignments that are due soon. I was caught up in a West bubble, and even though I'm fairly certain I didn't let anything slip, at least doing this is keeping my mind off what's happening a couple of blocks from here.

Though, it's hard to ignore the people walking past the house blowing horns and using noisemakers. And the cars lining the streets because the parking lot couldn't contain them all.

Everyone is enjoying this but me.

I reread the same paragraph three times before groaning and slamming the book shut.

I try my hand at watching TV, but my mind keeps wandering to how West is doing. It's a big day for him. I'd be lying if I said I hadn't checked my phone to see if he reached out.

"This is stupid!"

A line from the TV catches my attention. I don't even know what I have on, but there's a nicely tailored guy on the screen. The camera cuts to a woman in sweatpants and a sweatshirt who has her chin in the air.

"You love me, and I love you. That's all that matters."

"We lead different lives," the woman argues.

I lean toward the TV, engrossed by the Hallmark-like movie.

"And I said that's stupid."

"No, you're being naïve."

Say it girl. It's like he's the devil on my shoulder, and she's the rational part of my brain. I bet he works for some major company in the city that goes directly against what she believes in.

He walks toward her, grabbing her hands.

Oh... I stand up straighter. The look in his eyes.

He's determined, I can tell. For a moment, I picture me and West, and my heart begins to hammer.

"You've changed my life. What if I don't want to be that person anymore? I don't care where we live, I just want to be with you."

Aww. My eyes start to tear.

The girl is waffling, I can see it. My hand grips the remote tighter...

And then my phone rings.

I gasp at the intrusion, and then lean forward. *Sydney* scrolls across the screen, so I hurry to pick it up. "SOS," she says as soon as I have the phone to my ear. "I forgot my glitter scrunchies in my room!" The stress in her voice bleeds through. "If I don't have them, it's going to completely throw off my outfit. Please, Kenna, I beg you."

"Whoa, okay. No problem. Glitter scrunchies, I got it."

I'm already moving toward her room when she says, "Go to the east gate. They're going to let you in, I gave them your name, so just make sure you have your student ID with you."

"You got it," I tell her, scanning her room. It's no wonder that she forgot her glitter scrunchies. It looks like her closet threw up in here.

"Hurry, please!"

"On it," I tell her as I start throwing clothes around. She hangs up, and I shove my phone in my back pocket while I search. I finally find them on her dresser, which had not only clothes on it but her bathroom towel.

I grab the scrunchies and stuff them in my pocket. A pang of guilt hits me that I kept her up last night talking about West when she was obviously super nervous about today. I grab my keys and head outside. A sea of royal blue hits me. Banners on cars. People walking with our school colors. What a madhouse.

Before I leave, I check my small purse to make sure my ID is in there, and then I take off, dodging people as I go. The closer I get to campus, the stronger the smell of food wafts my way. Smoke and charcoal. Delicious barbecue. I've never seen the stadium area so busy. I've always avoided homecoming like the plague, and now I remember why. It's a madhouse.

I'm forced to walk once I get closer to the east gate, the area is so packed. To my right, the cheerleaders are rallying the onlookers into the Bulldog fight song, blue and white striped cones pressed against their mouths. "Fight, fight, fight!"

My mom told me never to budge a line, but I make an exception for today. I bypass as many people as I can until I get to the east gate attendant, who looks at me annoyedly. Before she can send me to the back of the line, I say, "Kenna Knowles. I'm here for the half-time show performer."

She nods. "ID?"

I pull it out of my wallet and show it to her. She stamps a big blue dot on my hand. "No reentry."

"Yes, ma'am," I say, taking off again. It's almost worse inside the stadium. The food vendors are lined against the wall. People are walking around, looking for their seats or just plain meandering. The smell of popcorn is overwhelming, and because of all the buzz, I almost don't hear my name being called.

A guy holds on to a metal exit door and waves at me. He's wearing a bright-gold shirt that says *Stadium Staff* on it. I recognize him as someone Sydney introduced me to briefly once.

I head his way, speed walking, and he rushes me through a back tunnel, shutting the door behind him. "Thank God you made it. Sydney's a wreck."

"She has nervous energy on a good day," I tell him with a smile.

Sweat dots his temples as he shakes his head. It sounds like Sydney is being a handful, but I never expected anything less.

"Do you want to see her first, and then you can take your seat?"

"Oh, I don't have a ticket."

"Sydney got you one. She didn't tell you? When she won the competition, she got free tickets to the game, too."

"Oh. Okay." My stomach twists in knots. I hadn't

planned on watching the game at all. I was just going to drop in for the show and leave.

He must recognize my apprehension. "They're great seats. Fifty-yard line. Perfect view of the show, too. Sydney looks amazing."

Now I remember who this guy is. One of the production dudes. It's part of their class grade to help run the homecoming show. I can't remember if he's lighting, sound, or set, but he's one or the other.

He turns a corner, and we start to slope down. At the end of the hall, people are milling around, some of them wearing headsets and others holding clipboards they're staring at as they exit one of the rooms.

"She's in here," he says, guiding me that way.

I take out her glitter scrunchies because I don't want to be accused of deforming them. When we get to the end of the hall, my guide goes right into the room, but a commotion to the left draws my attention.

My heart grinds to a halt.

At the end of the tunnel walks the entire Warner University football team. All the men dressed in their uniforms, standing shoulder-to-shoulder, reminds me of an army. They walk down a ramp like they're heading toward the battlefield. Sunlight slices through the tunnel, illuminating half the players. Here, I can hear and smell the same things going on outside, so this must be the entrance to the field.

The lead player waves, and it takes me a moment

to recognize Aidan. I wave back. He jumps up and down, his head almost hitting a mounted TV at the junction between the two hallways. The whole team has come to a stop, helmets in their hands. Some of them are stretching out, some have their heads bowed. None of them really talk to one another.

I start to scan the crowd, looking for *him*, but I stop myself before I get too far.

A sudden jolt hits my chest, and I realize it would be too much to see him like this, right now. So shortly after we'd ended things.

"Kenna, thank God!" Sydney runs up to me and grabs her scrunchies out of my hand. She wraps me up in a hug. "Thank you." She must spot Aidan over my head because she calls his name and waves furiously. "Good luck!"

He gives her a thumbs up back, coupled with a cocky smile. Above his head, the TV starts playing. Just like I'm used to seeing when my dad watches sports, a panel of men sit behind a long table and start talking about the game. I don't really hear what they're saying until they show a picture of West. Then, it cuts to a full screen of West speaking with a woman reporter.

Captions scroll across, but I hear him loud and clear. "I thought I should set the record straight."

My mind immediately focuses, intent on him. I'm trying to decipher whether this is an old interview or a new one. The well-dressed West on screen is confident and sure. "My father isn't a nice man..."

The football team quiets, the whole tunnel silenced like they're as engrossed as I am. Some of the players watch the TV while others turn inward until there's a large, sentinel-like body standing tall...and staring right at me.

My breath hitches. In the background, I can still hear his interview, which was obviously given earlier today. West accuses his father of extortion, and my pulse starts to race. His gaze locks with mine, and even though he's tethering me to this spot, it feels like the ground is uneven.

"I would like to ask everyone to stop sharing it, please. If you've posted it to your social media, please delete it, and I would appreciate it if news outlets stop running it as well. My father doesn't deserve any more of your time."

"I'm sure your girlfriend was very upset."

My body trembles.

"I won't be answering any questions about her."

Her.

I swallow the lump in my throat, but still, we don't stop staring at one another. The whole world is looking at him, and he's focused on me. Still.

His teammates start rallying around him. They pat his back. They say things to him, but he doesn't take his eyes off me.

Goosebumps spread over my body in waves. He nods at me, and I know West Brooks well enough to understand that he did some of that for me. He told people to stop sharing the video. Sydney and I had decided that I should delete my socials last night, so I hadn't even been on them to know. Maybe people haven't stopped. Maybe they're still sharing his father's hateful words, but just knowing that West asked... It means so much.

I nod back at him and bite the inside of my cheek. Tears prick my eyes, and then Aidan starts to jump up and down again, yelling, "Are we going to let them get away with that?"

"No!" the team yells.

"Do we protect our own?" he screams, doubling over at the waist.

"Yes!" the chorus calls back.

It's so primal. Even more electricity sparks through me.

"What are we going to do about it?"

"Win, win, win!"

Another guy in a gold shirt at the mouth of the tunnel signals for the team to go, and they start running up the ramp, battle cries ripping from their throats. Their coach walks next to them, but then he does a double take when he sees me. He changes direction, and I shuffle back and forth on my feet as he makes his way toward me. "McKenna?"

I nod, nerves fluttering in my stomach.

"I wanted to personally apologize to you about the thoughtless incident that occurred last year that injured you. I've often had sleepless nights thinking about you and wondering how you were doing. I have a daughter of my own and would've been just as furious as your parents."

His fingers grip a whiteboard in front of him fiercely.

"As my family likes to remind me, I can get overzealous about the sport I love. Football is like a living, breathing thing to me, but I would never put that over someone's well-being."

More tears prick my eyes.

"I had the pleasure of seeing you dive, and I can only imagine the hard work and dedication it took to get you back on the diving board. Kudos to you, young lady. I can see why West dedicated the game to you."

My heart skips a beat. "He dedicated the game to me?"

Coach nods, and his expression morphs into one of fondness. "We have a tradition in our pregame that if one of our players wants to share about someone or something that has really influenced and motivated them, they can do so. I've never seen West get up and talk in front of the whole team before, but today he spoke about how brave you are."

"Oh," I murmur, my gaze falling to my feet.

West's coach claps me on the shoulder, nearly toppling me over. He grimaces. "Sorry, you're a lot lighter than most of the players I work with. Good luck to you, Miss Knowles. You're welcome at a Bulldog practice any time. We could use people like you. Sometimes these players don't realize how easy they really have it."

I can barely wrap my head around what's happened, but I manage to call out, "Good luck!" as he walks away. He gives me a wave and continues to jog up the ramp. The school band is playing, people are still clapping, and the announcer's words echo off the stadium walls. On the TV screen near the ramp, a shot of the audience pans, and as soon as West runs out on the field, the entire place starts to chant "Hulk, Hulk, Hulk!"

It's electric. Chills run up and down my arms, and a well of emotion builds until tears prick my eyes.

So, this is football?

CHAPTER THIRTY-ONE

West

WHY DID she have to be right there? I didn't know they were going to replay the interview I gave this morning before we took the field, but worse was when Kenna was staring right at me when I evaded the girl-friend question. My mind wasn't ready for that.

Hell, my heart wasn't ready for that.

Seeing her and hearing the crowd scream my name makes it difficult to remember why I put up all those barriers. When I talked about her in the locker room, I laid out a story about a goddess who could conquer anything. At first, I thought I was just ramping up my teammates, but when my voice cracked, I realized I was talking about her because I missed her. Sure, she is all those things. Brave and beautiful and smart. She looks fear in the eyes and challenges it every day.

And what did I do? Fuck it up.

The whole crowd groans, and I snap my attention back to the field. Sweat pours down the side of my face while I spot the officials on the side moving the chains. Hamilton got a first down. They're winning 7–0, something I didn't think would be a possibility.

"Come on!" I shout from the sidelines before squirting water from a bottle over my face.

To my left, Aidan approaches. He already has a grass stain on his shoulder from when I missed a block. He eyes me but keeps walking. Then he turns again, keeping his attention on me. I try to avoid him, but when Aidan has something to say, he's going to say it.

"What?" I grind out. Behind him, Hamilton's quarterback passes off for a run and gains five yards. My legs jump up and down.

He moves up to me, the face guard of his helmet clenched in his hands. "I need you in this fucking game." His words are raw and gravelly.

"I *am* in the game."

He gestures out on the field. "Really? Because it seems to me you're in your head. Missing tackles. You missed a freaking handoff, West."

I wish I could place the blame back on him, but I can't. It was all me. I grind my teeth together. Seeing Kenna right before we started play fucked me up.

The crowd groans again, and I peer around Aidan to find that Hamilton has gotten another first down.

Fuck. They're marching right down the field, and I really don't want to be two touchdowns in the hole before offense can get back on the field.

He bends to one knee in front of me. "I know what's going through your head. You've been a zombie all day, and the only time you perked up was when you talked about Kenna to the guys. It's so obvious. I don't know why you can't see it."

What if I *can* see it now? What if I realize I was just scared to put my issues on her, so I backed away? I put those concrete walls up and pretended everything would be better without her in it. It was stupid. "I see it."

Aidan rears back, surprised.

"I bet you didn't expect me to say that."

"No, because you're a stubborn dick. Everyone can see it," he says, gesturing around the sidelines. When he does so, my fellow offensive players glance away.

Have they been looking at me this entire time? They're probably wondering what my problem is. I'm supposed to be a leader on the field, and I'm leading everyone to a fucking loss.

"You talked about how courageous Kenna was earlier, but you've been acting scared. You could've fought for her. You could've said something."

"Are we really going to do this during the game?" I snap. It's not him that I'm mad at, though. I'm furious with myself.

"Yes!" He shoves my knees. "Because you're losing it. And because you look like a damn coward in front of her."

I pull back. *In front of her?*

His jaw tenses. "I didn't want to tell you, but she's sitting on the fifty, first row. Sydney got her the seats."

"But she doesn't like football." It takes everything in me not to look behind me to search for her. I'm on the forty-five right now. We're so close.

"But maybe she likes a football player," he says, finally standing. He shakes his head. "I get it, man. She's gotten under your skin. The good news is you can get a second chance. You can make this right, but I'm begging you. Don't screw up this game because you're mad at yourself for how you've acted. You have plenty of time. She's. Right. There."

I blink up at him as his words settle like a warm blanket around my shoulders. Peering out at the field, I take in the collision of our D-line. Above them is a sea of blue, and beyond that, there's the vast, lighter-blue sky filled with white puffy clouds.

I know what I did now. I backed myself into a refined space where I could only count on myself. It was like being in that closet all those years ago.

But look where I am now. There are more Brooks jerseys out there than any other player on the team. They chanted *my* name when I walked out. If I scan the crowd for signs, I read their words, take in their response to me.

#TeamWest

No One Puts Brooks in a Corner

In the End, #WestWins

Brooks: True Blue

Keep Your Head Up, 53

They made those for me. Some of them sound like they're in direct response to the interview I gave just hours ago.

I am no longer the scared little boy, and I don't have to silence myself.

Aidan's still watching me, so I give him a short nod. "I'm in it."

"Good," he sighs. "Now, if we can get a stop on defense."

Aidan turns to stare at the field, and I hate the way I've let him down. There's so much riding on this game for him. It's hard being the quarterback after a great one gets drafted. He needs wins. He needs to start his legacy, and I've been screwing it up for him.

I stand, clapping him on the shoulder pads across his name. "I got you, man." I hold out my fist. "Let's turn this shit around."

He touches my fist with his. "I should be a motivational speaker. That was pretty damn good."

A grin spreads my lips apart. "You should, asshole."

"I mean, seriously," he says, "I think I could've stopped wars with that speech."

"We start the war on the field next time we're up."

He lets out an excited shout. "Oh, it's happening!"

Luckily, Hamilton doesn't score. We stop them on downs on the five-yard line.

I jog out onto the field, putting on my helmet.

It's time to get down to business. Gotta show my girl what I can do.

Kenna

I WORRY OVER MY LIP. The first quarter wasn't good for West. He made a few mistakes, but I spied Aidan talking to him on the sidelines, and since he went back out, he's been an unstoppable force. Play after play, the announcer echoes Brooks.

Brooks with the first down.

Brooks with fifteen yards on the play.

The Bulldog crowd is loving it. I can't get over all the signs that people made supporting West. I know it had to have taken so much out of him to do that interview, and now he's seeing that love reflected back to him.

In my head, I can understand why West would tell everyone else that I'm his inspiration but not tell me. It's his way. I let him go silent. I could've pushed. I could've shown up at his place, just like he did the night his father said all those awful things.

I have to fight for him. No one else ever has. He was so touched when I came to his game before, and here I sit now. Waiting. Watching. Cheering for him.

The game clock starts to count down to halftime. Soon, Sydney will be taking the stage, and I'm super pumped for her, but I'm also on eggshells about losing sight of West again. The way his stare bore into me when he saw me earlier... The connection is still there. It didn't fade just because he pulled back.

The young girl next to me bumps into me with her elbow. "Sorry," she giggle-yells. She waves a sign in the air that I haven't been able to read yet, but she keeps switching out from one sign to the other, leaving one at her feet at all times.

"Who's your favorite player?" I ask.

"West!" she exclaims, affronted. "Is there anyone else on the team?" She laughs to herself, and over her head, her father rolls his eyes while looking at me.

I give him a sincere smile.

An idea clicks into place. On the field, West rams into a defensive player and ends up on top of him while Aidan throws a short pass to Cade.

The girl next to me jumps up and down.

When she finally relaxes, I say, "Hey, what would you say if I said I could get West to come over here?"

She side-eyes me, and I turn toward her, lifting my brows in hope.

"I'd say you were full of it. He's playing a game."

"Okay, maybe I can't get him to come over during the game, but what about before halftime?"

She frowns, scrutinizing me. Her mouth drops open. "You— You're the girl from the video."

She's staring directly at my scar as I nod.

"My dad told me what happened to you, and I'm sorry. I'm sure Brooks didn't have anything to do with it."

I grin. "You're right. He didn't."

She looks me up and down. "So, he's going to come over here before halftime. There's only two minutes left."

I drum my fingers over the wall in front of us that leads down to the sidelines where the Bulldogs' defense is currently being instructed by their coach. "He will, but I need your help."

"What can *I* do? He doesn't even know I exist."

I chuckle into my hand. "Well, I was hoping you might have a marker like you used to make one of your signs, and then I was going to ask if I can write on the back."

She peers at the blank side of her sign. "You can, but I don't have a marker."

I groan inwardly.

The girl, however, takes action right away. She

turns, facing the rest of the crowd. I nearly get a head rush at the dizzying number of people behind us. "I need a marker. Does anyone have a marker?"

Some people shake their heads, but others start asking people next to them and behind them. Soon, there's a bit of a buzz. Butterflies dance around my insides. People stare down at me and the girl, but I look on hopefully.

"I do!" someone shouts. They produce a marker, holding it into the air.

The girl next to me takes action again. "Throw it!"

The guy looks around, but shrugs, tossing the marker our way. I reach out, and by some miracle, I actually catch it.

"Hurry," the girl shouts as I pop the cap off. She hands me her poster. "There's only one minute left!"

Goodness, this girl is not good for my nerves.

I don't even have time to think about what I'm going to say, I just start to write.

I write from the heart. I write what I want him to know: I'm still here. I'm still fighting for us. I won't be his dad. Or his mom. Or anyone else who's let him down.

"You don't need to write a book," the girl scolds.

I laugh, the sound coming out squeaky.

When I finish, I stand back. "Oh," she says. "Ohhhh."

I look at her, and she nods at me. Lord help me, but

she gives me the confidence I need to hold the sign up high.

I take a deep breath, closing my eyes briefly before reminding myself that if I'm all the things West thinks I am, then I can do this. I can be brave. I can be a fighter...even when everyone else is looking at me. I own everything about myself, especially the hard parts.

West

"LET'S GO!" I roar as I run the football in for a touchdown seconds before the end of the half. The crowd goes nuts. Royal-blue-and-white poms wave in the air. Cow bells are highlighted by the answering cheers from spectators.

Tied going into halftime. We have a chance. We have a really good chance.

Aidan runs toward me, and we both lift into the air to chest bump each other before falling back to our feet. He grabs my face guard and gets in my face. "That's what I'm talking about, brother."

I knock him in the helmet, and then we run toward the ramp to take us back down to the locker room for halftime.

Energy races through me. I can already feel that we're going to dominate the second half. We're going to blow Hamilton away, give them what they deserve.

A few fans call my name, but I ignore them to keep my head in the game, still reassured by Aidan's words that Kenna will be there waiting.

And she is watching. She's here again. Even when I broke it off with her, she still showed up.

God, this girl.

"West, West, West!" a chant starts out. I wave my hand in the air in acknowledgment.

Aidan elbows me. "Shit, dude."

He's stopped. I run a few steps farther but stop, too. Glancing up, I scan the crowd. The middle section of the stadium is all pointing to one area, echoing my name again and again.

And then I see her. My beautiful, fierce McKenna.

She's biting her lip like she does, arms extended straight out in the air, holding up a sign.

I met this guy...
And even though he doesn't talk,
even though he's a football player,
I think I'm in love with him.

THE WORLD STOPS. A reverberation hits me right in the core; a resounding, earth-shattering answer to her words. We were always an inevitability. I may have gotten lost in the weeds, but this is the final quarter, the closing minutes of play.

I was never one to think about my romantic future —my parents weren't the best role models. But if I had to choose the most epic feeling to coincide with a moment in my life that would change me forever, it would feel like this. Like I could run the fastest marathon in the world. Like I could climb Everest hours before anyone else, then stand on top and plant my flag. A profound moment where I know that I'm completely, utterly, deeply in love with this woman. And that's the final score.

My legs start running before I realize it. Somewhere along the way, I lose my helmet. The crowd's cheers fade away until all I see is Kenna, standing there, her eyes shining and glassy.

I jump up the wall, grabbing the metal handrail on top and holding myself there. "You think you love me?"

She hands off the poster to a girl next to her and steps toward me. "I *know* I love you, West Brooks."

Her hands come up to cup my cheeks, and I yank myself forward, sealing my lips to hers in a desperate kiss. The rioting in my brain rivals the chaos occurring around us. Fans cheer. Silly String cascades down us like royal-blue confetti. We laugh into each other's lips.

Pulling away, she stares into my eyes. "Now the whole world knows."

"Knows what?"

"That I'll never stop fighting for you."

The parts of me that weren't stitched up knit together in that moment. It's like when the quarterback calls the right play at the right time for a historic win.

"Then they know I won't stop fighting for you either."

The soft smile she gives me is everything. She grips my neck, tugging me forward until we kiss once more to the delight of the crowd. I'll be pulling Silly String out of her hair for days.

She places soft kisses across my cheeks until she says in my ear, "I kind of promised this little girl that you'd say hi to her. She lent me the sign and got me a marker."

I peek at the young girl beside Kenna who's beaming, lit up like the sun. "So, I have her to thank?" I ask.

Kenna grips my forearm as we both face the girl. "I guess so."

The girl is already answering for Kenna, nodding intensely.

I hold my hand out, keeping my grip on the railing so I don't fall backward. "I'm West Brooks."

She puts her hand in mine, and I give it a gentle shake.

"I'm Lyndsey, but my friends call me Lyn-Z. Without the *d* and just a *z* on the end." She enunciates the Z like she's giving her own professional interview.

"Nice to meet you, Lyn-Z." I notice she has another poster in her hands that reads West is My Hero. The words hit me right in the heart. "Tell you what, if I sign your poster, do you think you could give me this one Kenna made for me? I promise to keep it forever."

She nods happily.

Kenna hands me a blue marker, and then has to help hold me up while I write: Lyn-Z, you're MY hero. Then scribble my name and end it with #53.

"You mean it?" she asks.

"You bet I do."

Then I smile at Kenna. Anyone who helped bring Kenna and I together is my hero.

Behind me, I hear the first few notes of a song before it gets cut off. The halftime show is setting up, and I'm about to be on Coach's shit list. Kenna reads my apprehension. "I'll still be here," she says.

"Promise?"

She makes a cross over her heart.

I give one last lunge forward to kiss her on the cheek and then I drop down, scooping up my helmet as I haul ass down the ramp and toward the locker room.

This just might be the best day ever. I'm playing great, we're going to beat Hamilton, and when all of this is over, I get to see the girl I'm in love with. What could be better?

CHAPTER THIRTY-TWO

Kenna

THE NEW WEIGHT room in the football complex is state-of-the-art. Banners of each first-string player line the room along with the biggest banner announcing the Warner Bulldogs as homecoming champs. I stand in front of West's poster, wondering if I could get away with stealing it and hanging it up in my room. I have the perfect place for it.

Large hands wind around me from behind, and I lay my head back on his shoulder. "What are the odds?"

"Of?" he asks, his sweaty hands gripping me tighter.

"Of me climbing up there to take that."

I feel him grin against my cheek. "I think we can arrange it. No more David Booty."

I don't even correct him. David who? My mind has been wrapped up in West Brooks for weeks, and he's going to stay there, consuming me.

After catching the highlight reel of our home-coming game on ESPN, my parents demanded they meet West. That all went down last week, and it went even better than I imagined. They were wary at first, but by the end of the night, they took to him just like I have.

Anyone who meets him can't doubt his sincerity, and when the two of us are together, it feels like we're glowing from the inside out.

Behind us, the door opens and more players file in. They wave at us as we break apart, and we head back over to the squat rack where West has already deloaded the bar for my much lighter weights. He doesn't need to coach me nearly as much as he used to, but he's always there...just in case.

I drop down for my set and then rerack the bar. West loads another five-pound plate on each side. "So, how would you feel about flying to Atlanta with me on Tuesday?"

My brow furrows. "Fly to Atlanta? Tuesday?"

He shrugs. "That new NIL deal will probably come through."

I beam up at him. Not only did all of the compa-nies West was already partnering with pull back on their reticence to associate with him after his interview, but even more reached out. One is an abuse charity that he's going to work pro bono with, but there are other ones, too. Like an online mental health app that connects patients and doctors through the internet for easier access to healthcare.

I couldn't be prouder of him. "That's great. I'm so happy, but—"

"They want you to come, too."

I drop my shoulders. "Tell me you didn't ask to bring me."

He shakes his head. "No, they specifically requested me to bring you. They saw us on ESPN... and they want to work with both of us." He places the clip on the end of the bar, then glances up. My brain has stopped functioning. He smiles at me. Probably at the lost look on my face. "They specifically asked for both of us, I didn't do a thing. In fact, they said if you had an agent, they would've asked your agent directly."

"But I don't get NIL deals," I say, voice wavering.

"You do now."

I press my lips together. Excitement unfurls in my stomach, making it hard to think. To breathe.

He moves closer, grasping my cheeks. "And I already told them I'm not stealing the spotlight. This is for you. They want you to bring your suit and your dive gear. We're going to do a photo shoot by the pool."

"But—"

He shakes his head. "Stop doubting this. It's real.

My agent will handle the contracts, and you'll just have to sign. Unless you want to get your own lawyer?"

Goosebumps spread over my body. I've never had to think of any of this stuff before. "I-I don't know," I stammer out.

"I don't either. That's why we hire people smarter than us to do it."

My stomach flops. Tears prick my eyes. I didn't realize how much I wanted something like this. To be seen as an athlete. *Oh my God.* "This is all because of you."

He presses a kiss to my lips. "They just see what I see. Someone brave and fierce and passionate. Exactly who they want to represent them." He pats my butt. "Now, one more set and we're done. I have to get to practice."

My mind races as I bust out the last set. My legs quiver. I grit my teeth. But I've come so far. I used to have the same reaction when I started with half the weight, and now I can do so much more.

I rerack the bar, and then we both unload it. Afterward, he picks up his hoodie and wraps it around my shoulders. One of the first things I did was ask for it back. He takes both our gym bags and slings them over his shoulder as we walk out of the weight room and down the hall. Before we get to the exit, he guides me into an empty corridor and presses me against the wall, his wide chest pressing into mine.

His hot breath blows across my lips. "Your place or mine after practice?"

I bite my lip momentarily. "We can decide that later." He pulls away, brows knitted together. "I'm coming to practice with you today." His green eyes take on even more confusion. "Coach invited me. Plus, I have a pact to fulfill."

"You don't—"

"I do." I no longer think poorly of football players. There are good ones and bad ones. Immature and mature ones, just like regular people. The football player in front of me is one of the best men I've ever known, and he's most definitely changed my mind. "We had a deal, West Brooks. You get me in shape for diving, and I come to one of your practices. A deal is a promise, and I fulfill my promises."

He searches my gaze, and I can almost see a sliver of relief lift from him. I accept football. I have to because I accept West for who he is. Football is his passion, and I would never want to take that away from him. "Have I told you today that I love you?"

I wind my arms around him. "Not in the last few hours."

He grins, the inner light that pours from him growing brighter. "I must be the worst boyfriend."

"The worst," I agree.

He hikes my legs up over his hips. "Let me fix it, then. I fucking love you, McKenna Knowles. Tonight, let's sneak into the hot springs again, and I'll show you exactly how much."

"It's a date."

"No, it's a promise."

He seals his lips to mine, kissing me like two souls intertwined.

Loving West Brooks is going to be an adventure. Nights spent under the glow of stadium lights with thousands of people screaming his name, and days of just us where I make sure he knows that he is loved, and he reminds me that I am brave.

...And I'm so ready for the next chapter.

EPILOGUE

West

I GLARE at the ringing phone. Kenna takes my hands, making me focus on her. She gives me a small smile. "Do you think we should turn the ringer off?"

My nerves go from a plague of butterflies to a low buzz just looking at her. "I wish."

"Everyone wants a piece," she says, squeezing my hands. "The great West 'the Hulk' Brooks's draft day."

Her saying it out loud amps up the electricity in my veins. I got invited to Union Station for the selection, but I turned it down. I wanted to be here. With my friends. With Kenna.

I tug on my college jersey—the one I gave her a year and a half ago. I can still remember the way my stomach flipped when I saw her in the stands. She wasn't obligated to come, but there she was, anyway. "I'm so glad we decided to do this."

She bites her lip and peers around mischievously. "What? Con everyone into coming over for a draft party when really we're forcing them to watch us get married?"

"Shh," I tease, pulling her in close and nibbling on her ear. "You're terrible at keeping secrets."

"I've not said a single thing, which is really hard because you don't know Sydney like I do. She's like a Chihuahua with her favorite slipper." Backing away, she gives me a stern look. "And you know I'm fine waiting. We can just make this your day."

I give her the same look I gave my phone. "I don't need a day. I need us to be official."

"Silly me, I thought we were."

Her snark makes me grin. She always does this. Whenever I'm the least bit worried or stressed, she turns on her charm to get me out of my own head.

"Just know it's not happening if you get dropped to the second round."

I grimace. I'm not one for acting, but I try. "What if I go in the third?"

"Oh, then we're officially broken up. I can't have you ruining my street cred. McKenna Knowles doesn't marry third-round draft picks." She doesn't even get all the words out before she's chuckling.

"Maybe I should call my prospects again to make sure?"

My façade falls, and the worry creeps back in. No one really knows for sure when they'll be drafted. It's all about what position the team needs and what pick they get. Add in traded picks, and the whole day will be an absolute gamble on the player's part.

I've spoken with a few teams and worked out with a few, but I've tried not to pick favorites. When ESPN starts discussing team strategy and which players they think will go one through twenty, I turn it off.

"Hey," Kenna says, drawing me back to her. "For what it's worth, I'll always choose you as my number one."

And this is why I love her. I pick her up, and she winds her legs around my hips as I grab the back of her neck to pull her in for a kiss.

Sydney walks into the room and groans. "Oh, this again. I swear something is up with you two."

The doorbell rings, and instead of waiting to be welcomed in, a few of my teammates walk in, including Aidan. "Kenna, your parents just got here. Also, there's about five reporters on the sidewalk."

I place Kenna on her feet, and she stares up at me with round eyes. She hasn't even told her parents our plan, but they love me.

She hurries to the door, scooting around my team-mates as they come to greet me. The house is small to begin with, but with them in here, the living room seems so much smaller.

Sydney sets a few appetizers out on the coffee table, side-eyeing Aidan, and I check my phone again to see if my mom has texted. My relationship with her is strained still but moving in the right direction. I've set boundaries that she's had a hard time adjusting to, but everything is improving, and honestly, I think they're making her a better person, too. She even started seeing a therapist to deal with some of her trauma, and I can see the positive impacts. Maybe she won't ever be the perfect mom I wished I had, but she's trying, and sometimes, that's all we can ask for.

Kenna ushers her parents in, and her dad comes right up to shake my hand. "Big day."

"Yes, sir." I squeeze his hand and hope he's not furious with me when Kenna and I break the news. It's what we wanted.

Her mom comes over next, giving me a hug. "I have a few dishes in the car."

My teammates perk right up. "On the way."

Kenna's mom goes into the kitchen with Sydney, leaving Kenna and I alone again as her dad picks at the vegetable tray.

"How many more are we waiting for?" she asks.

"Coach," I tell her.

"Your mom?"

"She hasn't texted."

345

"She'll be here," she says with more confidence than I feel right now. My mom isn't known for punctuality.

"If she's not here on time, we're doing it, anyway."

"If that's what you want."

"I'm not waiting on anybody."

A ball of mixed emotions clogs my throat. I'm nervous, scared, and happy balled into one. When I told Kenna a few weeks ago that I didn't want to go into the next phase of my life without her, I meant it more than anything.

Today's the draft.

Today's my wedding day.

Next week, we're both graduating and heading off to wherever the NFL deems my fate.

Neither one of us needed a big wedding. We just wanted the two of us along with everyone who has always supported us.

The door opens again, and Aidan calls out, "Look who we found."

Coach comes striding in. His wife follows behind him, the other players taking in the rear.

Coach has been my father figure since I was a freshman, and when he shakes my hand, I feel it. All the love. All the encouragement.

He slaps my back. "This day has been a long time coming."

More food gets set on the table. More bodies crowd

around. Kenna and I are forced to squeeze together, and when she takes my hand, I know she's feeling the nerves, too. It's not every day you surprise people with a wedding.

I check my watch. If my mother doesn't get here in the next five minutes, she's going to miss it.

The minutes tick by. There's happy laughter and people trying to talk to me, but I'm completely consumed. Everyone thinks it's draft nerves, but it's not.

It's...expectation.

I always felt like Kenna and I were an inevitability, and that feeling has only grown stronger.

Aidan peeks up at me, and I nod. He moves to come talk to me. "Your mom?"

I shrug. "I'm not waiting."

"West," he cautions.

He's the only one who knows what's going down today. Someone had to get the license to marry us, so here he is.

"I—"

The doorbell rings, and I hold a breath in my throat while Kenna beams. She runs to the door, and in walks my mom.

I try to hold it in, but emotion overpowers me. I clear my throat, swallowing. The one thing I needed her to be here for, and she actually came.

Kenna gives me the brightest smile as she leads her

in. Mom walks right up to me. Like Kenna, she barely comes up to my shoulders. Her thin, frail hands surround me with a little more strength than they have in the past. "I'm so proud of you."

"I'm proud of you," I tell her. If she keeps showing up for me, I'll continue to show up for her.

Now, everything feels complete.

Kenna and I link hands. The strength we draw from one another is calming. The tension in the room has only increased, brought on by all the nervous, excited energy with every newcomer.

"So, are we turning the TV on?" Coach asks, rocking back on his heels while he stands next to Kenna's dad.

"Before we do that," Kenna states, smiling up at me, unshed tears making her eyes shine.

I turn toward our friends and family. "We brought you here under false pretenses."

The room goes quiet.

I don't know how to do this. Kenna and I didn't plan it out. We just kind of decided and leaped.

I peer at her. In her eyes, I gain all the strength I need. In her face, I know I'll always find comfort. In her love, so deep that sometimes I can barely catch my breath, I'll always feel mine mirrored back. In understanding. In patience. In bravery.

Sydney's the first to get it. She gasps, then screams out, "I knew it!"

Kenna chuckles, still keeping my stare. "I didn't tell her, I promise."

"What?" her mom asks, clearly confused.

"Today, I'm getting drafted," I say for everyone else's benefit, but I still only have eyes for the girl who loves me when no one else did. "But I'm also going to marry my best friend."

Mrs. Knowles gasps now, too. Coach's wife *oohs* and *ahhs*, and my mom? She starts to cry.

"Like, right now?" one of my teammates asks.

"Like right now," Kenna agrees.

"There's no way I was going to start the next phase of my life without making sure I had Kenna with me. Forever and always."

And then the real best day of my life kicks off. With Kenna by my side, I'll have so many more.

I'm convinced that the greatest lives are tallied by how many best days one can cram into them. Mine only started when I met Kenna. And they'll end with Kenna, too.

About the Author

E. M. Moore is a USA Today Bestselling author of Contemporary and Paranormal Romance. She's drawn to write within the teen and college-aged years where her characters get knocked on their asses, torn inside out, and put back together again by their first loves. Whether it's in a fantastical setting where human guards protect the creatures of the night or a realistic high school backdrop where social cliques rule the halls, the emotions are the same. Dark. Twisty. Angsty. Raw.

When Erin's not writing, you can find her dreaming up vacations for her family, watching murder mystery shows, or dancing in her kitchen while she pretends to cook.